CLASSIC SCIENCE FICTION STORIES

More short stories available
from Macmillan Collector's Library

Classic Dog Stories
Classic Cat Stories
Irish Ghost Stories
Classic Hallowe'en Stories
Classic Locked Room Mysteries
Round About the Christmas Tree
Ghost Stories by Charles Dickens
Complete Ghost Stories by M. R. James
Best Short Stories by W. Somerset Maugham
Prelude & Other Stories by Katherine Mansfield
The Awakening & Other Stories by Kate Chopin
In the Ravine & Other Stories by Anton Chekhov
The Third Man & Other Stories by Graham Greene
The Happy Prince & Other Stories by Oscar Wilde
The Best of Sherlock Holmes by Arthur Conan Doyle
Tales of Mystery and Imagination by Edgar Allan Poe
A Glove Shop in Vienna & Other Stories
by Eva Ibbotson
Standing Her Ground: Classic Short Stories
by Trailblazing Women
Sleepily Ever After: Bedtime Stories for Grown Ups
Tales and Poems by Edgar Allan Poe
All the Mowgli Stories by Rudyard Kipling
Just So Stories by Rudyard Kipling
Dubliners by James Joyce

CLASSIC SCIENCE FICTION STORIES

Selection and introduction by
ADAM ROBERTS

MACMILLAN COLLECTOR'S LIBRARY

This collection first published 2022 by Macmillan Collector's Library
an imprint of Pan Macmillan
The Smithson, 6 Briset Street, London ECIM 5NR
Associated companies throughout the world
www.panmacmillan.com

ISBN 978-1-5290-6907-5

The Permissions Acknowledgements on p. 393 constitute an extension of this copyright page.

The text of this book remains true to the original in every way and is reflective of the language and period in which it was originally written. Readers should be aware that there may be hurtful or indeed harmful phrases and terminology that were prevalent at the time these stories were written and in the context of the historical setting of the stories. Macmillan believes changing the text to reflect today's world would undermine the authenticity of the original, so has chosen to leave the text in its entirety. This does not, however, constitute an endorsement of the characterization, content or language used.

1 3 5 7 9 8 6 4 2

A CIP catalogue record for this book is available from the British Library.

Casing design and endpaper pattern by Andrew Davidson
Typeset in Plantin by Jouve (UK), Milton Keynes
Printed and bound in China by Imago

FSC
www.fsc.org
MIX
Paper from responsible sources
FSC® C116313

Contents

Introduction

ADAM ROBERTS

Science fiction is older than you think. People think of it as a literature about 'the future', imaginative extrapolations into the 'to come'. In fact, the genre is larger than that (alternate histories and speculative presents are also part of science fiction's empire), but projected futurity has a long pedigree. People in the eighteenth century were as interested in what tomorrow might hold as we are today. This collection gathers together a range of 'classic' science-fiction stories, from the 1750s to the early twentieth century, and it shows not just the range, inventiveness and sheer wonder of science fiction, but also that science fiction has been around for a very long time.

Ask a dozen scholars of science fiction when the genre begins and you'll get a dozen different answers. Some argue that it is a relatively recent development, and it's true that the name 'science fiction' was coined by the Luxembourgish-American editor and writer Hugo Gernsback, who founded the world's first dedicated science-fiction magazine, *Amazing Stories*, in 1926. The success of this led to many imitators: the newsstands of the 1920s and 1930s soon thronged with SF 'pulp' magazines, with their garish, brightly coloured, exotic covers. And something certainly happened to SF over this period: it boomed, growing from a small-scale interest into a major cultural form. The 'age of pulps' grew into what is still called the 'golden age' of SF – the 1940s and 1950s – through the 'new wave' of the 1960s and 1970s, and via the huge success of SF cinema, beginning with *Star Wars* (1977), and up to the present day, where SF is everywhere; a global phenomenon spanning books and films, TV shows and video games, fandoms, cosplay and cultures.

But although the name 'science fiction' dates to 1926, stories of space aliens visiting Earth, immortality, strange new technologies, time travel and so on – known as 'scientific romances' or 'fantastical tales' or 'strange stories' – predate the year the phrase was coined. Some critics push science fiction's origin date back to the nineteenth century: to the 1890s with H. G. Wells in the UK, further back to Jules Verne in France in the 1860s, or further still to Edgar Allan Poe in the USA in the 1840s. Great writers all, and enormously influential, but not the first. Voltaire's celebrated *conte philosophique* – his 'philosophical tale' – about visiting extraterrestrials, 'Micromégas', was published in 1752. The German astronomer Johannes Kepler wrote a detailed speculative fiction called *Somnium* ('The Dream') in 1634, about the bizarre non-humanoid forms of life that might be inhabiting our moon. I would have liked to include *Somnium* in this collection, although in the end it proved too long. But its date and the scientific career of its author point to something important about the origins of science fiction as a mode.

The point is that fantasy is the default mode of human storytelling. By 'fantasy' I mean stories of magic and monsters, tales that don't merely reproduce the mundanity of the world in which we live but instead populate their story-worlds with ghosts and marvels, wizards and sorceresses, that focus on an enchanted, more wondrous version of existence. The *Epic of Gilgamesh* and Homer's *Odyssey* are both fantasies in this sense; so are *Beowulf* and medieval romances. It is possible to find stories that follow a logic of verisimilitude, tales set in story-worlds that more closely resemble the actual world, but across the large scale of history these are very much the exception. Humans have always preferred something grander, something more magical and amazing: heroes battling monsters, a universe animated by the strange and sublime and extraordinary.

Science fiction is a new kind of fantasy story, one based not on 'magic' but on the extrapolated possibilities of science. And when we see it in those terms, we will not be surprised to discover that these sorts of story began to appear at the same time as the Renaissance fed through into the Enlightenment, as science itself was being forged and refined as a method and discourse. As scientists like Kepler expanded our understanding of the cosmos, and as new scientific understandings fed technological advance, a version of fantasy predicated not on nostalgic enchantment but rather on a forward-looking materialist sublime, a new cosmic sense of wonder, came into being.

You can trace the excitement, the thrill and the terror of this new logic in the stories collected in this volume. Medieval Europe, on the authority of the Church, believed (mostly) that the Earth was the centre of the universe. Dante's *Divine Comedy* (early fourteenth century) takes place in such a location: a solar system comprised of concentric crystal spheres all rotating around our world, with all the stars embedded in the outmost sphere. In the early sixteenth century, Copernicus showed that this wasn't the reality of things, and although it took a while for his ideas to become accepted – the Church was still persecuting scientists like Galileo into the 1630s – by the time Kepler was writing, a whole new cosmos had grown up around us, strange and wonderful, but also, in its sheer size and indifference to human affairs, alarming. 'The eternal silence of these infinite spaces terrifies me' wrote French philosopher and scientist Blaise Pascal in his *Pensées* (1670). Kepler's *Somnium* captures something of the unsettling grandeur and inhumanity of these new cosmic dimensions.

For Voltaire, whose 'Micromégas' is included here, these new vastnesses provide the occasion not so much for awestruck sense of wonder as for a satirical reminder of our own relativeness, smallness and triviality. His two gigantic space aliens are amazed to find creatures so minuscule as human beings swarming over this insignificant little planet, and more amazed to discover that these creatures consider the universe created and arranged for *their* benefit. It's a splendid and funny tale.

Mary Shelley's *Frankenstein* (1818) – another popular pick for the 'first' science fiction story among scholars – styles the new creative possibilities opened up by science and technology as a cautionary tale. Shelley's scientist hopes to bless humanity with a new species to serve it, but instead he is blindsided by the unintended consequences of his act, as his 'creature', abandoned and reviled, causes havoc. *Frankenstein* is a story of hubris meeting nemesis, but that ancient moral is made fresh for the era of science, darkly enlivened by the sheer sublimity of Shelley's vision, the splendour and horror of her monster – intelligent, eloquent, wronged, yet violent and dangerous. In her story selected here, Shelley imagines immortality, or something like it, with a similar dark glamour, the remorselessness of time, the appalling wonder of the wilderness. Poe also used the forms of Gothic literature to cast out the humanly familiar and reassuring into a compellingly strange and unsettling zone

By the mid-nineteenth century, science fiction had moved beyond the Gothic, exploring a wide range of effective and tonal registers. Fitz-James O'Brien's witty speculation, Florence McLandburgh's ingenious time-travel conceit and Edward Page Mitchell's splendid mathematical extrapolation in this collection are three examples of the variety of which SF is capable. James Clerk Maxwell's poem shows that the mode was still attractive to scientists, and Ambrose Bierce's satire utilized the speculative and self-reflective possibilities of the mode.

All these stories are interesting, though some are more of their time than others. But it was not until the end of the nineteenth century, and the arrival on the scene of Herbert George Wells, a writer and imaginer of genius, deservedly known as the father of British science fiction, that SF came into its own.

Wells did not invent SF as such, but he was a prolific writer of it, with an extraordinary gift for invention. From his mind, fully armed, like Athena from the forehead of Zeus, came the first time-travel story (*The Time Machine*, 1895), the first story of 'uplifted' or augmented animals (*The Island of Doctor Moreau*, 1896), the first story of technologically facilitated invisibility (*The Invisible Man*, 1897), the first great alien-invasion story (*The War of the Worlds*, 1898) and the first dystopia (*When the Sleeper Wakes*, 1899), to name only a few. Each of these works established a different, still-popular sub-genre of science fiction. For this collection, a couple of Wellsian short stories have been selected, and choosing which to include from his myriad brilliant shorts was the hardest editorial task of the volume.

Much of Wells's best SF – indeed, much of the best SF ever written – has appeared in the short-story format, and it's worth dwelling for a moment on the affinity between the genre of science fiction and the form of the short story. The salient factor of any short story is brevity, of course, and the dangers brevity inevitably entail are triviality and evanescence. One way of avoiding those consequences is for a writer to structure their story around a central trope or metaphor that stays with the reader after the events and characters have been forgotten. SF is just better at doing that than other modes of writing, because SF is a fundamentally metaphorical form of art. It is a fundamentally metaphorical form of art because it aims at representing the world without simply reproducing it. Sometimes these metaphors are tropes or props: a robot, a time machine, a walking plant, a planet-killing space station. Sometimes they are conceptual reworkings: new ways of thinking about gender or society. Sometimes they are ways of intimating the vastness of space, or the enormities of time, apprehensions of the 'sense of wonder' so prized by SF fans. But in all such modes of SF writing, the piercing eloquence of the *moment*, the shortness of the story form, is the best way of unlocking these metaphors.

Indeed, I would argue that, for these reasons, the SF short is the key mode of short story in the twentieth century. Walter Allen's critical survey *The Short Story in English* (1981) argues that 'the short story is rooted in a single incident or perception', and that therefore its effect 'is nearer to that of lyric poetry than the novel'. V. S. Pritchett (in his introduction to *The Oxford Book of Short Stories*) agrees: 'the novel tends to tell us everything whereas the short story tells us only one thing, and that, intensely . . . the short story springs from a spontaneously poetic, as distinct from a prosaic, impulse.' Where prose narrative is a fundamentally metonymic progression of A → B → C, the lyric poem makes a metaphoric leap into some new, and affecting, location. SF, though often embodied in narrative form, is much more centrally about this metaphorical jump. Think of the ape-man's bone in *2001: A Space Odyssey*, thrown up into the wide blue sky, followed by the camera, reaching its apogee, starting to fall back down and then, unexpectedly, turning into an orbiting space-craft; it's powerful and beautiful and affecting, and its power, beauty and effect cannot really be rationally described, in that it is a poetic, rather than a narrative, moment. And Wells, for all his witty garrulity, is capable of piercing moments of real poetry. 'The Door in the Wall' is a resonantly haunting evocation of what is lost in growing up, and 'The Star' – short, beautifully focused – generates a potent, cosmic-scale 'sense of wonder'.

Partly because of the influence of Wells's shorts, and partly reflecting the exigencies of publication, in which full-length books were relatively expensive and magazine short fiction relatively cheap, twentieth-century science fiction moved along a path in which the short story was dominant. It was a mode both accessible and flexible; it allowed Bengali writer Rokeya Sakhawat Hossain to elegantly explore her thought-experiment about gender, but also allowed the very different sensibility of H. P. Lovecraft to construe a weird, frightening and dream-haunting vibe of terrors lurking in the backwoods, in the remotenesses of the world – and in the corner of the eye. Lovecraft's apprehension of 'the alien' could not be more different than Stanley Weinbaum's rationally extrapolated and crisply delineated alien Martians, although both in their own way are marvellous creations. And Arthur Conan Doyle is able to pick a middle lane: the comprehensible technology of airplanes, but traversing a strange, almost Lovecraftian territory in the stratosphere.

The larger story – the growth and development of science fiction as a mode – continues beyond the remit of this present collection, and short fiction remained at the heart of the genre for many decades. The dominant markets for SF writers in the 1930s and 1940s were pulp magazines, so writers wrote a lot of short stories, the staple of the format. After the Second World War things changed a little: the magazine market shrank sharply through the 1950s and 1960s (for several reasons: home TV, wider and cheaper access to movies, more people buying comics and fewer buying mags). So, in the 1950s, SF writers addressed themselves to a new market, one created by SF book clubs and civic libraries: hardback books. This in turn created one of the distinctive textual forms of SF – the 'fix up'. Asimov, Bradbury and Van Vogt reworked their older stories into longer books. Bradbury's *The Martian Chronicles* (1950) and Asimov's *Foundation* (1951), to name only two, are both congeries of disparate 1940s short stories glued together with paragraphs of linking exposition, and both are acclaimed as being great classics of SF.

Since then the market has shifted again several times, away from hardbacks to cheap paperbacks, and thence to ebooks and audiobooks, not to mention jumping mode to TV, film and video games. But I'd argue that the 'fix up' has had a much larger, perhaps even a shaping, effect on the entire later development of SF than is realized. I don't just mean those occasional SF novels today that are made up of discrete elements tessellated, like Dan Simmons's *Hyperion* (1989) or Jennifer Egan's *A Visit from the Goon Squad* (2011). It's also in the way TV shows like *Doctor Who* or *Star Trek* assemble mega-texts out of lots of short-story-esque discrete elements, something (as per the Marvel Comics Universe movies) increasingly mimicked by cinema. Only die-hard fans read new SF short stories today, but the *form* of the short story feeds directly into contemporary SF in fundamental ways.

In this collection I have assembled some of the

best examples of short stories from SF's deeper past. They're enjoyable to read in their own right, but more than that, they give insight into the roots, and therefore into the present delights, of science fiction.

CLASSIC SCIENCE FICTION STORIES

H. G. Wells

Herbert George Wells, known as 'the father of British science fiction', is, uniquely in this collection, represented by more than one story. He was indeed a prolific and prodigiously gifted writer of science fiction, and his best work embodies the focus and concision of the short story and the novella. Born in 1866 into a lower-middle-class family in south-east London, he worked as a draper and schoolteacher before achieving remarkable success as a writer and journalist. His first decade as a writer, the 1890s, saw him produce a string of enduring masterpieces of science fiction: novels like *The Time Machine* (1895) and *The War of the Worlds* (1898), and scores of brilliant short stories. These early pieces remain dazzling examples of the mode. 'The Star', published in *Graphic* magazine (December 1897) and very often reprinted, is a potent slug of the dark espresso of 'sense-of-wonder' cosmic-scale SF.

The Star

It was on the first day of the New Year that the announcement was made, almost simultaneously from three observatories, that the motion of the planet Neptune, the outermost of all the planets that wheel about the sun, had become very erratic. Ogilvy had already called attention to a suspected retardation in its velocity in December. Such a piece of news was scarcely calculated to interest a world the greater portion of whose inhabitants were unaware of the existence of the planet Neptune, nor outside the astronomical profession did the subsequent discovery of a faint remote speck of light in the region of the perturbed planet cause any very great excitement. Scientific people, however, found the intelligence remarkable enough, even before it became known that the new body was rapidly growing larger and brighter, that its motion was quite different from the orderly progress of the planets, and that the deflection of Neptune and its satellite was becoming now of an unprecedented kind.

Few people without a training in science can realise the huge isolation of the solar system. The sun with its specks of planets, its dust of planetoids, and its impalpable comets, swims in a vacant immensity that almost defeats the imagination. Beyond the orbit of Neptune there is space, vacant so far as human observation has penetrated, without warmth or light or sound, blank emptiness, for twenty million times a million miles. That is the smallest estimate of the distance to be traversed before the very nearest of the stars is attained. And, saving a few comets more unsubstantial than the thinnest flame, no matter had ever to human knowledge crossed this gulf of space, until early in the twentieth century this strange wanderer appeared. A vast mass of matter it was, bulky, heavy, rushing without warning out of the black mystery of the sky into the radiance of the sun. By the second day it was clearly visible to any decent instrument, as a speck with a barely sensible diameter, in the constellation Leo near Regulus. In a little while an opera glass could attain it.

On the third day of the new year the newspaper readers of two hemispheres were made aware for the first time of the real importance of this unusual apparition in the heavens. "A Planetary Collision," one London paper headed the news, and proclaimed Duchaine's opinion that this strange new planet would probably collide with Neptune. The leader writers enlarged upon the topic; so that in most of the capitals of the world, on January 3rd, there was an expectation, however vague, of some imminent phenomenon in the sky; and as the night followed the sunset round the globe, thousands of men turned their eyes skyward to see—the old familiar stars just as they had always been.

Until it was dawn in London and Pollux setting and the stars overhead grown pale. The Winter's dawn it was, a sickly filtering accumulation of day-light, and the light of gas and candles shone yellow in the windows to show where people were astir. But the yawning policeman saw the thing, the busy crowds in the markets stopped agape, workmen going to their work betimes, milkmen, the drivers of new-carts, dissipation going home jaded and pale, homeless wanderers, sentinels on their beats, and in the country, labourers trudging afield, poachers slinking home, all over the dusky quickening country it could be seen—and out at sea by seamen watching for the day—a great white star, come suddenly into the westward sky!

Brighter it was than any star in our skies; brighter than the evening star at its brightest. It still glowed out white and large, no mere twinkling spot of light, but a small round clear shining disc, an hour after the day had come. And where science has not reached, men stared and feared, telling one another of the wars and pestilences that are foreshadowed by these fiery signs in the Heavens. Sturdy Boers, dusky Hottentots, Gold Coast Negroes, Frenchmen,

Spaniards, Portuguese, stood in the warmth of the sunrise watching the setting of this strange new star.

And in a hundred observatories there had been suppressed excitement, rising almost to shouting pitch, as the two remote bodies had rushed together; and a hurrying to and fro, to gather photographic apparatus and spectroscope, and this appliance and that, to record this novel astonishing sight, the destruction of a world. For it was a world, a sister planet of our earth, far greater than our earth indeed, that had so suddenly flashed into flaming death. Neptune it was, had been struck, fairly and squarely, by the strange planet from outer space and the heat of the concussion had incontinently turned two solid globes into one vast mass of incandescence. Round the world that day, two hours before the dawn, went the pallid great white star, fading only as it sank westward and the sun mounted above it. Everywhere men marvelled at it, but of all those who saw it none could have marvelled more than those sailors, habitual watchers of the stars, who far away at sea had heard nothing of its advent and saw it now rise like a pigmy moon and climb zenithward and hang overhead and sink westward with the passing of the night.

And when next it rose over Europe everywhere were crowds of watchers on hilly slopes, on house-roofs, in open spaces, staring eastward for the rising of the great new star. It rose with a white glow in front of it, like the glare of a white fire, and those who had seen it come into existence the night before cried out at the sight of it. "It is larger," they cried. "It is brighter!" And, indeed the moon a quarter full and sinking in the west was in its apparent size beyond comparison, but scarcely in all its breadth had it as much brightness now as the little circle of the strange new star.

"It is brighter!" cried the people clustering in the streets. But in the dim observatories the watchers held their breath and peered at one another "*It is nearer*," they said. "*Nearer!*"

And voice after voice repeated, "It is nearer," and the clicking telegraph took that up, and it trembled along telephone wires, and in a thousand cities grimy compositors fingered the type. "It is nearer." Men writing in offices, struck with a strange realisation, flung down their pens, men talking in a thousand places suddenly came upon a grotesque possibility in those words, "It is nearer." It hurried along wakening streets, it was shouted down the frost-stilled ways of quiet villages; men who had read these things from the throbbing tape stood in yellow-lit doorways shouting the news to the passers-by. "It is nearer." Pretty women, flushed and glittering, heard the news told jestingly between the dances, and feigned an intelligent interest they did not feel. "Nearer! Indeed. How curious! How very, very clever people must be to find out things like that!"

Lonely tramps faring through the wintry night murmured those words to comfort themselves—looking skyward. "It has need to be nearer, for the night's as cold as charity. Don't seem much warmth from it if it *is* nearer, all the same."

"What is a new star to me?" cried the weeping woman kneeling beside her dead.

The schoolboy, rising early for his examination work, puzzled it out for himself—with the great white star shining broad and bright through the frost-flowers of his window. "Centrifugal, centripetal," he said, with his chin on his fist. "Stop a planet in its flight, rob it of its centrifugal force, what then? Centripetal has it, and down it falls into the sun! And this—!"

"Do *we* come in the way? I wonder—"

The light of that day went the way of its brethren, and with the later watches of the frosty darkness rose the strange star again. And it was now so bright that the waxing moon seemed but a pale yellow ghost of itself, hanging huge in the sunset. In a South African City a great man had married, and the streets were alight to welcome his return with his bride. "Even the skies have illuminated," said the flatterer. Under

Capricorn, two negro lovers, daring the wild beasts and evil spirits, for love of one another, crouched together in a cane brake where the fire-flies hovered. "That is our star," they whispered, and felt strangely comforted by the sweet brilliance of its light.

The master mathematician sat in his private room and pushed the papers from him. His calculations were already finished. In a small white phial there still remained a little of the drug that had kept him awake and active for four long nights. Each day, serene, explicit, patient as ever, he had given his lecture to his students, and then had come back at once to this momentous calculation. His face was grave, a little drawn and hectic from his drugged activity. For some time he seemed lost in thought. Then he went to the window, and the blind went up with a click. Half way up the sky, over the clustering roofs, chimneys and steeples of the city, hung the star.

He looked at it as one might look into the eyes of a brave enemy. "You may kill me," he said after a silence. "But I can hold you—and all the universe for that matter—in the grip of this little brain. I would not change. Even now."

He looked at the little phial. "There will be no need of sleep again," he said. The next day at noon—punctual to the minute, he entered his lecture theatre, put his hat on the end of the table as his habit was, and carefully selected a large piece of chalk. It was a joke among his students that he could not lecture without that piece of chalk to fumble in his fingers, and once he had been stricken to impotence by their hiding his supply. He came and looked under his grey eyebrows at the rising tiers of young fresh faces, and spoke with his accustomed studied commonness of phrasing. "Circumstances have arisen—circumstances beyond my control," he said and paused, "which will debar me from completing the course I had designed. It would seem, gentlemen, if I may put the thing clearly and briefly, that—Man has lived in vain."

The students glanced at one another. Had they heard aright? Mad? Raised eyebrows and grinning lips there were, but one or two faces remained intent upon his calm grey-fringed face. "It will be interesting," he was saying, "to devote this morning to an exposition, so far as I can make it clear to you, of the calculations that have led me to this conclusion. Let us assume—"

He turned towards the blackboard, meditating a diagram in the way that was usual to him. "What was that about 'lived in vain?'" whispered one student to another. "Listen," said the other, nodding towards the lecturer.

And presently they began to understand.

That night the star rose later, for its proper eastward motion had carried it some way across Leo towards Virgo, and its brightness was so great that the sky became a luminous blue as it rose, and every star was hidden in its turn, save only Jupiter near the zenith, Capella, Aldebaran, Sirius and the pointers of the Bear. It was very white and beautiful. In many parts of the world that night a pallid halo encircled it about. It was perceptibly larger; in the clear refractive sky of the tropics it seemed as if it were nearly a quarter the size of the moon. The frost was still on the ground in England, but the world was as brightly lit as if it were midsummer moonlight. One could see to read quite ordinary print by that cold clear light, and in the cities the lamps burnt yellow and wan.

And everywhere the world was awake that night, and throughout Christendom a sombre murmur hung in the keen air over the country side like the belling of bees in the heather, and this murmurous tumult grew to a clangour in the cities. It was the tolling of the bells in a million belfry towers and steeples, summoning the people to sleep no more, to sin no more, but to gather in their churches and pray. And overhead, growing larger and brighter as the earth rolled on its way and the night passed, rose the dazzling star.

And the streets and houses were alight in all the

cities, the shipyards glared, and whatever roads led to high country were lit and crowded all night long. And in all the seas about the civilised lands, ships with throbbing engines, and ships with bellying sails, crowded with men and living creatures, were standing out to ocean and the north. For already the warning of the master mathematician had been telegraphed all over the world, and translated into a hundred tongues. The new planet and Neptune, locked in a fiery embrace, were whirling headlong, ever faster and faster towards the sun. Already every second this blazing mass flew a hundred miles, and every second its terrific velocity increased. As it flew now, indeed, it must pass a hundred million of miles wide of the earth and scarcely affect it. But near its destined path, as yet only slightly perturbed, spun the mighty planet Jupiter and his moons sweeping splendid round the sun. Every moment now the attraction between the fiery star and the greatest of the planets grew stronger. And the result of that attraction? Inevitably Jupiter would be deflected from its orbit into an elliptical path, and the burning star, swung by his attraction wide of its sunward rush, would "describe a curved path" and perhaps collide with, and certainly pass very close to, our earth. "Earthquakes, volcanic outbreaks, cyclones, sea waves, floods, and a steady rise in temperature to

I know not what limit"—so prophesied the master mathematician.

And overhead, to carry out his words, lonely and cold and livid, blazed the star of the coming doom.

To many who stared at it that night until their eyes ached, it seemed that it was visibly approaching. And that night, too, the weather changed, and the frost that had gripped all Central Europe and France and England softened towards a thaw.

But you must not imagine because I have spoken of people praying through the night and people going aboard ships and people fleeing toward mountainous country that the whole world was already in a terror because of the star. As a matter of fact, use and wont still ruled the world, and save for the talk of idle moments and the splendour of the night, nine human beings out of ten were still busy at their common occupations. In all the cities the shops, save one here and there, opened and closed at their proper hours, the doctor and the undertaker plied their trades, the workers gathered in the factories, soldiers drilled, scholars studied, lovers sought one another, thieves lurked and fled, politicians planned their schemes. The presses of the newspapers roared through the night, and many a priest of this church and that would not open his holy building to further what he considered a foolish panic. The newspapers insisted on the lesson of the year 1000—for then, too, people had anticipated the end. The star was no star—mere gas—a comet; and were it a star it could not possibly strike the earth. There was no precedent for such a thing. Common sense was sturdy everywhere, scornful, jesting, a little inclined to persecute the obdurate fearful. That night, at seven-fifteen by Greenwich time, the star would be at its nearest to Jupiter. Then the world would see the turn things would take. The master mathematician's grim warnings were treated by many as so much mere elaborate self-advertisement. Common sense at last, a little heated by argument, signified its unalterable convictions by going to bed. So, too, barbarism and savagery, already tired of the novelty, went about their nightly business, and save for a howling dog here and there, the beast world left the star unheeded.

And yet, when at last the watchers in the European States saw the star rise, an hour later it is true, but no larger than it had been the night before, there were still plenty awake to laugh at the master mathematician—to take the danger as if it had passed.

But hereafter the laughter ceased. The star grew—it grew with a terrible steadiness hour after hour, a little larger each hour, a little nearer the midnight zenith, and brighter and brighter, until it had turned night into a second day. Had it come straight to the earth instead of in a curved path, had it lost no velocity to Jupiter, it must have leapt the intervening gulf in a day, but as it was it took five days altogether to come by our planet. The next night it had become a third the size of the moon before it set to English eyes, and the thaw was assured. It rose over America near the size of the moon, but blinding white to look at, and *hot*; and a breath of hot wind blew now with its rising and gathering strength, and in Virginia, and Brazil, and down the St. Lawrence valley, it shone intermittently through a driving reek of thunder-clouds, flickering violet lightning, and hail unprecedented. In Manitoba was a thaw and devastating floods. And upon all the mountains of the earth the snow and ice began to melt that night, and all the rivers coming out of high country flowed thick and turbid, and soon—in their upper reaches—with swirling trees and the bodies of beasts and men. They rose steadily, steadily in the ghostly brilliance, and came trickling over their banks at last, behind the flying population of their valleys.

And along the coast of Argentina and up the South Atlantic the tides were higher than had ever been in the memory of man, and the storms drove the waters in many cases scores of miles inland, drowning whole cities. And so great grew the heat during the night that the rising of the sun was like the coming of a shadow. The earthquakes began and grew until all down America, from the Arctic Circle to Cape Horn, hillsides were sliding, fissures were opening, and houses and walls crumbling to destruction. The whole side of Cotopaxi slipped out in one vast convulsion, and a tumult of lava poured out so high and broad and swift and liquid that in one day it reached the sea.

So the star, with the wan moon in its wake, marched across the Pacific, trailed the thunderstorms like the hem of a robe, and the growing tidal wave that toiled behind it, frothing and eager, poured over island and island and swept them clear of men. Until that wave came at last—in a blinding light and with the breath of a furnace, swift and terrible it came—a wall of water, fifty feet high, roaring hungrily, upon the long coasts of Asia, and swept inland across the plains of China. For a space the star, hotter now and larger and brighter than the sun in its strength, showed with pitiless brilliance the wide and populous country; towns and villages with their pagodas and trees, roads, wide cultivated fields, millions of sleepless people staring in helpless terror at the incandescent sky; and then, low and growing, came the murmur of the flood. And thus it was with millions of men that night—a flight nowhither, with limbs heavy with heat and breath fierce and scant, and the flood like a wall swift and white behind. And then death.

China was lit glowing white, but over Japan and Java and all the islands of Eastern Asia the great star was a ball of dull red fire because of the steam and smoke and ashes the volcanoes were spouting forth to salute its coming. Above was the lava, hot gases and ash, and below the seething floods, and the whole earth swayed and rumbled with the earthquake shocks. Soon the immemorial snows of Thibet and the Himalaya were melting and pouring down by ten million deepening converging channels upon the plains of Burmah and Hindostan. The tangled summits of the Indian jungles were aflame in a thousand places, and below the hurrying waters around the stems were dark objects that still struggled feebly and reflected the blood-red tongues of fire. And in a rudderless confusion a multitude of men and women fled down the broad river ways to that one last hope of men—the open sea.

Larger grew the star, and larger, hotter, and brighter with a terrible swiftness now. The tropical ocean had lost its phosphorescence, and the whirling steam rose in ghostly wreaths from the black waves that plunged incessantly, speckled with storm-tossed ships.

And then came a wonder. It seemed to those who in Europe watched for the rising of the star that the world must have ceased its rotation. In a thousand open spaces of down and upland the people who had fled thither from the floods and the falling houses and sliding slopes of hill watched for that rising in vain. Hour followed hour through a terrible suspense, and the star rose not. Once again men set their eyes upon the old constellations they had counted lost to them forever. In England it was hot and clear overhead, though the ground quivered perpetually, but in the tropics, Sirius and Capella and Aldebaran showed through a veil of steam. And when at last the great star rose near ten hours late, the sun rose close upon it, and in the centre of its white heart was a disc of black.

Over Asia it was the star had begun to fall behind the movement of the sky, and then suddenly, as it hung over India, its light had been veiled. All the plain of India from the mouth of the Indus to the mouths of the Ganges was a shallow waste of shining water that night, out of which rose temples and palaces, mounds and hills, black with people. Every minaret was a clustering mass of people, who fell one by one into the turbid waters, as heat and terror overcame them. The whole land seemed a-wailing and suddenly there a swept a shadow across that furnace of despair, and a breath of cold wind, and a gathering of clouds, out of the cooling air. Men looking up, near blinded, at the star, saw that a black disc was creeping across the light. It was the moon, coming between the star and the earth. And even as men cried to God at this respite, out of the East with a strange inexplicable swiftness sprang the sun. And then star, sun and moon rushed together across the heavens.

So it was that presently, to the European watchers, star and sun rose close upon each other, drove headlong for a space and then slower, and at last came to rest, star and sun merged into one glare of flame at the zenith of the sky. The moon no longer eclipsed the star but was lost to sight in the brilliance of the sky. And though those who were still alive regarded it for the most part with that dull stupidity that hunger, fatigue, heat and despair engender, there were still men who could perceive the meaning of these signs. Star and earth had been at their nearest, had swung about one another, and the star had passed. Already it was receding, swifter and swifter, in the last stage of its headlong journey downward into the sun.

And then the clouds gathered, blotting out the

vision of the sky, the thunder and lightning wove a garment round the world; all over the earth was such a downpour of rain as men had never before seen, and where the volcanoes flared red against the cloud canopy there descended torrents of mud. Everywhere the waters were pouring off the land, leaving mud-silted ruins, and the earth littered like a storm-worn beach with all that had floated, and the dead bodies of the men and brutes, its children. For days the water streamed off the land, sweeping away soil and trees and houses in the way, and piling huge dykes and scooping out Titanic gullies over the country side. Those were the days of darkness that followed the star and the heat. All through them, and for many weeks and months, the earthquakes continued.

But the star had passed, and men, hunger-driven and gathering courage only slowly, might creep back to their ruined cities, buried granaries, and sodden fields. Such few ships as had escaped the storms of that time came stunned and shattered and sounding their way cautiously through the new marks and shoals of once familiar ports. And as the storms subsided men perceived that everywhere the days were hotter than of yore, and the sun larger, and the moon, shrunk to a third of its former size, took now fourscore days between its new and new.

But of the new brotherhood that grew presently among men, of the saving of laws and books and machines, of the strange change that had come over Iceland and Greenland and the shores of Baffin's Bay, so that the sailors coming there presently found them green and gracious, and could scarce believe their eyes, this story does not tell. Nor of the movement of mankind now that the earth was hotter, northward and southward towards the poles of the earth. It concerns itself only with the coming and the passing of the Star.

The Martian astronomers—for there are astronomers on Mars, although they are very different beings from men—were naturally profoundly interested by these things. They saw them from their own standpoint of course. "Considering the mass and temperature of the missile that was flung through our solar system into the sun," one wrote, "it is astonishing what a little damage the earth, which it missed so narrowly, has sustained. All the familiar continental markings and the masses of the seas remain intact, and indeed the only difference seems to be a shrinkage of the white discoloration (supposed to be frozen water) round either pole." Which only shows how small the vastest of human catastrophes may seem, at a distance of a few million miles.

Stanley Weinbaum

This famous story of a human–alien encounter, set on Mars, astonished contemporary readers and critics by the degree to which it was – by 1930s understanding – realistically evoked. Published in the SF pulp magazine *Wonder Stories* (July 1934), it had an immediate impact. In *Before the Golden Age*, Isaac Asimov recalls how Weinbaum's 'easy style and his realistic description of extra-terrestrial scenes and life-forms were better than anything yet seen', adding, 'it had the effect on the field of an exploding grenade. With this single story, Weinbaum was instantly recognized as the world's best living science-fiction writer, and at once almost every writer in the field tried to imitate him.' Weinbaum died of lung cancer in his early thirties in 1935. Though aspects of this style of SF feel dated now, he is a fitting figure to mark the transition from the older styles of SF short story, standing at the threshold of a new golden age of SF writing.

Jarvis stretched himself as luxuriously as he could in the cramped general quarters of the *Ares*.

"Air you can breathe!" he exulted. "It feels as thick as soup after the thin stuff out there!" He nodded at the Martian landscape stretching flat and desolate in the light of the nearer moon, beyond the glass of the port.

The other three stared at him sympathetically—Putz, the engineer, Leroy, the biologist, and Harrison, the astronomer and captain of the expedition. Dick Jarvis was chemist of the famous crew, the *Ares* expedition, first human beings to set foot on the mysterious neighbor of the earth, the planet Mars. This, of course, was in the old days, less than twenty years after the mad American Doheny perfected the atomic blast at the cost of his life, and only a decade after the equally mad Cardoza rode on it to the moon. They were true pioneers, these four of the *Ares*. Except for a half-dozen moon expeditions and the ill-fated de Lancey flight aimed at the seductive orb of Venus, they were the first men to feel other gravity than earth's, and certainly the first successful crew to leave the earth–moon system. And they deserved that success when one considers the difficulties and discomforts—the months spent in acclimatization chambers back on earth, learning to breathe the air as tenuous as that of Mars, the challenging of the void in the tiny rocket driven by the cranky reaction motors of the twenty-first century, and mostly the facing of an absolutely unknown world.

Jarvis stretched and fingered the raw and peeling tip of his frost-bitten nose. He sighed again contentedly.

"Well," exploded Harrison abruptly, "are we going to hear what happened? You set out all shipshape in an auxiliary rocket, we don't get a peep for ten days, and finally Putz here picks you out of a lunatic ant-heap with a freak ostrich as your pal! Spill it, man!"

"Speel?" queried Leroy perplexedly. "Speel what?"

"He means '*spiel*'," explained Putz soberly. "It iss to tell."

Jarvis met Harrison's amused glance without the shadow of a smile. "That's right, Karl," he said in grave agreement with Putz. "*Ich spiel es!*" He grunted comfortably and began.

"According to orders," he said, "I watched Karl here take off toward the North, and then I got into my flying sweat-box and headed South. You'll remember, Cap—we had orders not to land, but just scout about for points of interest. I set the two cameras clicking and buzzed along, riding pretty high—about two thousand feet—for a couple of reasons. First, it gave the cameras a greater field, and second, the under-jets travel so far in this half-vacuum they call air here that they stir up dust if you move low."

"We know all that from Putz," grunted Harrison. "I wish you'd saved the films, though. They'd have paid the cost of this junket; remember how the public mobbed the first moon pictures?"

"The films are safe," retorted Jarvis. "Well," he resumed, "as I said, I buzzed along at a pretty good clip; just as we figured, the wings haven't much lift in this air at less than a hundred miles per hour, and even then I had to use the under-jets.

"So, with the speed and the altitude and the blurring caused by the under-jets, the seeing wasn't any too good. I could see enough, though, to distinguish that what I sailed over was just more of this grey plain that we'd been examining the whole week since our landing—same blobby growths and the same eternal carpet of crawling little plant-animals, or biopods, as Leroy calls them. So I sailed along, calling back my position every hour as instructed, and not knowing whether you heard me."

"I did!" snapped Harrison.

"A hundred and fifty miles south," continued

Jarvis imperturbably, "the surface changed to a sort of low plateau, nothing but desert and orange-tinted sand. I figured that we were right in our guess, then, and this grey plain we dropped on was really the Mare Cimmerium, which would make my orange desert the region called Xanthus. If I were right, I ought to hit another grey plain, the Mare Chronium, in another couple of hundred miles, and then another orange desert, Thyle I or II. And so I did."

"Putz verified our position a week and a half ago!" grumbled the captain. "Let's get to the point."

"Coming!" remarked Jarvis. "Twenty miles into Thyle—believe it or not—I crossed a canal!"

"Putz photographed a hundred! Let's hear something new!"

"And did he also see a city?"

"Twenty of 'em, if you call those heaps of mud cities!"

"Well," observed Jarvis, "from here on I'll be telling a few things Putz didn't see!" He rubbed his tingling nose, and continued. "I knew that I had sixteen hours of daylight at this season, so eight hours—eight hundred miles—from here, I decided to turn back. I was still over Thyle, whether I or II I'm not sure, not more than twenty-five miles into it. And right there, Putz's pet motor quit!"

"Quit? How?" Putz was solicitous.

"The atomic blast got weak. I started losing altitude right away, and suddenly there I was with a thump right in the middle of Thyle! Smashed my nose on the window, too!" He rubbed the injured member ruefully.

"Did you maybe try vashing der combustion chamber mit acid sulphuric?" inquired Putz. "Sometimes der lead giffs a secondary radiation—"

"Naw!" said Jarvis disgustedly. "I wouldn't try that, of course—not more than ten times! Besides, the bump flattened the landing gear and busted off the under-jets. Suppose I got the thing working—what then? Ten miles with the blast coming right out of the bottom and I'd have melted the floor from under me!" He rubbed his nose again. "Lucky for me a pound only weighs seven ounces here, or I'd have been mashed flat!"

"I could have fixed!" ejaculated the engineer. "I bet it vas not serious."

"Probably not," agreed Jarvis sarcastically. "Only it wouldn't fly. Nothing serious, but I had my choice of waiting to be picked up or trying to walk back—eight hundred miles, and perhaps twenty days before we had to leave! Forty miles a day! Well," he concluded, "I chose to walk. Just as much chance of being picked up, and it kept me busy."

"We'd have found you," said Harrison.

"No doubt. Anyway, I rigged up a harness from some seat straps, and put the water tank on my back, took a cartridge belt and revolver, and some iron rations, and started out."

"Water tank!" exclaimed the little biologist, Leroy. "She weigh one-quarter ton!"

"Wasn't full. Weighed about two hundred and fifty pounds earth-weight, which is eighty-five here. Then, besides, my own personal two hundred and ten pounds is only seventy on Mars, so, tank and all, I grossed a hundred and fifty-five, or fifty-five pounds less than my everyday earth-weight. I figured on that when I undertook the forty-mile daily stroll. Oh—of course I took a thermo-skin sleeping bag for these wintry Martian nights.

"Off I went, bouncing along pretty quickly. Eight hours of daylight meant twenty miles or more. It got tiresome, of course—plugging along over a soft sand desert with nothing to see, not even Leroy's crawling biopods. But an hour or so brought me to the canal—just a dry ditch about four hundred feet wide, and straight as a railroad on its own company map.

"There'd been water in it sometime, though. The ditch was covered with what looked like a nice green lawn. Only, as I approached, the lawn moved out of my way!"

"Eh?" said Leroy.

"Yeah, it was a relative of your biopods. I caught one—a little grass-like blade about as long as my finger, with two thin, stemmy legs."

"He is where?" Leroy was eager.

"He is let go! I had to move, so I plowed along with the walking grass opening in front and closing behind. And then I was out on the orange desert of Thyle again.

"I plugged steadily along, cussing the sand that made going so tiresome, and, incidentally, cussing that cranky motor of yours, Karl. It was just before twilight that I reached the edge of Thyle, and looked down over the gray Mare Chronium. And I knew there was seventy-five miles of *that* to be walked over, and then a couple of hundred miles of that Xanthus desert, and about as much more Mare Cimmerium. Was I pleased? I started cussing you fellows for not picking me up!"

"We were trying, you sap!" said Harrison.

"That didn't help. Well, I figured I might as well use what was left of daylight in getting down the cliff that bounded Thyle. I found an easy place, and down I went. Mare Chronium was just the same sort of place as this—crazy leafless plants and a bunch of crawlers; I gave it a glance and hauled out my sleeping bag. Up to that time, you know, I hadn't seen anything worth worrying about on this half-dead world—nothing dangerous, that is."

"Did you?" queried Harrison.

"*Did I!* You'll hear about it when I come to it. Well, I was just about to turn in when suddenly I heard the wildest sort of shenanigans!"

"Vot iss shenanigans?" inquired Putz.

"He says, 'Je ne sais quoi,'" explained Leroy. "It is to say, 'I don't know what.'"

"That's right," agreed Jarvis. "I didn't know what, so I sneaked over to find out. There was a racket like a flock of crows eating a bunch of canaries—whistles, cackles, caws, trills, and what have you. I rounded a clump of stumps, and there was Tweel!"

"Tweel?" said Harrison, and "Tveel?" said Lerov and Putz.

"That freak ostrich," explained the narrator. "At least, Tweel is as near as I can pronounce it without sputtering. He called it something like 'Trrrweerrlll.'"

"What was he doing?" asked the captain.

"He was being eaten! And squealing, of course, as any one would."

"Eaten! By what?"

"I found out later. All I could see then was a bunch of black ropy arms tangled around what looked like, as Putz described it to you, an ostrich.

I wasn't going to interfere, naturally; if both creatures were dangerous, I'd have one less to worry about.

"But the bird-like thing was putting up a good battle, dealing vicious blows with an eighteen-inch beak, between screeches. And besides, I caught a glimpse or two of what was on the end of those arms!" Jarvis shuddered. "But the clincher was when I noticed a little black bag or case hung about the neck of the bird-thing! It was intelligent! That or tame, I assumed. Anyway, it clinched my decision. I pulled out my automatic and fired into what I could see of its antagonist.

"There was a flurry of tentacles and a spurt of black corruption, and then the thing, with a disgusting sucking noise, pulled itself and its arms into a hole in the ground. The other let out a series of clacks, staggered around on legs about as thick as golf sticks, and turned suddenly to face me. I held my weapon ready, and the two of us stared at each other.

"The Martian wasn't a bird, really. It wasn't even bird-like, except just at first glance. It had a beak all right, and a few feathery appendages, but the beak wasn't really a beak. It was somewhat flexible; I could see the tip bend slowly from side to side; it was almost like a cross between a beak and a trunk. It had four-toed feet, and four fingered things—hands, you'd have to call them, and a little roundish body, and a long neck ending in a tiny head—and that beak. It stood an inch or so taller than I, and—well, Putz saw it!"

The engineer nodded. "*Ja!* I saw!"

Jarvis continued. "So—we stared at each other. Finally the creature went into a series of clackings and twitterings and held out its hands toward me, empty. I took that as a gesture of friendship."

"Perhaps," suggested Harrison, "it looked at that nose of yours and thought you were its brother!"

"Huh! You can be funny without talking! Anyway, I put up my gun and said 'Aw, don't mention it,' or something of the sort, and the thing came over and we were pals.

"By that time, the sun was pretty low and I knew that I'd better build a fire or get into my thermo-skin. I decided on the fire. I picked a spot at the base of the Thyle cliff, where the rock could reflect a little heat on my back. I started breaking off chunks of this desiccated Martian vegetation, and my companion caught the idea and brought in an armful. I reached for a match, but the Martian fished into his pouch and brought out something that looked like a glowing coal; one touch of it, and the fire was blazing—and you all know what a job we have starting a fire in this atmosphere!

"And that bag of his!" continued the narrator. "That was a manufactured article, my friends; press an end and she popped open—press the middle and she sealed so perfectly you couldn't see the line. Better than zippers.

"Well, we stared at the fire a while and I decided to attempt some sort of communication with the Martian. I pointed at myself and said 'Dick'; he caught the drift immediately, stretched a bony claw at me and repeated 'Tick.' Then I pointed at him, and he gave that whistle I called Tweel; I can't imitate his accent. Things were going smoothly; to emphasize the names, I repeated 'Dick,' and then, pointing at him, 'Tweel.'

"There we stuck! He gave some clacks that sounded negative, and said something like 'P-p-p-proot.' And that was just the beginning; I was always 'Tick,' but as for him—part of the time he was 'Tweel,' and part of the time he was 'P-p-p-proot,' and part of the time he was sixteen other noises!

"We just couldn't connect. I tried 'rock,' and I tried 'star,' and 'tree,' and 'fire,' and Lord knows what else, and try as I would, I couldn't get a single word! Nothing was the same for two successive minutes, and if that's a language, I'm an alchemist! Finally I gave it up and called him Tweel, and that seemed to do.

"But Tweel hung on to some of my words. He remembered a couple of them, which I suppose is a great achievement if you're used to a language you have to make up as you go along. But I couldn't get the hang of his talk; either I missed some subtle point or we just didn't *think* alike—and I rather believe the latter view.

"I've other reasons for believing that. After a while I gave up the language business, and tried mathematics. I scratched two plus two equals four on the ground, and demonstrated it with pebbles. Again Tweel caught the idea, and informed me that three plus three equals six. Once more we seemed to be getting somewhere.

"So, knowing that Tweel had at least a grammar school education, I drew a circle for the sun, pointing first at it, and then at the last glow of the sun. Then I sketched in Mercury, and Venus, and Mother Earth, and Mars, and finally, pointing to Mars, I swept my hand around in a sort of inclusive gesture to indicate that Mars was our current environment. I was working up to putting over the idea that my home was on the earth.

"Tweel understood my diagram all right. He poked his beak at it, and with a great deal of trilling and clucking, he added Deimos and Phobos to Mars, and then sketched in the earth's moon!

"Do you see what that proves? It proves that Tweel's race uses telescopes—that they're civilized!"

"Does not!" snapped Harrison. "The moon is visible from here as a fifth magnitude star. They could see its revolution with the naked eye."

"The moon, yes!" said Jarvis. "You've missed my point. Mercury isn't visible! And Tweel knew of Mercury because he placed the Moon at the *third* planet, not the second. If he didn't know Mercury, he'd put the earth second, and Mars third, instead of fourth! See?"

"Humph!" said Harrison.

"Anyway," proceeded Jarvis, "I went on with my lesson. Things were going smoothly, and it looked as if I could put the idea over. I pointed at the earth on my diagram, and then at myself, and then, to clinch it, I pointed to myself and then to the earth itself shining bright green almost at the zenith.

"Tweel set up such an excited clacking that I was certain he understood. He jumped up and down, and suddenly he pointed at himself and then at the sky, and then at himself and at the sky again. He pointed at his middle and then at Arcturus, at his head and then at Spica, at his feet and then at half a dozen stars, while I just gaped at him. Then, all of a sudden, he gave a tremendous leap. Man, what a hop! He shot straight up into the starlight, seventy-five feet if an inch! I saw him silhouetted against the sky, saw him turn and come down at me head first, and land smack on his beak like a javelin! There he stuck square in the center of my sun-circle in the sand—a bull's eye!"

"Nuts!" observed the captain. "Plain nuts!"

"That's what I thought, too! I just stared at him open-mouthed while he pulled his head out of the sand and stood up. Then I figured he'd missed my point, and I went through the whole blamed rigamarole again, and it ended the same way, with Tweel on his nose in the middle of my picture!"

"Maybe it's a religious rite," suggested Harrison.

"Maybe," said Jarvis dubiously. "Well, there we were. We could exchange ideas up to a certain point, and then—blooey! Something in us was different, unrelated; I don't doubt that Tweel thought me just as screwy as I thought him. Our minds simply looked at the world from different viewpoints, and perhaps his viewpoint is as true as ours. But—we couldn't get together, that's all. Yet, in spite of all difficulties, I *liked* Tweel, and I have a queer certainty that he liked me."

"Nuts!" repeated the captain. "Just daffy!"

"Yeah? Wait and see. A couple of times I've thought that perhaps we—" He paused, and then resumed his narrative. "Anyway, I finally gave it up, and got into my thermo-skin to sleep. The fire hadn't kept me any too warm, but that damned sleeping bag did. Got stuffy five minutes after I closed myself in. I opened it a little and bingo! Some eighty-below-zero air hit my nose, and that's when I got this pleasant little frostbite to add to the bump I acquired during the crash of my rocket.

"I don't know what Tweel made of my sleeping. He sat around, but when I woke up, he was gone. I'd just crawled out of my bag, though, when I heard some twittering, and there he came, sailing down from that three-story Thyle cliff to alight on his beak beside me. I pointed to myself and toward the north, and he pointed at himself and toward the south, but when I loaded up and started away, he came along.

"Man, how he traveled! A hundred and fifty feet at a jump, sailing through the air stretched out like a spear, and landing on his beak. He seemed surprised at my plodding, but after a few moments he fell in beside me, only every few minutes he'd go into one of his leaps, and stick his nose into the sand a block ahead of me. Then he'd come shooting back at me; it made me nervous at first to see that beak of his coming at me like a spear, but he always ended in the sand at my side.

"So the two of us plugged along across the Mare Chronium. Same sort of place as this—same crazy plants and same little green biopods growing in the sand, or crawling out of your way. We talked—not that we understood each other, you know, but just for company. I sang songs, and I suspect Tweel did too; at least, some of his trillings and twitterings had a subtle sort of rhythm.

"Then, for variety, Tweel would display his smattering of English words. He'd point to an outcropping and say 'rock,' and point to a pebble and say it again; or he'd touch my arm and say 'Tick,' and then repeat it. He seemed terrifically amused that the same word meant the same thing twice in succession, or that the same word could apply to two different objects. It set me wondering if perhaps his language wasn't like the primitive speech of some earth people—you know, Captain, like the Negritoes, for instance, who haven't any generic words. No word for food or water or man—words for good food and bad food, or rain water and sea water, or strong man and weak man—but no names for general classes. They're too primitive to understand that rain water and sea water are just different aspects of the same thing. But that wasn't the case with Tweel; it was just that we were somehow mysteriously different—our minds were alien to each other. And yet—we *liked* each other!"

"Looney, that's all," remarked Harrison. "That's why you two were so fond of each other."

"Well, I like *you!*" countered Jarvis wickedly. "Anyway," he resumed, "don't get the idea that there was anything screwy about Tweel. In fact, I'm not so sure but that he couldn't teach our highly praised human intelligence a trick or two. Oh, he wasn't an intellectual superman, I guess; but don't overlook the point that he managed to understand a little of my mental workings, and I never even got a glimmering of his."

"Because he didn't have any!" suggested the captain, while Putz and Leroy blinked attentively.

"You can judge of that when I'm through," said Jarvis. "Well, we plugged along across the Mare Chronium all that day, and all the next. Mare Chronium—Sea of Time! Say, I was willing to agree with Schiaparelli's name by the end of that march! Just that grey, endless plain of weird plants, and never a sign of any other life. It was so monotonous that I was even glad to see the desert of Xanthus toward the evening of the second day.

"I was fair worn out, but Tweel seemed as fresh as ever, for all I never saw him drink or eat. I think he could have crossed the Mare Chronium in a couple of hours with those block-long nose dives of his, but he stuck along with me. I offered him some water once or twice; he took the cup from me and sucked the liquid into his beak, and then carefully squirted it all back into the cup and gravely returned it.

"Just as we sighted Xanthus, or the cliffs that bounded it, one of those nasty sand clouds blew along, not as bad as the one we had here, but mean to travel against. I pulled the transparent flap of my thermo-skin bag across my face and managed pretty well, and I noticed that Tweel used some feathery appendages growing like a mustache at the base of his beak to cover his nostrils, and some similar fuzz to shield his eyes."

"He is a desert creature!" ejaculated the little biologist, Leroy.

"Huh? Why?"

"He drink no water—he is adapt' for sand storm—"

"Proves nothing! There's not enough water to waste any where on this desiccated pill called Mars. We'd call all of it desert on earth, you know." He paused. "Anyway, after the sand storm blew over, a little wind kept blowing in our faces, not strong enough to stir the sand. But suddenly things came drifting along from the Xanthus cliffs—small, transparent spheres, for all the world like glass tennis balls! But light—they were almost light enough to float even in this thin air—empty, too; at least, I cracked open a couple and nothing came out but a bad smell. I asked Tweel about them, but all he said was 'No, no, no,' which I took to mean that he knew nothing about them. So they went bouncing by like tumbleweeds, or like soap bubbles, and we plugged on toward Xanthus. Tweel pointed at one of the crystal balls once and said 'rock,' but I was too tired to argue with him. Later I discovered what he meant.

"We came to the bottom of the Xanthus cliffs finally, when there wasn't much daylight left. I decided to sleep on the plateau if possible; anything dangerous, I reasoned, would be more likely to prowl through the vegetation of the Mare Chronium than the sand of Xanthus. Not that I'd seen a single sign of menace, except the rope-armed black thing that had trapped Tweel, and apparently that didn't prowl at all, but lured its victims within reach. It couldn't lure me while I slept, especially as Tweel didn't seem to sleep at all, but simply sat patiently around all night. I wondered how the creature had managed to trap Tweel, but there wasn't any way of asking him. I found that out too, later; it's devilish!

"However, we were ambling around the base of the Xanthus barrier looking for an easy spot to climb. At least, I was. Tweel could have leaped it easily, for the cliffs were lower than Thyle—perhaps sixty feet. I found a place and started up, swearing at the water tank strapped to my back—it didn't bother me except when climbing—and suddenly I heard a sound that I thought I recognized!

"You know how deceptive sounds are in this thin air. A shot sounds like the pop of a cork. But this sound was the drone of a rocket, and sure enough, there went our second auxiliary about ten miles to westward, between me and the sunset!"

"Vas me!" said Putz. "I hunt for you."

"Yeah; I knew that, but what good did it do me? I hung on to the cliff and yelled and waved with one hand. Tweel saw it too, and set up a trilling and twittering, leaping to the top of the barrier and then high into the air. And while I watched, the machine droned on into the shadows to the south.

"I scrambled to the top of the cliff. Tweel was still pointing and trilling excitedly, shooting up toward the sky and coming down head-on to stick upside down on his beak in the sand. I pointed toward the south and at myself, and he said, 'Yes—Yes—Yes'; but somehow I gathered that he thought the flying thing was a relative of mine, probably a parent. Perhaps I did his intellect an injustice; I think now that I did.

"I was bitterly disappointed by the failure to attract attention. I pulled out my thermo-skin bag and crawled into it, as the night chill was already apparent. Tweel stuck his beak into the sand and drew up his legs and arms and looked for all the world like one of those leafless shrubs out there. I think he stayed that way all night."

"Protective mimicry!" ejaculated Leroy. "See? He is desert creature!"

"In the morning," resumed Jarvis, "we started off again. We hadn't gone a hundred yards into Xanthus when I saw something queer! This is one thing Putz didn't photograph, I'll wager!

"There was a line of little pyramids—tiny ones, not more than six inches high, stretching across Xanthus as far as I could see! Little buildings made of pygmy bricks, they were, hollow inside and truncated, or at least broken at the top and empty. I pointed at them and said 'What?' to Tweel, but he gave some negative twitters to indicate, I suppose, that he didn't know. So off we went, following the row of pyramids because they ran north, and I was going north.

"Man, we trailed that line for hours! After a while, I noticed another queer thing: they were getting larger. Same number of bricks in each one, but the bricks were larger.

"By noon they were shoulder high. I looked into a couple—all just the same, broken at the top and empty. I examined a brick or two as well; they were silica, and old as creation itself!"

"How you know?" asked Leroy.

"They were weathered—edges rounded. Silica doesn't weather easily even on earth, and in this climate—!"

"How old you think?"

"Fifty thousand—a hundred thousand years. How can I tell? The little ones we saw in the morning were older—perhaps ten times as old. Crumbling. How old would that make *them?* Half a million years? Who knows?" Jarvis paused a moment. "Well," he resumed, "we followed the line. Tweel pointed at them and said 'rock' once or twice, but he'd done that many times before. Besides, he was more or less right about these.

"I tried questioning him. I pointed at a pyramid and asked 'People?' and indicated the two of us. He set up a negative sort of clucking and said, 'No, no, no. No one-one-two. No two-two-four,' meanwhile rubbing his stomach. I just stared at him and he went through the business again. 'No one-one-two. No two-two-four.' I just gaped at him."

"That proves it!" exclaimed Harrison. "Nuts!"

"You think so?" queried Jarvis sardonically. "Well, I figured it out different! 'No one-one-two!' You don't get it, of course, do you?"

"Nope—nor do you!"

"I think I do! Tweel was using the few English words he knew to put over a very complex idea. What, let me ask, does mathematics make you think of?"

"Why—of astronomy. Or—or logic!"

"That's it! 'No one-one-two!' Tweel was telling me that the builders of the pyramids weren't people—or that they weren't intelligent, that they weren't reasoning creatures! Get it?"

"Huh! I'll be damned!"

"You probably will."

"Why," put in Leroy, "he rub his belly?"

"Why? Because, my dear biologist, that's where his brains are! Not in his tiny head—in his middle!"

"*C'est impossible!*"

"Not on Mars, it isn't! This flora and fauna aren't earthly; your biopods prove that!" Jarvis grinned and took up his narrative. "Anyway, we plugged along across Xanthus and in about the middle of the afternoon, something else queer happened. The pyramids ended."

"Ended!"

"Yeah; the queer part was that the last one—and now they were ten-footers—was capped! See? Whatever built it was still inside; we'd trailed 'em from their half-million-year-old origin to the present.

"Tweel and I noticed it about the same time. I yanked out my automatic (I had a clip of Boland explosive bullets in it) and Tweel, quick as a sleight-of-hand trick, snapped a queer little glass revolver out of his bag. It was much like our weapons, except that the grip was larger to accommodate his four-taloned hand. And we held our weapons ready while we sneaked up along the lines of empty pyramids.

"Tweel saw the movement first. The top tiers of bricks were heaving, shaking, and suddenly slid down the sides with a thin crash. And then—something—something was coming out!

"A long, silvery-grey arm appeared, dragging after it an armored body. Armored, I mean, with scales, silver-grey and dull-shining. The arm heaved the body out of the hole; the beast crashed to the sand.

"It was a nondescript creature—body like a big grey cask, arm and a sort of mouth-hole at one end; stiff, pointed tail at the other—and that's all. No other limbs, no eyes, ears, nose—nothing! The thing dragged itself a few yards, inserted its pointed tail in the sand, pushed itself upright, and just sat.

"Tweel and I watched it for ten minutes before it moved. Then, with a creaking and rustling like—oh, like crumpling stiff paper—its arm moved to the mouth-hole and out came a brick! The arm placed the brick carefully on the ground, and the thing was still again.

"Another ten minutes—another brick. Just one of Nature's bricklayers. I was about to slip away and move on when Tweel pointed at the thing and said 'rock'! I went 'huh?' and he said it again. Then, to the accompaniment of some of his trilling, he said, 'No—no—,' and gave two or three whistling breaths.

"Well, I got his meaning, for a wonder! I said, 'No breath?' and demonstrated the word. Tweel was ecstatic; he said, 'Yes, yes, yes! No, no, no breet!' Then he gave a leap and sailed out to land on his nose about one pace from the monster!

"I was startled, you can imagine! The arm was going up for a brick, and I expected to see Tweel caught and mangled, but—nothing happened! Tweel pounded on the creature, and the arm took the brick and placed it neatly beside the first. Tweel rapped on its body again, and said 'rock,' and I got up nerve enough to take a look myself.

"Tweel was right again. The creature was rock, and it didn't breathe!"

"How you know?" snapped Leroy, his black eyes blazing interest.

"Because I'm a chemist. The beast was made of silica! There must have been pure silicon in the sand, and it lived on that. Get it? We, and Tweel, and those plants out there, and even the biopods are *carbon* life; this thing lived by a different set of chemical reactions. It was silicon life!"

"*La vie silicieuse!*" shouted Leroy. "I have suspect, and now it is proof! I must go see! *Il faut que je—*"

"All right! All right!" said Jarvis. "You can go see. Anyhow, there the thing was, alive and yet not alive, moving every ten minutes, and then only to remove a brick. Those bricks were its waste matter. See, Frenchy? We're carbon, and our waste is carbon dioxide, and this thing is silicon, and its waste is silicon dioxide—silica. But silica is a solid, hence the bricks. And it builds itself in, and when it is covered, it moves over to a fresh place to start over. No wonder it creaked! A living creature half a million years old!"

"How you know how old?" Leroy was frantic.

"We trailed its pyramids from the beginning, didn't we? If this weren't the original pyramid builder, the series would have ended somewhere before we found him, wouldn't it?—ended and started over with the small ones. That's simple enough, isn't it?

"But he reproduces, or tries to. Before the third brick came out, there was a little rustle and out popped a whole stream of those little crystal balls.

They're his spores, or eggs, or seeds—call 'em what you want. They went bouncing by across Xanthus just as they'd bounced by us back in the Mare Chronium. I've a hunch how they work, too—this is for your information, Leroy. I think the crystal shell of silica is no more than a protective covering, like an eggshell, and that the active principle is the smell inside. It's some sort of gas that attacks silicon, and if the shell is broken near a supply of that element, some reaction starts that ultimately develops into a beast like that one."

"You should try!" exclaimed the little Frenchman. "We must break one to see!"

"Yeah? Well, I did. I smashed a couple against the sand. Would you like to come back in about ten thousand years to see if I planted some pyramid monsters? You'd most likely be able to tell by that time!" Jarvis paused and drew a deep breath. "Lord! That queer creature! Do you picture it? Blind, deaf, nerveless, brainless—just a mechanism, and yet—immortal! Bound to go on making bricks, building pyramids, as long as silicon and oxygen exist, and even afterwards it'll just stop. It won't be dead. If the accidents of a million years bring it its food again, there it'll be, ready to run again, while brains and civilizations are part of the past. A queer beast—yet I met a stranger one!"

"If you did, it must have been in your dreams!" growled Harrison.

"You're right!" said Jarvis soberly. "In a way, you're right. The dream-beast! That's the best name for it—and it's the most fiendish, terrifying creation one could imagine! More dangerous than a lion, more insidious than a snake!"

"Tell me!" begged Leroy. "I must go see!"

"Not this devil!" He paused again. "Well," he resumed, "Tweel and I left the pyramid creature and plowed along through Xanthus. I was tired and a little disheartened by Putz's failure to pick me up, and Tweel's trilling got on my nerves, as did his flying nosedives. So I just strode along without a word, hour after hour across that monotonous desert.

"Toward mid-afternoon we came in sight of a low dark line on the horizon. I knew what it was. It was a canal; I'd crossed it in the rocket and it meant that we were just one-third of the way across Xanthus. Pleasant thought, wasn't it? And still, I was keeping up to schedule.

"We approached the canal slowly; I remembered that this one was bordered by a wide fringe of vegetation and that Mudheap City was on it.

"I was tired, as I said. I kept thinking of a good hot meal, and then from that I jumped to reflections of how nice and home-like even Borneo would seem after this crazy planet, and from that, to thoughts of little old New York, and then to thinking about a girl I know there—Fancy Long. Know her?"

"Vision entertainer," said Harrison. "I've tuned her in. Nice blonde—dances and sings on the *Yerba Mate* hour."

"That's her," said Jarvis ungrammatically. "I know her pretty well—just friends, get me?—though she came down to see us off in the *Ares*. Well, I was thinking about her, feeling pretty lonesome, and all the time we were approaching that line of rubbery plants.

"And then—I said, 'What 'n Hell!' and stared. And there she was—Fancy Long, standing plain as day under one of those crack-brained trees, and smiling and waving just the way I remembered her when we left!"

"Now you're nuts, too!" observed the captain.

"Boy, I almost agreed with you! I stared and pinched myself and closed my eyes and then stared again—and every time, there was Fancy Long smiling and waving! Tweel saw something, too; he was trilling and clucking away, but I scarcely heard him. I was bounding toward her over the sand, too amazed even to ask myself questions.

"I wasn't twenty feet from her when Tweel caught me with one of his flying leaps. He grabbed my arm, yelling, 'No—no—no!' in his squeaky voice. I tried to shake him off—he was as light as if he were built of bamboo—but he dug his claws in and yelled. And finally some sort of sanity returned to me and I stopped less than ten feet from her. There she stood, looking as solid as Putz's head!"

"Vot?" said the engineer.

"She smiled and waved, and waved and smiled, and I stood there dumb as Leroy, while Tweel squeaked and chattered. I *knew* it couldn't be real, yet—there she was!

"Finally I said, 'Fancy! Fancy Long!' She just kept on smiling and waving, but looking as real as if I hadn't left her thirty-seven million miles away.

"Tweel had his glass pistol out, pointing it at her. I grabbed his arm, but he tried to push me away. He pointed at her and said, 'No breet! No breet!' and I understood that he meant that the Fancy Long thing wasn't alive. Man, my head was whirling!

"Still, it gave me the jitters to see him pointing his weapon at her. I don't know why I stood there watching him take careful aim, but I did. Then he squeezed the handle of his weapon; there was a little puff of steam, and Fancy Long was gone! And in her place was one of those writhing, black, rope-armed horrors like the one I'd saved Tweel from!

"The dream-beast! I stood there dizzy, watching

it die while Tweel trilled and whistled. Finally he touched my arm, pointed at the twisting thing, and said, 'You one-one-two, he one-one-two.' After he'd repeated it eight or ten times, I got it. Do any of you?"

"*Oui!*" shrilled Leroy. "*Moi—je le comprends!* He mean you think of something, the beast he know, and you see it! *Un chien*—a hungry dog, he would see the big bone with meat! Or smell it—not?"

"Right!" said Jarvis. "The dream-beast uses its victim's longings and desires to trap its prey. The bird at nesting season would see its mate, the fox, prowling for its own prey, would see a helpless rabbit!"

"How he do?" queried Leroy.

"How do I know? How does a snake back on earth charm a bird into its very jaws? And aren't there deep-sea fish that lure their victims into their mouths? Lord!" Jarvis shuddered. "Do you see how insidious the monster is? We're warned now—but henceforth we can't trust even our eyes. You might see me—I might see one of you—and back of it may be nothing but another of those black horrors!"

"How'd your friend know?" asked the captain abruptly.

"Tweel? I wonder! Perhaps he was thinking of something that couldn't possibly have interested me, and when I started to run, he realized that I saw something different and was warned. Or perhaps the dream-beast can only project a single vision, and Tweel saw what I saw—or nothing. I couldn't ask him. But it's just another proof that his intelligence is equal to ours or greater."

"He's daffy, I tell you!" said Harrison. "What makes you think his intellect ranks with the human?"

"Plenty of things! First, the pyramid-beast. He hadn't seen one before; he said as much. Yet he recognized it as a dead-alive automaton of silicon."

"He could have heard of it," objected Harrison. "He lives around here, you know."

"Well how about the language? I couldn't pick up a single idea of his and he learned six or seven words of mine. And do you realize what complex ideas he put over with no more than those six or seven words? The pyramid-monster—the dream-beast! In a single phrase he told me that one was a harmless automaton and the other a deadly hypnotist. What about that?"

"Huh!" said the captain.

"*Huh* if you wish! Could you have done it knowing only six words of English? Could you go even further, as Tweel did, and tell me that another creature was of a sort of intelligence so different from ours that understanding was impossible—even more impossible than that between Tweel and me?"

"Eh? What was that?"

"Later. The point I'm making is that Tweel and his race are worthy of our friendship. Somewhere on Mars—and you'll find I'm right—is a civilization and culture equal to ours, and maybe more than equal. And communication is possible between them and us; Tweel proves that. It may take years of patient trial, for their minds are alien, but less alien than the next minds we encountered—if they are minds."

"The next ones? What next ones?"

"The people of the mud cities along the canals." Jarvis frowned, then resumed his narrative. "I thought the dream-beast and the silicon-monster were the strangest beings conceivable, but I was wrong. These creatures are still more alien, less understandable than either and far less comprehensible than Tweel, with whom friendship is possible, and even, by patience and concentration, the exchange of ideas.

"Well," he continued, "We left the dream-beast dying, dragging itself back into its hole, and we moved toward the canal. There was a carpet of that queer walking-grass scampering out of our way, and when we reached the bank, there was a yellow trickle of water flowing. The mound city I'd noticed from the rocket was a mile or so to the right and I was curious enough to want to take a look at it.

"It had seemed deserted from my previous glimpse of it, and if any creatures were lurking in it—well, Tweel and I were both armed. And by the way, that crystal weapon of Tweel's was an interesting device; I took a look at it after the dream-beast episode. It fired a little glass splinter, poisoned, I suppose, and I guess it held at least a hundred of 'em to a load. The propellant was steam—just plain steam!"

"Shteam!" echoed Putz. "From vot come, shteam?"

"From water, of course! You could see the water through the transparent handle and about a gill of another liquid, thick and yellowish. When Tweel squeezed the handle—there was no trigger—a drop of water and a drop of the yellow stuff squirted into the firing chamber, and the water vaporized—pop!—like that. It's not so difficult; I think we could develop the same principle. Concentrated sulphuric acid will heat water almost to boiling, and so will quicklime, and there's potassium and sodium—

"Of course, his weapon hadn't the range of mine, but it wasn't so bad in this thin air, and it *did* hold as many shots as a cowboy's gun in a Western movie. It was effective, too, at least against Martian life; I tried it out, aiming at one of the crazy plants, and darned if the plant didn't wither up and fall apart! That's why I think the glass splinters were poisoned.

"Anyway, we trudged along toward the mud-heap city and I began to wonder whether the city builders dug the canals. I pointed to the city and then at the canal, and Tweel said 'No—no—no!' and gestured toward the south. I took it to mean that some other race had created the canal system, perhaps Tweel's people. I don't know; maybe there's still another intelligent race on the planet, or a dozen others. Mars is a queer little world.

"A hundred yards from the city we crossed a sort of road—just a hard-packed mud trail, and then, all of a sudden, along came one of the mound builders!

"Man, talk about fantastic beings! It looked rather like a barrel trotting along on four legs with four other arms or tentacles. It had no head, just body and members and a row of eyes completely around it. The top end of the barrel-body was a diaphragm stretched as tight as a drum head, and that was all. It was pushing a little coppery cart and tore right past us like the proverbial bat out of Hell. It didn't even notice us, although I thought the eyes on my side shifted a little as it passed.

"A moment later another came along, pushing another empty cart. Same thing—it just scooted past us. Well, I wasn't going to be ignored by a bunch of barrels playing train, so when the third one approached, I planted myself in the way—ready to jump, of course, if the thing didn't stop.

"But it did. It stopped and set up a sort of drumming from the diaphragm on top. And I held out both hands and said, 'We are friends!' And what do you suppose the thing did?"

"Said, 'Pleased to meet you,' I'll bet!" suggested Harrison.

"I couldn't have been more surprised if it had! It drummed on its diaphragm, and then suddenly boomed out, 'We are v-r-r-riends!' and gave its pushcart a vicious poke at me! I jumped aside, and away it went while I stared dumbly after it.

"A minute later another one came hurrying along. This one didn't pause, but simply drummed out, 'We are v-r-r-riends!' and scurried by. How did it learn the phrase? Were all of the creatures in some sort of communication with each other? Were they all parts of some central organism? I don't know, though I think Tweel does.

"Anyway, the creatures went sailing past us, every one greeting us with the same statement. It got to be funny; I never thought to find so many friends on this God-forsaken ball! Finally I made a puzzled gesture to Tweel; I guess he understood, for he said, 'One-one-two—yes!—two-two-four—no!' Get it?"

"Sure," said Harrison. "It's a Martian nursery rhyme."

"Yeah! Well, I was getting used to Tweel's symbolism, and I figured it out this way. 'One-one-two—yes!' The creatures were intelligent. 'Two-two-four—no!' Their intelligence was not of our order, but something different and beyond the logic of two and two is four. Maybe I missed his meaning. Perhaps he meant that their minds were of low degree, able to figure out the simple things—'One-one-two—yes!'—but not more difficult things—'Two-two-four—no!' But I think from what we saw later that he meant the other.

"After a few moments, the creatures came rushing back—first one, then another. Their pushcarts were full of stones, sand, chunks of rubbery plants, and such rubbish as that. They droned out their friendly greeting, which didn't really sound so friendly, and dashed on. The third one I assumed to be my first acquaintance and I decided to have another chat with him. I stepped into his path again and waited.

"Up he came, booming out his 'We are v-r-riends' and stopped. I looked at him; four or five of his eyes looked at me. He tried his password again and gave a shove on his cart, but I stood firm. And then the—the dashed creature reached out one of his arms, and two finger-like nippers tweaked my nose!"

"Haw!" roared Harrison. "Maybe the things have a sense of beauty!"

"Laugh!" grumbled Jarvis. "I'd already had a nasty bump and a mean frostbite on that nose. Anyway, I yelled 'Ouch!' and jumped aside and the creature dashed away; but from then on, their greeting was 'We are v-r-r-riends! Ouch!' Queer beasts!

"Tweel and I followed the road squarely up to the nearest mound. The creatures were coming and going, paying us not the slightest attention, fetching their loads of rubbish. The road simply dived into an opening, and slanted down like an old mine, and in and out darted the barrel-people, greeting us with their eternal phrase.

"I looked in; there was a light somewhere below, and I was curious to see it. It didn't look like a flame or torch, you understand, but more like a civilized light, and I thought that I might get some clue as to the creatures' development. So in I went and Tweel tagged along, not without a few trills and twitters, however.

"The light was curious; it sputtered and flared like an old arc light, but came from a single black rod set in the wall of the corridor. It was electric, beyond doubt. The creatures were fairly civilized, apparently.

"Then I saw another light shining on something that glittered and I went on to look at that, but it was only a heap of shiny sand. I turned toward the entrance to leave, and the Devil take me if it wasn't gone!

"I suppose the corridor had curved, or I'd stepped into a side passage. Anyway, I walked back in that direction I thought we'd come, and all I saw was more dimlit corridor. The place was a labyrinth! There was nothing but twisting passages running every way, lit by occasional lights, and now and then a creature running by, sometimes with a pushcart, sometimes without.

"Well, I wasn't much worried at first. Tweel and I had only come a few steps from the entrance. But every move we made after that seemed to get us in deeper. Finally I tried following one of the creatures with an empty cart, thinking that he'd be going out for his rubbish, but he ran around aimlessly, into one passage and out another. When he started dashing around a pillar like one of those Japanese waltzing mice, I gave up, dumped my water tank on the floor, and sat down.

"Tweel was as lost as I. I pointed up and he said 'No—no—no!' in a sort of helpless trill. And we couldn't get any help from the natives. They paid no attention at all, except to assure us they were friends—ouch!

"Lord! I don't know how many hours or days we wandered around there! I slept twice from sheer exhaustion; Tweel never seemed to need sleep. We tried following only the upward corridors, but they'd run uphill a ways and then curve downwards. The temperature in that damned ant hill was constant; you couldn't tell night from day and after my first sleep I didn't know whether I'd slept one hour or thirteen, so I couldn't tell from my watch whether it was midnight or noon.

"We saw plenty of strange things. There were machines running in some of the corridors, but they didn't seem to be doing anything—just wheels turning. And several times I saw two barrel-beasts with a little one growing between them, joined to both."

"Parthenogenesis!" exulted Leroy. "Parthenogenesis by budding like *les tulipes!*"

"If you say so, Frenchy," agreed Jarvis. "The things never noticed us at all, except, as I say, to greet us with 'We are v-r-r-riends! Ouch!' They seemed to have no home-life of any sort, but just scurried around with their pushcarts, bringing in rubbish. And finally I discovered what they did with it.

"We'd had a little luck with a corridor, one that

slanted upwards for a great distance. I was feeling that we ought to be close to the surface when suddenly the passage debouched into a domed chamber, the only one we'd seen. And man!—I felt like dancing when I saw what looked like daylight through a crevice in the roof.

"There was a—a sort of machine in the chamber, just an enormous wheel that turned slowly, and one of the creatures was in the act of dumping his rubbish below it. The wheel ground it with a crunch—sand, stones, plants, all into powder that sifted away somewhere. While we watched, others filed in, repeating the process, and that seemed to be all. No rhyme nor reason to the whole thing—but that's characteristic of this crazy planet. And there was another fact that's almost too bizarre to believe.

"One of the creatures, having dumped his load, pushed his cart aside with a crash and calmly shoved himself under the wheel! I watched him being crushed, too stupefied to make a sound, and a moment later, another followed him! They were perfectly methodical about it, too; one of the cartless creatures took the abandoned pushcart.

"Tweel didn't seem surprised; I pointed out the next suicide to him, and he just gave the most human-like shrug imaginable, as much as to say,

'What can I do about it?' He must have known more or less about these creatures.

"Then I saw something else. There was something beyond the wheel, something shining on a sort of low pedestal. I walked over; there was a little crystal about the size of an egg, fluorescing to beat Tophet. The light from it stung my hands and face, almost like a static discharge, and then I noticed another funny thing. Remember that wart I had on my left thumb? Look!" Jarvis extended his hand. "It dried up and fell off—just like that! And my abused nose—say, the pain went out of it like magic! The thing had the property of hard x-rays or gamma radiations, only more so; it destroyed diseased tissue and left healthy tissue unharmed!

"I was thinking what a present *that'd* be to take back to Mother Earth when a lot of racket interrupted. We dashed back to the other side of the wheel in time to see one of the pushcarts ground up. Some suicide had been careless, it seems.

"Then suddenly the creatures were booming and drumming all around us and their noise was decidedly menacing. A crowd of them advanced toward us; we backed out of what I thought was the passage we'd entered by, and they came rumbling after us, some pushing carts and some not. Crazy brutes! There was a whole chorus of 'We are v-r-r-riends! Ouch!' I didn't like the 'ouch'; it was rather suggestive.

"Tweel had his glass gun out and I dumped my water tank for greater freedom and got mine. We backed up the corridor with the barrel-beasts following—about twenty of them. Queer thing—the ones coming in with loaded carts moved past us inches away without a sign.

"Tweel must have noticed that. Suddenly, he snatched out that glowing coal cigar-lighter of his and touched a cart-load of plant limbs. Puff! The whole load was burning—and the crazy beast pushing it went right along without a change of pace! It created some disturbance among our 'V-r-r-riends,' however—and then I noticed the smoke eddying and swirling past us, and sure enough, there was the entrance!

"I grabbed Tweel and out we dashed and after us our twenty pursuers. The daylight felt like Heaven, though I saw at first glance that the sun was all but set, and that was bad, since I couldn't live outside my thermo-skin bag in a Martian night—at least, without a fire.

"And things got worse in a hurry. They cornered us in an angle between two mounds, and there we stood. I hadn't fired, nor had Tweel; there wasn't any use in irritating the brutes. They stopped a little distance away and began their booming about friendship and ouches.

"Then things got still worse! A barrel-brute came out with a pushcart and they all grabbed into it and came out with handfuls of foot-long copper darts—sharp-looking ones—and all of a sudden one sailed past my ear—zing! And it was shoot or die then.

"We were doing pretty well for a while. We picked off the ones next to the pushcart and managed to keep the darts at a minimum, but suddenly there was a thunderous booming of 'v-r-r-riends' and 'ouches,' and a whole army of 'em came out of their hole.

"Man! We were through and I knew it! Then I realized that Tweel wasn't. He could have leaped the mound behind us as easily as not. He was staying for me!

"Say, I could have cried if there'd been time! I'd liked Tweel from the first, but whether I'd have had gratitude to do what he was doing—suppose I *had* saved him from the first dream-beast—he'd done as much for me, hadn't he? I grabbed his arm, and said 'Tweel,' and pointed up, and he understood. He said, 'No—no—no, Tick!' and popped away with his glass pistol.

"What could I do? I'd be a goner anyway when the sun set, but I couldn't explain that to him. I said, 'Thanks, Tweel. You're a man!' and felt that I wasn't paying him any compliment at all. A man! There are mighty few men who'd do that.

"So I went 'bang' with my gun and Tweel went 'puff' with his, and the barrels were throwing darts and getting ready to rush us, and booming about being friends. I had given up hope. Then suddenly an angel dropped right down from Heaven in the shape of Putz, with his under-jets blasting the barrels into very small pieces!

"Wow! I let out a yell and dashed for the rocket; Putz opened the door and in I went, laughing and crying and shouting! It was a moment or so before I remembered Tweel; I looked around in time to see him rising in one of his nosedives over the mound and away.

"I had a devil of a job arguing Putz into following! By the time we got the rocket aloft, darkness was down; you know how it comes here—like turning off a light. We sailed out over the desert and put down once or twice. I yelled 'Tweel!' and yelled it a hundred times, I guess. We couldn't find him; he could travel like the wind and all I got—or else I imagined it—was a faint trilling and twittering drifting out of the south. He'd gone, and damn it! I wish—I wish he hadn't!"

The four men of the *Ares* were silent—even the

sardonic Harrison. At last little Leroy broke the stillness.

"I should like to see," he murmured.

"Yeah," said Harrison. "And the wart-cure. Too bad you missed that; it might be the cancer cure they've been hunting for a century and a half."

"Oh, that!" muttered Jarvis gloomily. "That's what started the fight!" He drew a glistening object from his pocket.

"Here it is."

Fitz-James O'Brien

Michael O'Brien was born in Ireland in 1826. After a colourful youth in which he burned through an inheritance of £8,000 – a lot of money back then – and served for a time in the army, he emigrated to the USA in 1852, taking the opportunity to reinvent himself under a new name, the more aristocratic-sounding Fitz-James. He made a living writing stories for magazines such as *Harper's Magazine*, *Vanity Fair* and the *Atlantic Monthly*. A number of his stories had strikingly original science-fiction premises. 'The Diamond Lens', a strange and wondrous combination of microscopy, spiritualism and love, is probably his most famous short story, but 'The Wonder Smith' (1859), about some toys who become possessed by evil spirits and rise up against humanity, is an early example of the 'robot rebellion' trope, and 'What Was It? A Mystery' (1859) is an early example of invisibility fiction. When the American Civil War began, O'Brien enlisted for the North, and died of wounds in 1862.

The Diamond Lens

I

THE BENDING OF THE TWIG

From a very early period of my life the entire bent of my inclinations had been towards microscopic investigations. When I was not more than ten years old, a distant relative of our family, hoping to astonish my inexperience, constructed a simple microscope for me, by drilling in a disk of copper a small hole, in which a drop of pure water was sustained by capillary attraction. This very primitive apparatus, magnifying some fifty diameters, presented, it is true, only indistinct and imperfect forms, but still sufficiently wonderful to work up my imagination to a preternatural state of excitement.

Seeing me so interested in this rude instrument, my cousin explained to me all that he knew about the principles of the microscope, related to me a few of the wonders which had been accomplished through its agency, and ended by promising to send me one regularly constructed, immediately on his return to the city. I counted the days, the hours, the minutes, that intervened between that promise and his departure.

Meantime I was not idle. Every transparent substance that bore the remotest resemblance to a lens

I eagerly seized upon, and employed in vain attempts to realise that instrument, the theory of whose construction I as yet only vaguely comprehended. All panes of glass containing those oblate spheroidal knots familiarly known as "bull's-eyes" were ruthlessly destroyed, in the hope of obtaining lenses of marvellous power. I even went so far as to extract the crystalline humour from the eyes of fishes and animals, and endeavoured to press it into the microscopic service. I plead guilty to having stolen the glasses from my Aunt Agatha's spectacles, with a dim idea of grinding them into lenses of wondrous magnifying properties,—in which attempt it is scarcely necessary to say that I totally failed.

At last the promised instrument came. It was of that order known as Field's simple microscope, and had cost perhaps about fifteen dollars. As far as educational purposes went, a better apparatus could not have been selected. Accompanying it was a small treatise on the microscope,—its history, uses, and discoveries. I comprehended then for the first time the "Arabian Nights' Entertainments." The dull veil of ordinary existence that hung across the world seemed suddenly to roll away, and to lay bare a land of enchantments. I felt towards my companions as the seer might feel towards the ordinary masses of men. I held conversations with nature in a tongue which they could not understand. I was in daily communication with living wonders, such as they never imagined in their wildest visions. I penetrated beyond the external portal of things, and roamed through the sanctuaries. Where they beheld only a drop of rain slowly rolling down the window-glass, I saw a universe of beings animated with all the passions common to physical life, and convulsing their minute sphere with struggles as fierce and protracted as those of men. In the common spots of mould, which my mother, good housekeeper that she was, fiercely scooped away from her jam pots, there abode for me, under the name of mildew, enchanted gardens, filled with dells and avenues of the densest foliage and most astonishing verdure, while from the fantastic boughs of these microscopic forests hung strange fruits glittering with green, and silver, and gold.

It was no scientific thirst that at this time filled my mind. It was the pure enjoyment of a poet to whom a world of wonders has been disclosed. I talked of my solitary pleasures to none. Alone with my microscope, I dimmed my sight, day after day and night after night, poring over the marvels which it unfolded to me. I was like one who, having discovered the ancient Eden still existing in all its primitive glory, should resolve to enjoy it in solitude, and never betray to mortal the secret of its locality. The rod of my life was bent at this moment. I destined myself to be a microscopist.

Of course, like every novice, I fancied myself a discoverer. I was ignorant at the time of the thousands of acute intellects engaged in the same pursuit as myself, and with the advantage of instruments a thousand times more powerful than mine. The names of Leeuwenhoek, Williamson, Spencer, Ehrenberg, Schultz, Dujardin, Schact, and Schleiden were then entirely unknown to me, or if known, I was ignorant of their patient and wonderful researches. In every fresh specimen of cryptogamia which I placed beneath my instrument I believed that I discovered wonders of which the world was as yet ignorant. I remember well the thrill of delight and admiration that shot through me the first time that I discovered the common wheel animalcule (*Rotifera vulgaris*) expanding and contracting its flexible spokes, and seemingly rotating through the water. Alas! as I grew older, and obtained some works treating of my favourite study, I found that I was only on the threshold of a science to the investigation of which some of the greatest men of the age were devoting their lives and intellects.

As I grew up, my parents, who saw but little likelihood of anything practical resulting from the examination of bits of moss and drops of water through a brass tube and a piece of glass, were anxious that I should choose a profession. It was their desire that I should enter the counting-house of my uncle, Ethan Blake, a prosperous merchant, who carried on business in New York. This suggestion I decisively combated. I had no taste for trade; I should only make a failure; in short, I refused to become a merchant.

But it was necessary for me to select some pursuit. My parents were staid New England people, who insisted on the necessity of labour; and therefore, although, thanks to the bequest of my poor Aunt Agatha, I should, on coming of age, inherit a small fortune sufficient to place me above want, it was decided that, instead of waiting for this, I should act the nobler part, and employ the intervening years in rendering myself independent.

After much cogitation I complied with the wishes of my family, and selected a profession. I determined to study medicine at the New York Academy. This disposition of my future suited me. A removal from my relatives would enable me to dispose of my time as I pleased without fear of detection. As long as I paid my Academy fees, I might shirk attending the lectures if I chose; and, as I never had the remotest intention of standing an examination, there was no danger of my being "plucked". Besides, a metropolis was the place for me. There I could obtain excellent instruments, the newest publications, intimacy with men of pursuits kindred with my own,—in short, all things necessary to insure a profitable devotion of my life to my beloved science. I had an abundance of money, few desires that were not bounded by my illuminating mirror on one side and my object-glass on the other; what, therefore, was to prevent my becoming an illustrious investigator of the veiled worlds? It was with the most buoyant hope that I left my New England home and established myself in New York.

II

THE LONGING OF A MAN OF SCIENCE

My first step, of course, was to find suitable apartments. These I obtained, after a couple of days' search, in Fourth Avenue; a very pretty second-floor unfurnished, containing sitting-room, bedroom, and a smaller apartment which I intended to fit up as a laboratory. I furnished my lodgings simply, but rather elegantly, and then devoted all my energies to the adornment of the temple of my worship. I visited Pike, the celebrated optician, and passed in review his splendid collection of microscopes,—Field's Compound, Hingham's, Spencer's, Nachet's Binocular, (that founded on the principles of the stereoscope,) and at length fixed upon that form known as Spencer's Trunnion Microscope, as combining the greatest number of improvements with an almost perfect freedom from tremor. Along with this I purchased every possible accessory,—draw-tubes, micrometers, a *camera-lucida*, lever-stage, achromatic condensers, white cloud illuminators, prisms, parabolic condensers, polarising apparatus, forceps, aquatic boxes, fishing-tubes, with a host of other articles, all of which would have been useful in the hands of an experienced microscopist, but, as I afterwards discovered, were not of the slightest present value to me. It takes years of practice to know how to use a complicated microscope. The optician looked suspiciously at me as I made these wholesale purchases. He evidently was uncertain whether to set me down as some scientific celebrity or a madman. I think he inclined to the latter belief. I suppose I was mad. Every great genius is mad upon the subject in which he is greatest. The unsuccessful madman is disgraced and called a lunatic.

Mad or not, I set myself to work with a zeal which few scientific students have ever equalled. I had everything to learn relative to the delicate study upon which I had embarked,—a study involving the most earnest patience, the most rigid analytic powers, the steadiest hand, the most untiring eye, the most refined and subtle manipulation.

For a long time half my apparatus lay inactively on the shelves of my laboratory, which was now most amply furnished with every possible contrivance for facilitating my investigations. The fact was that I did not know how to use some of my scientific implements,—never having been taught microscopics,—and those whose use I understood theoretically were of little avail, until by practice I could attain the necessary delicacy of handling. Still, such was the fury of my ambition, such the untiring perseverance of my experiments, that, difficult of credit as it may be, in the course of one year I became theoretically and practically an accomplished microscopist.

During this period of my labours, in which I submitted specimens of every substance that came under my observation to the action of my lenses, I became a discoverer,—in a small way, it is true, for I was very young, but still a discoverer. It was I who destroyed Ehrenberg's theory that the *Volvox globator* was an animal, and proved that his "monads" with stomachs and eyes were merely phases of the formation of a vegetable cell, and were, when they reached their mature state, incapable of the act of conjugation, or any true generative act, without which no organism rising to any stage of life higher than vegetable can be said to be complete. It was I who resolved the singular problem of rotation in the cells and hairs of plants into ciliary attraction, in spite of the assertions of Mr. Wenham and others, that my explanation was the result of an optical illusion.

But notwithstanding these discoveries, laboriously and painfully made as they were, I felt horribly dissatisfied. At every step I found myself stopped by the imperfections of my instruments. Like all active microscopists, I gave my imagination full play. Indeed, it is a common complaint against many such, that they supply the defects of their instruments with the creations of their brains. I imagined depths beyond depths in nature which the limited power of my lenses prohibited me from exploring. I lay awake at night constructing imaginary microscopes of immeasurable power, with which I seemed to pierce through all the envelopes of matter down to its original atom. How I cursed those imperfect mediums which necessity through ignorance compelled me to use! How I longed to discover the secret of some perfect lens, whose magnifying power should be limited only by the resolvability of the object, and which at the same time should be free from spherical and chromatic aberrations, in short from all the obstacles over which the poor microscopist finds himself continually stumbling! I felt convinced that the simple microscope, composed of a single lens of such vast yet perfect power, was possible of construction. To attempt to bring the compound microscope up to such a pitch would have been commencing at the wrong end; this latter being simply a partially successful endeavour to remedy those very defects of the simple instrument, which, if conquered, would leave nothing to be desired.

It was in this mood of mind that I became a constructive microscopist. After another year passed in this new pursuit, experimenting on every imaginable substance,—glass, gems, flints, crystals, artificial crystals formed of the alloy of various vitreous materials,—in short, having constructed as many varieties of lenses as Argus had eyes, I found myself precisely where I had started, with nothing gained save an extensive knowledge of glass-making. I was almost dead with despair. My parents were surprised at my apparent want of progress in my medical studies, (I had not attended one lecture since my arrival in the city,) and the expenses of my mad pursuit had been so great as to embarrass me very seriously.

I was in this frame of mind one day, experimenting in my laboratory on a small diamond,—that stone, from its great refracting power, having always occupied my attention more than any other,—when a young Frenchman, who lived on the second floor above me, and who was in the habit of occasionally visiting me, entered the room.

I think that Jules Simon was a Jew. He had many traits of the Hebrew character: a love of jewelry, of dress, and of good living. There was something mysterious about him. He always had something to sell, and yet went into excellent society. When I say sell, I should perhaps have said peddle; for his operations were generally confined to the disposal of single articles,—a picture, for instance, or a rare carving in ivory, or a pair of duelling-pistols, or the dress of a Mexican *caballero*. When I was first furnishing my rooms, he paid me a visit, which ended in my purchasing an antique silver lamp, which he assured me was a Cellini,—it was handsome enough even for that,—and some other knickknacks for my sitting-room. Why Simon should pursue this petty trade I never could imagine. He apparently had plenty of money, and had the *entrée* of the best houses in the city,—taking care, however, I suppose, to drive no bargains within the enchanted circle of the Upper Ten. I came at length to the conclusion that this peddling was but a mask to cover some greater object, and even went so far as to believe my young acquaintance to be implicated in the slave-trade. That, however, was none of my affair.

On the present occasion, Simon entered my room in a state of considerable excitement.

'*Ah! mon ami!*' he cried, before I could even offer him the ordinary salutation, 'it has occurred to me to be the witness of the most astonishing things in the world. I promenade myself to the house of Madame . . . How does the little animal—*le renard*—name himself in the Latin?'

'Vulpes,' I answered.

'Ah! yes,—Vulpes. I promenade myself to the house of Madame Vulpes.'

'The spirit medium?'

'Yes, the great medium. Great heavens! what a woman! I write on a slip of paper many of questions concerning affairs the most secret,—affairs that conceal themselves in the abysses of my heart the most profound; and behold! by example! what occurs?—This devil of a woman makes me replies the most truthful to all of them. She talks to me of things that I do not love to talk of to myself. What am I to think? I am fixed to the earth!'

'Am I to understand you, M. Simon, that this Mrs. Vulpes replied to questions secretly written by you, which questions related to events known only to yourself?'

'Ah! more than that, more than that,' he answered with an air of some alarm. 'She related to me things—But,' he added, after a pause, and suddenly changing his manner, 'why occupy ourselves with these follies? It was all the biology, without doubt. It goes without saying that it has not my credence. —But why are we here, *mon ami*? It has occurred to me to discover the most beautiful thing as you can imagine,—a vase with green lizards on it, composed by the great Bernard Palissy. It is in my apartment; let us mount. I go to show it to you.'

I followed Simon mechanically; but my thoughts were far from Palissy and his enamelled ware, although I, like him, was seeking in the dark a great discovery. This casual mention of the spiritualist, Madame Vulpes, set me on a new track. What if this spiritualism should be really a great fact? What if, through communication with more subtile organisms than my own, I could reach at a single bound the goal, which perhaps a life of agonising mental toil would never enable me to attain?

While purchasing the Palissy vase from my friend Simon, I was mentally arranging a visit to Madame Vulpes.

III

THE SPIRIT OF LEEUWENHOEK

Two evenings after this, thanks to an arrangement by letter and the promise of an ample fee, I found

Madame Vulpes awaiting me at her residence alone. She was a coarse-featured woman, with keen and rather cruel dark eyes, and an exceedingly sensual expression about her mouth and under-jaw. She received me in perfect silence, in an apartment on the ground floor, very sparely furnished. In the centre of the room, close to where Mrs. Vulpes sat, there was a common round mahogany table. If I had come for the purpose of sweeping her chimney, the woman could not have looked more indifferent to my appearance. There was no attempt to inspire the visitor with awe. Everything bore a simple and practical aspect. This intercourse with the spiritual world was evidently as familiar an occupation with Mrs. Vulpes as eating her dinner or riding in an omnibus.

'You come for a communication, Mr. Linley?' said the medium, in a dry, business-like tone of voice.

'By appointment,—yes.'

'What sort of communication do you want?—a written one?'

'Yes,—I wish for a written one.'

'From any particular spirit?'

'Yes.'

'Have you ever known this spirit on this earth?'

'Never. He died long before I was born. I wish merely to obtain from him some information which he ought to be able to give better than any other.'

'Will you seat yourself at the table, Mr. Linley,' said the medium, 'and place your hands upon it?'

I obeyed,—Mrs. Vulpes being seated opposite to me, with her hands also on the table. We remained thus for about a minute and a half, when a violent succession of raps came on the table, on the back of my chair, on the floor immediately under my feet, and even on the windowpanes. Mrs. Vulpes smiled composedly.

'They are very strong tonight,' she remarked. 'You are fortunate.' She then continued, 'Will the spirits communicate with this gentleman?'

Vigorous affirmative.

'Will the particular spirit he desires to speak with communicate?'

A very confused rapping followed this question.

'I know what they mean,' said Mrs. Vulpes, addressing herself to me; 'they wish you to write down the name of the particular spirit that you desire to converse with. Is that so?' she added, speaking to her invisible guests.

That it was so was evident from the numerous affirmatory responses. While this was going on, I tore a slip from my pocket-book, and scribbled a name, under the table.

'Will this spirit communicate in writing with this gentleman?' asked the medium once more.

After a moment's pause, her hand seemed to be seized with a violent tremor, shaking so forcibly that the table vibrated. She said that a spirit had seized her hand and would write. I handed her some sheets of paper that were on the table and a pencil. The latter she held loosely in her hand, which presently began to move over the paper with a singular and seemingly involuntary motion. After a few moments had elapsed, she handed me the paper, on which I found written, in a large uncultivated hand, the words, 'He is not here, but has been sent for.' A pause of a minute or so now ensued, during which Mrs. Vulpes remained perfectly silent, but the raps continued at regular intervals. When the short period I mentioned had elapsed, the hand of the medium was again seized with its convulsive tremor, and she wrote, under this strange influence, a few words on the paper, which she handed to me. They were as follows:-

I am here. Question me.

Leeuwenhoek.

I was astounded. The name was identical with that I had written beneath the table, and carefully kept concealed. Neither was it at all probable that an uncultivated woman like Mrs. Vulpes should know even the name of the great father of microscopics. It may have been biology; but this theory was soon doomed to be destroyed. I wrote on my slip—still concealing it from Mrs. Vulpes—a series of questions, which, to avoid tediousness, I shall place with the responses in the order in which they occurred:

I.—Can the microscope be brought to perfection?

Spirit.—Yes.

I.—Am I destined to accomplish this great task?

Spirit.—You are.

I.—I wish to know how to proceed to attain this end. For the love which you bear to science, help me!

Spirit.—A diamond of one hundred and forty carats, submitted to electro-magnetic currents for a long period, will experience a rearrangement of its atoms *inter se*, and from that stone you will form the universal lens.

I.—Will great discoveries result from the use of such a lens?

Spirit.—So great that all that has gone before is as nothing.

I.—But the refractive power of the diamond is so immense, that the image will be formed within the lens. How is that difficulty to be surmounted?

Spirit.—Pierce the lens through its axis, and the difficulty is obviated. The image will be formed in the pierced space, which will itself serve as a tube to look through. Now I am called. Good night.

I cannot at all describe the effect that these extraordinary communications had upon me. I felt completely bewildered. No biological theory could account for the *discovery* of the lens. The medium might, by means of biological *rapport* with my mind, have gone so far as to read my questions, and reply to them coherently. But biology could not enable her to discover that magnetic currents would so alter the crystals of the diamond as to remedy its previous defects, and admit of its being polished into a perfect lens. Some such theory may have passed through my head, it is true; but if so, I had forgotten it. In my excited condition of mind there was no course left but to become a convert, and it was in a state of the most painful nervous exaltation that I left the medium's house that evening. She accompanied me to the door, hoping that I was satisfied. The raps followed us as we went through the hall, sounding on the balusters, the flooring, and even the lintels of the door. I hastily expressed my satisfaction, and escaped hurriedly into the cool night air. I walked home with but one thought possessing me,—how to obtain a diamond of the immense size required. My entire means multiplied a hundred times over would have been inadequate to its purchase. Besides, such stones are rare, and become historical. I could find such only in the regalia of Eastern or European monarchs.

IV

THE EYE OF MORNING

There was a light in Simon's room as I entered my house. A vague impulse urged me to visit him. As I opened the door of his sitting-room unannounced, he was bending, with his back toward me, over a carcel lamp, apparently engaged in minutely examining some object which he held in his hands. As I entered, he started suddenly, thrust his hand into his breast pocket, and turned to me with a face crimson with confusion.

'What!' I cried, 'poring over the miniature of some fair lady? Well, don't blush so much; I won't ask to see it.'

Simon laughed awkwardly enough, but made none of the negative protestations usual on such occasions. He asked me to take a seat.

'Simon,' I said, 'I have just come from Madame Vulpes.'

This time Simon turned as white as a sheet, and seemed stupefied, as if a sudden electric shock had smitten him. He babbled some incoherent words, and went hastily to a small closet where he usually kept his liquors. Although astonished at his emotions, I was too preoccupied with my own idea to pay much attention to anything else.

'You say truly when you call Madame Vulpes a devil of a woman,' I continued. 'Simon, she told me wonderful things tonight, or rather was the means of telling me wonderful things. Ah! if I could only get a diamond that weighed one hundred and forty carats!'

Scarcely had the sigh with which I uttered this desire died upon my lips, when Simon, with the aspect of a wild beast, glared at me savagely, and, rushing to the mantelpiece, where some foreign weapons hung on the wall, caught up a Malay creese, and brandished it furiously before him.

'No!' he cried in French, into which he always broke when excited. 'No! you shall not have it! You are perfidious! You have consulted with that demon, and desire my treasure! But I will die first! Me! I am brave! You cannot make me fear!'

All this, uttered in a loud voice trembling with excitement, astounded me. I saw at a glance that I had accidentally trodden upon the edges of Simon's secret, whatever it was. It was necessary to reassure him.

'My dear Simon,' I said, 'I am entirely at a loss to know what you mean. I went to Madame Vulpes to consult with her on a scientific problem, to the solution of which I discovered that a diamond of the size I just mentioned was necessary. You were never alluded to during the evening, nor, so far as I was concerned, even thought of. What can be the meaning of this outburst? If you happen to have a set of valuable diamonds in your possession, you need fear nothing from me. The diamond which I require you could not possess; or, if you did possess it, you would not be living here.'

Something in my tone must have completely reassured him; for his expression immediately changed to a sort of constrained merriment, combined, however, with a certain suspicious attention to my movements. He laughed, and said that I must bear with him; that he was at certain moments subject to a species of vertigo, which betrayed itself in incoherent speeches, and that the attacks passed off as rapidly as they came. He put his weapon aside while making this explanation, and endeavoured, with some success, to assume a more cheerful air.

All this did not impose on me in the least. I was too much accustomed to analytical labours to be baffled by so flimsy a veil. I determined to probe the mystery to the bottom.

'Simon,' I said, gayly, 'let us forget all this over a bottle of burgundy. I have a case of Lausseure's *Clos Vougeot* downstairs, fragrant with the odours and ruddy with the sunlight of the Côte d'Or. Let us have up a couple of bottles. What say you?'

'With all my heart,' answered Simon, smilingly.

I produced the wine and we seated ourselves to drink. It was a famous vintage, that of 1848, a year when war and wine throve together,—and its pure but powerful juice seemed to impart renewed vitality to the system. By the time we had half finished the second bottle, Simon's head, which I knew was a weak one, had begun to yield, while I remained calm as ever, only that every draught seemed to send a flush of vigour through my limbs. Simon's utterance became more and more indistinct. He took to singing French *chansons* of a not very moral tendency. I rose suddenly from the table just at the conclusion of one of those incoherent verses, and, fixing my eyes on him with a quiet smile, said: 'Simon, I have deceived you. I learned your secret this evening. You may as well be frank with me. Mrs. Vulpes, or rather one of her spirits, told me all.'

He started with horror. His intoxication seemed for the moment to fade away, and he made a movement towards the weapon that he had a short time before laid down. I stopped him with my hand.

'Monster!' he cried passionately, 'I am ruined! What shall I do? You shall never have it! I swear by my mother!'

'I don't want it,' I said; 'rest secure, but be frank with me. Tell me all about it.'

The drunkenness began to return. He protested with maudlin earnestness that I was entirely mistaken,—that I was intoxicated; then asked me to swear eternal secrecy, and promised to disclose the mystery to me. I pledged myself, of course, to all. With an uneasy look in his eyes, and hands unsteady with drink and nervousness, he drew a small case from his breast and opened it. Heavens! How the mild lamp-light was shivered into a thousand prismatic arrows, as it fell upon a vast rose-diamond that glittered in the case! I was no judge of diamonds, but I saw at a glance that this was a gem of rare size and purity. I looked at Simon with wonder, and—must I confess it?—with envy. How could he have obtained this treasure? In reply to my question, I could just gather from his drunken statements (of which, I fancy, half the incoherence was affected) that he had been superintending a gang of slaves engaged in diamond washing in Brazil; that he had seen one of them secrete a diamond, but, instead of informing his employers, had quietly watched the negro until he saw him bury his treasure; that he had dug it up and fled with it, but that as yet he was afraid to attempt to dispose of it publicly,—so valuable a gem being almost certain to attract too much attention to its owner's antecedents,—and he had not been able to discover any of those obscure channels by which such matters are conveyed away safely. He added that, in accordance with oriental practice, he had named his diamond with the fanciful title of 'The Eye of Morning.'

While Simon was relating this to me, I regarded the great diamond attentively. Never had I beheld anything so beautiful. All the glories of light, ever imagined or described, seemed to pulsate in its crystalline chambers. Its weight, as I learned from Simon, was exactly one hundred and forty carats. Here was an amazing coincidence. The hand of destiny seemed in it. On the very evening when the spirit of Leeuwenhoek communicates to me the great secret of the microscope, the priceless means which he directs me to employ start up within my easy reach! I determined, with the most perfect deliberation, to possess myself of Simon's diamond.

I sat opposite to him while he nodded over his glass, and calmly revolved the whole affair. I did not for an instant contemplate so foolish an act as a common theft, which would of course be discovered, or at least necessitate flight and concealment, all of which must interfere with my scientific plans. There was but one step to be taken,—to kill Simon. After all, what was the life of a little peddling Jew, in comparison with the interests of science? Human beings are taken every day from the condemned prisons to be experimented on by surgeons. This man, Simon, was by his own confession a criminal, a robber, and I believed on my soul a murderer. He deserved death quite as much as any felon condemned by the laws: why should I not, like government, contrive that his punishment should contribute to the progress of human knowledge?

The means for accomplishing everything I desired lay within my reach. There stood upon the mantelpiece a bottle half full of French laudanum. Simon was so occupied with his diamond, which I had just restored to him, that it was an affair of no difficulty to drug his glass. In a quarter of an hour he was in a profound sleep.

I now opened his waistcoat, took the diamond from the inner pocket in which he had placed it, and removed him to the bed, on which I laid him so that his feet hung down over the edge, I had possessed myself of the Malay creese, which I held in my right hand, while with the other I discovered as accurately as I could by pulsation the exact location of the heart. It was essential that all the aspects of his death should lead to the surmise of self-murder. I calculated the exact angle at which it was probable that the weapon, if levelled by Simon's own hand, would enter his breast; then with one powerful blow I thrust it up to the hilt in the very spot which I desired to penetrate. A convulsive thrill ran through Simon's limbs. I heard a smothered sound issue from his throat, precisely like the bursting of a large air-bubble, sent up by a diver, when it reaches the surface of the water; he turned half round on his side, and, as if to assist my plans more effectually, his right hand, moved by some mere spasmodic impulse, clasped the handle of the creese, which it remained holding with extraordinary muscular tenacity. Beyond this there was no apparent struggle. The laudanum, I presume, paralysed the usual nervous action. He must have died instantly.

There was yet something to be done. To make it certain that all suspicion of the act should be diverted from any inhabitant of the house of Simon himself, it was necessary that the door should be found in the morning *locked on the inside*. How to do this, and afterwards escape myself? Not by the window; that was a physical impossibility. Besides, I was determined that the windows *also* should be found bolted. The solution was simple enough. I descended softly to my own room for a peculiar instrument which I had used for holding small slippery substances, such as minute spheres of glass, etc. This instrument was nothing more than a long slender hand-vice, with a very powerful grip, and a considerable leverage, which last was accidentally owing to the shape of the handle. Nothing was simpler than, when the key was in the lock, to seize the end of its stem in this vice, through the keyhole, from the outside, and so lock the door. Previously, however, to doing this, I burned a number of papers on Simon's hearth. Suicides almost always burn papers before they destroy themselves. I also emptied some more laudanum into Simon's glass,—having first removed from it all traces of wine,—cleaned the other wine glass, and brought the bottles away with me. If traces of two persons drinking had been found in the room, the question naturally would have arisen, who was the second? Besides, the wine bottles might have been identified as belonging to me. The laudanum I poured out to account for its presence in his stomach, in case of a *post-mortem* examination. The theory naturally would be, that he first intended to poison himself, but, after swallowing a little of the drug, was either disgusted with its taste, or changed his mind from other motives, and chose the dagger. These arrangements made, I walked out, leaving the gas burning, locked the door with my vice, and went to bed.

Simon's death was not discovered until nearly three in the afternoon. The servant, astonished at seeing the gas burning,—the light streaming on the dark landing from under the door,—peeped through the keyhole and saw Simon on the bed. She gave the alarm. The door was burst open, and the neighbourhood was in a fever of excitement.

Every one in the house was arrested, myself included. There was an inquest; but no clue to his death beyond that of suicide could be obtained. Curiously enough, he had made several speeches to his friends the preceding week, that seemed to point to self-destruction. One gentleman swore that Simon had said in his presence that 'he was tired of life.' His landlord affirmed that Simon, when paying him his last month's rent, remarked that 'he should not pay him rent much longer.' All the other evidence corresponded,—the door locked inside, the position of the corpse, the burnt papers. As I anticipated, no one knew of the possession of the diamond by Simon, so that no motive was suggested for his murder. The jury, after a prolonged examination, brought in the usual verdict, and the neighbourhood once more settled down into its accustomed quiet.

V

ANIMULA

The three months succeeding Simon's catastrophe I devoted night and day to my diamond lens. I had constructed a vast galvanic battery, composed of nearly two thousand pairs of plates,—a higher power

I dared not use, lest the diamond should be calcined. By means of this enormous engine I was enabled to send a power current of electricity continually through my great diamond, which it seemed to me gained in lustre every day. At the expiration of a month I commenced the grinding and polishing of the lens, a work of intense toil and exquisite delicacy. The great density of the stone, and the care required to be taken with the curvatures of the surfaces of the lens, rendered the labour the severest and most harassing that I had yet undergone.

At last the eventful moment came; the lens was completed. I stood trembling on the threshold of new worlds. I had the realisation of Alexander's famous wish before me. The lens lay on the table, ready to be placed upon its platform. My hand fairly shook as I enveloped a drop of water with a thin coating of oil of turpentine, preparatory to its examination,—a process necessary in order to prevent the rapid evaporation of the water. I now placed the drop on a thin slip of glass under the lens, and throwing upon it, by the combined aid of a prism and a mirror, a powerful stream of light, I approached my eye to the minute hole drilled through the axis of the lens. For an instant I saw nothing save what seemed to be an illuminated chaos, a vast luminous abyss. A pure white light, cloudless and serene, and seemingly limitless as space itself, was my first impression. Gently, and with the greatest care, I depressed the lens a few hair's-breadths. The wondrous illumination still continued, but as the lens approached the object a scene of indescribable beauty was unfolded to my view.

I seemed to gaze upon a vast space, the limits of which extended far beyond my vision. An atmosphere of magical luminousness permeated the entire field of view. I was amazed to see no trace of animalculous life. Not a living thing, apparently, inhabited that dazzling expanse. I comprehended instantly that, by the wondrous power of my lens, I had penetrated beyond the grosser particles of aqueous matter, beyond the realms of infusoria and protozoa, down to the original gaseous globule, into whose luminous interior I was gazing, as into an almost boundless dome filled with a supernatural radiance.

It was, however, no brilliant void into which I looked. On every side I beheld beautiful inorganic forms, of unknown texture, and coloured with the most enchanting hues. These forms presented the appearance of what might be called, for want of a more specific definition, foliated clouds of the highest rarity; that is, they undulated and broke into vegetable formations, and were tinged with splendours compared with which the gilding of our autumn woodlands is as dross compared with gold. Far away into the illimitable distance stretched long avenues of these gaseous forests, dimly transparent, and painted with prismatic hues of unimaginable brilliancy. The pendent branches waved along the fluid glades until every vista seemed to break through half-lucent ranks of many coloured drooping silken pennons. What seemed to be either fruits or flowers, pied with a thousand hues, lustrous and ever varying, bubbled from the crowns of this fairy foliage. No hills, no lakes, no rivers, no forms animate or inanimate, were to be seen, save those vast auroral copses that floated serenely in the luminous stillness, with leaves and fruits and flowers gleaming with unknown fires, unrealisable by mere imagination.

How strange, I thought, that this sphere should be thus condemned to solitude! I had hoped, at least, to discover some new form of animal life,—perhaps of a lower class than any with which we are at present acquainted, but still, some living organism. I found my newly discovered world, if I may so speak, a beautiful chromatic desert.

While I was speculating on the singular arrangements of the internal economy of Nature, with which she so frequently splinters into atoms our most compact theories, I thought, I beheld a form moving slowly through the glades of one of the prismatic forests. I looked more attentively, and found that I was not mistaken. Words cannot depict the anxiety with which I awaited the nearer approach of this mysterious object. Was it merely some inanimate substance, held in suspense in the attenuated atmosphere of the globule? or was it an animal endowed with vitality and motion? It approached, flitting behind the gauzy, coloured veils of cloud-foliage, for seconds dimly revealed, then vanishing. At last the violet pennons that trailed nearest to me vibrated; they were gently pushed aside, and the form floated out into the broad light.

It was a female human shape. When I say human, I mean it possessed the outlines of humanity,—but there the analogy ends. Its adorable beauty lifted it illimitable heights beyond the loveliest daughter of Adam.

I cannot, I dare not, attempt to inventory the charms of this divine revelation of perfect beauty. Those eyes of mystic violet, dewy and serene, evade my words. Her long, lustrous hair following her glorious head in a golden wake, like the track sown in heaven by a falling star, seems to quench my most burning phrases with its splendours. If all the bees of Hybla nestled upon my lips, they would still sing but hoarsely the wondrous harmonies of outline that enclosed her form.

She swept out from between the rainbow-curtains of the cloud-trees into the broad sea of light that lay beyond. Her motions were those of some graceful naiad, cleaving, by a mere effort of her will, the clear, unruffled waters that fill the chambers of the sea. She floated forth with the serene grace of a frail bubble ascending through the still atmosphere of a June day. The perfect roundness of her limbs formed suave and enchanting curves. It was like listening to the most spiritual symphony of Beethoven the divine, to watch the harmonious flow of lines. This, indeed, was a pleasure cheaply purchased at any price. What cared I, if I had waded to the portal of this wonder through another's blood? I would have given my own to enjoy one such moment of intoxication and delight.

Breathless with gazing on this lovely wonder, and forgetful for an instant of everything save her presence, I withdrew my eye from the microscope eagerly, — alas! As my gaze fell on the thin slide that lay beneath my instrument, the bright light from mirror and from prism sparkled on a colourless drop of water! There, in that tiny bead of dew, this beautiful being was forever imprisoned. The planet Neptune was not more distant from me than she. I hastened once more to apply my eye to the microscope.

Animula (let me now call her by that dear name

which I subsequently bestowed on her) had changed her position. She had again approached the wondrous forest, and was gazing earnestly upwards. Presently one of the trees—as I must call them—unfolded a long ciliary process, with which it seized one of the gleaming fruits that glittered on its summit, and, sweeping slowly down, held it within reach of Animula. The sylph took it in her delicate hand and began to eat. My attention was so entirely absorbed by her, that I could not apply myself to the task of determining whether this singular plant was or was not instinct with volition.

I watched her, as she made her repast, with the most profound attention. The suppleness of her motions sent a thrill of delight through my frame; my heart beat madly as she turned her beautiful eyes in the direction of the spot in which I stood. What would I have not given to have had the power to precipitate myself into that luminous ocean, and float with her through those groves of purple and gold! While I was thus breathlessly following her every movement, she suddenly started, seemed to listen for a moment, and then cleaving the brilliant ether in which she was floating, like a flash of light, pierced through the opaline forest, and disappeared.

Instantly a series of the most singular sensations attacked me. It seemed as if I had suddenly gone blind. The luminous sphere was still before me, but my daylight had vanished. What caused this sudden disappearance? Had she a lover or a husband? Yes, that was the solution! Some signal from a happy fellow-being had vibrated through the avenues of the forest, and she had obeyed the summons.

The agony of my sensations, as I arrived at this conclusion, startled me. I tried to reject the conviction that my reason forced upon me. I battled against the fatal conclusion,—but in vain. It was so. I had no escape from it. I loved an animalcule!

It is true that thanks to the marvellous power of my microscope, she appeared of human proportions. Instead of presenting the revolting aspect of the coarser creatures, that live and struggle and die, in the more easily resolvable portions of the water-drop, she was fair and delicate and of surpassing beauty. But of what account was all that? Every time that my eye was withdrawn from the instrument, it fell on a miserable drop of water, within which, I must be content to know, dwelt all that could make my life lovely.

Could she but see me once! Could I for one moment pierce the mystical walls that so inexorably rose to separate us, and whisper all that filled my soul, I might consent to be satisfied for the rest of my life with the knowledge of her remote sympathy. It would be something to have established even the faintest personal link to bind us together,—to know that at times, when roaming through those enchanted glades, she might think of the wonderful stranger, who had broken the monotony of her life with his presence, and left a gentle memory in her heart!

But it could not be. No invention of which human intellect was capable could break down the barriers that nature had erected. I might feast my soul upon her wondrous beauty, yet she must always remain ignorant of the adoring eyes that day and night gazed down upon her, and, even when closed, beheld her in dreams. With a bitter cry of anguish I fled from the room, and, flinging myself on my bed, sobbed myself to sleep like a child.

VI

THE SPILLING OF THE CUP

I arose the next morning almost at daybreak, and rushed to my microscope. I trembled as I sought the luminous world in miniature that contained my all. Animula was there. I had left the gas-lamp, surrounded by its moderators, burning, when I went to bed the night before. I found the sylph bathing, as it were, with an expression of pleasure animating her features, in the brilliant light which surrounded her. She tossed her lustrous golden hair over her shoulders with innocent coquetry. She lay at full length in the transparent medium, in which she supported herself with ease, and gambolled with the enchanting grace that the nymph Salmacis might have exhibited when she sought to conquer the modest Hermaphroditus. I tried an experiment to satisfy myself if her powers of reflection were developed. I lessened the lamp-light considerably. By the dim light that remained, I could see an expression of pain flit across her face. She looked upward suddenly, and her brows contracted. I flooded the stage of the microscope again with a full stream of light, and her whole expression changed. She sprang forward like some substance deprived of all weight. Her eyes sparkled and her lips moved. Ah! if science had only the means of conducting and reduplicating sounds, as it does the rays of light, what carols of happiness would then have entranced my ears! what jubilant hymns to Adonais would have thrilled the illumined air!

I now comprehended how it was that the Count de Gabalis peopled his mystic world with sylphs,—beautiful beings whose breath of life was lambent fire, and who sported forever in regions of purest ether and purest light. The Rosicrucian had anticipated the wonder that I had practically realised.

How long this worship of my divinity went on

thus I scarcely know. I lost all note of time. All day from early dawn, and far into the night, I was to be found peering through that wonderful lens. I saw no one, went nowhere, and scarce allowed myself sufficient time for my meals. My whole life was absorbed in contemplation as rapt as that of any of the Romish saints. Every hour that I gazed upon the divine form strengthened my passion,—a passion that was always overshadowed by the maddening conviction, that, although I could gaze on her at will, she never, never could behold me!

At length, I grew so pale and emaciated, from want of rest, and continual brooding over my insane love and its cruel conditions, that I determined to make some effort to wean myself from it. 'Come,' I said, 'this is at best but a fantasy. Your imagination has bestowed on Animula charms which in reality she does not possess. Seclusion from female society has produced this morbid condition of mind. Compare her with the beautiful women of your own world, and this false enchantment will vanish.'

I looked over the newspapers by chance. There I beheld the advertisement of a celebrated *danseuse* who appeared nightly at Niblo's. The Signorina Caradolce had the reputation of being the most beautiful as well as the most graceful woman in the world. I instantly dressed and went to the theatre.

The curtain drew up. The usual semicircle of fairies in white muslin were standing on the right toe around the enamelled flower-bank, of green canvas, on which the belated prince was sleeping. Suddenly a flute is heard. The fairies start. The trees open, the fairies all stand on the left toe, and the queen enters. It was the Signorina. She bounded forward amid thunders of applause, and, lighting on one foot, remained poised in the air. Heavens! was this the great enchantress that had drawn monarchs at her chariot-wheels? Those heavy muscular limbs, those thick ankles, those cavernous eyes, that stereotyped smile, those crudely painted cheeks! Where were the vermeil blooms, the liquid expressive eyes, the harmonious limbs of Animula?

The Signorina danced. What gross, discordant movements! The play of her limbs was all false and artificial. Her bounds were painful athletic efforts; her poses were angular and distressed the eye. I could bear it no longer; with an exclamation of disgust that drew every eye upon me, I rose from my seat in the very middle of the Signorina's *pas-de-fascination*, and abruptly quitted the house.

I hastened home to feast my eyes once more on the lovely form of my sylph. I felt that henceforth to combat this passion would be impossible. I applied my eye to the lens. Animula was there,—but what could have happened? Some terrible change seemed to have taken place during my absence. Some secret grief seemed to cloud the lovely features of her I gazed upon. Her face had grown thin and haggard; her limbs trailed heavily; the wondrous lustre of her golden hair had faded. She was ill!—ill, and I could not assist her! I believe at that moment I would have gladly forfeited all claims to my human birth-right, if I could only have been dwarfed to the size of an animalcule, and permitted to console her from whom fate had forever divided me.

I racked my brain for the solution of this mystery. What was it that afflicted the sylph? She seemed to suffer intense pain. Her features contracted, and she even writhed, as if with some internal agony. The wondrous forests appeared also to have lost half their beauty. Their hues were dim and in some places faded away altogether. I watched Animula for hours with a breaking heart, and she seemed absolutely to wither away under my very eye. Suddenly I remembered that I had not looked at the water-drop for several days. In fact I hated to see it; for it reminded me of the natural barrier between Animula and myself. I hurriedly looked down on the stage of the microscope. The slide was still there,—but, great heavens! the water-drop had vanished! The awful truth burst upon me; it had evaporated, until it had become so minute as to be invisible to the naked eye; I had been gazing on its last atom, the one that contained Animula, and she was dying!

I rushed again to the front of the lens, and looked through. Alas! the last agony had seized her. The rainbow-hued forests had all melted away, and Animula lay struggling feebly in what seemed to be a spot of dim light. Ah! the sight was horrible: the limbs once so round and lovely shrivelling up into nothings; the eyes—those eyes that shone like heaven—being quenched into black dust; the lustrous golden hair now lank and discoloured. The last throe came. I beheld that final struggle of the blackening form—and I fainted.

When I awoke out of a trance of many hours, I found myself lying amid the wreck of my instrument, myself as shattered in mind and body as it. I crawled feebly to my bed, from which I did not rise for months.

They say now that I am mad; but they are mistaken. I am poor, for I have neither the heart nor the will to work; all my money is spent, and I live on charity. Young men's associations that love a joke invite me to lecture on Optics before them, for which they pay me, and laugh at me while I lecture. "Linley, the mad microscopist," is the name I go by. I suppose that I talk incoherently while I lecture.

Who could talk sense when his brain is haunted by such ghastly memories, while ever and anon among the shapes of death I behold the radiant form of my lost Animula!

Voltaire

French writer and philosopher François-Marie Arouet (1694–1778), better known by his nom de plume Voltaire, was one of the first superstars of literature: famous for his wit and fearless in his criticism of Christianity. An advocate of freedom of speech, he wrote more than 20,000 letters and published nearly 2,000 books and pamphlets. Among the latter are various science-fictional stories, and 'Micromégas' – a name that means 'Littlebig' – is one of the best. In this tale Voltaire includes pointed satire on human folly and the pettiness and blindness of scientists and philosophers, but balances against this a sense-of-wonder, interstellar voyage of exploration.

Micromégas

CHAPTER I

VOYAGE OF AN INHABITANT OF THE STAR SIRIUS TO THE PLANET SATURN

On one of the planets that orbits the star named Sirius there lived a spirited young man, whom I had the honour of meeting on the last voyage he made to our little anthill. He was called Micromégas, a fitting name for anyone so great. He was eight leagues tall – 24,000 yards.

Certain mathematicians, always of use to the public, will immediately take up their pens and calculate that, since Mr Micromégas, inhabitant of the world of Sirius, is 24,000 yards tall, which is to say some paces of five feet each, and since we citizens of the Earth are hardly five feet tall, and our sphere 9,000 leagues around, they will find, I say, that it is absolutely necessary that the planet that produced him must be 21,600,000 times greater in circumference than our little Earth. Nothing in nature is simpler or more orderly. The sovereign states of Germany or Italy, which one can traverse in a half-hour, compared to the empires of Turkey, Moscow or China, are only feeble reflections of the prodigious differences that nature has placed in all beings.

His Excellency's size being as large as I have said, all our sculptors and all our painters will agree without protest that his belt must have been 50,000 feet in circumference, which gives him very good proportions. His nose taking up one-third of his attractive face, and his attractive face taking up one-seventh of his attractive body, it must be admitted that the nose of the Sirian is 6,333 feet long, give or take; which is hard to ignore.

As for his mind: well, it is one of the most cultivated that we have. He knows many things. He invented some of them. He was not even 250 years old when he studied, as is customary, at the most celebrated colleges of his planet, at which time he managed to figure out by pure willpower more than fifty of Euclid's propositions. That's eighteen more than Blaise Pascal, who, after having figured out thirty-two, just for fun (according to his sister's reports), later became a fairly mediocre mathematician and a very bad philosopher. Towards his 450th year, near the end of his infancy, he dissected many small insects no more than one hundred feet in diameter, which would evade ordinary microscopes. He wrote a very curious book about this, and it gave him some income. The mufti of his country, an extremely ignorant worrywart, found some suspicious, rash, disagreeable, and heretical propositions in the book, smelled heresy, and pursued it vigorously; it was a matter of finding out whether the substantial form of the fleas of Sirius were of the same nature as those of the snails. Micromégas gave a spirited defence. He brought in some women to testify in his favour; the trial lasted 220 years. Finally, the judge had the book condemned by jurisconsults who had not read it, and the author was ordered not to appear in court for 800 years.

He was thereby dealt the minor inconvenience of being banished from a court that consisted of nothing but harassment and pettiness. He wrote an amusing song at the expense of the judge, which the latter hardly deigned to notice. Then he took up voyaging from planet to planet in order to *develop his heart and mind*, as the saying goes. Those that travel only by stage-coach or sedan-chair will probably be surprised to learn of the carriage of this vessel; for we, on our little pile of mud, can conceive of only that to which we are accustomed. Our voyager was very familiar with the laws of gravity and with all the other attractive and repulsive forces. He utilized them so well that, whether with the help of a ray of sunlight or some comet, he jumped from globe to globe like a bird hopping from branch to branch. He quickly spanned the Milky Way, and I am obliged to report that he never saw, throughout its constitutive stars, the beautiful empyrean sky that the Reverend Mr Derham boasts of having seen at the other end of his telescope.* I do not claim that Mr Derham has defective eyesight, God forbid! But Micromégas was actually there, which makes him a reliable witness. Still, I do not want to contradict anyone.

Micromégas, after having toured around, arrived at the planet Saturn. As accustomed as he was to seeing new things, he could not, upon seeing the smallness of the planet and its inhabitants, stop himself from smiling with the superiority that occasionally betrays even the wisest of us. For in the end Saturn is hardly nine times bigger than Earth, and the citizens of this world are dwarfs, no more than a thousand fathoms tall, or thereabouts. He and his men poked fun at them at first, like Italian musicians laughing at the music of Lully when he comes to France. But, as the Sirian had a good heart, he understood very quickly that a thinking being is not necessarily ridiculous just because he is only 6,000 feet tall. He got to know the Saturnians, once their initial shock had worn off. Indeed, he cultivated a

* William Derham (1657–1735) was an English clergyman and scientist. Voltaire is here referencing his *Astro-Theology* (1714).

strong friendship with the secretary of the Academy of Saturn, a lively fellow who, though (to tell the truth) he had not invented anything, nonetheless understood the inventions of others very well, and who wrote some passable verses and carried out some complicated calculations. I will report here, for the reader's satisfaction, a singular conversation that Micromégas had with the secretary one day.

CHAPTER II

CONVERSATION BETWEEN THE INHABITANT OF SIRIUS AND THAT OF SATURN

It was after His Excellency had laid himself down for a rest that the secretary approached him.

'You have to admit,' said Micromégas, 'nature is extremely varied.'

'Yes,' said the Saturnian, 'nature is like a flower bed, in which the flowers—'

'Oh!' said the other. 'Don't talk to me about *flower beds*.'

The secretary began again. 'Nature is like a group of blonde and brunette girls, whose jewellery—'

'What am I supposed to do with your brunettes?' returned the other.

'Perhaps we could say that nature is like an art gallery, whose paintings—'

'None of that!' said the voyager. 'I tell you: nature is like nature. Why go searching after comparisons?'

'To please you,' replied the secretary.

'I do not want to be pleased,' answered the voyager. 'I want to be educated. Tell me how many senses the men of your planet have.'

'Only seventy-two, I'm afraid,' said the academic. 'We're always complaining about it. Our capacity for imagination is much larger than it needs to be, frankly. We find that with our seventy-two senses, our planetary ring, our five moons, we are too restricted; and despite all our curiosity and the expansive range of enthusiasms that result from our seventy-two senses, we have plenty of time to get bored.'

'I believe it,' said Micromégas. 'For on our planet we have almost a thousand senses; and yet we are still aware of a sort of vague feeling, a kind of worry, that warns us that there exists, somewhere, beings even more perfect than us. I have travelled a bit; and have seen mortal creatures that surpass us. Some, indeed, are far superior. But I have not seen any that desire only what they truly need, and whose needs perfectly match their lives. Maybe someday I will happen upon a country that lacks for nothing; but so far no one has given me any word of a place like that.'

The Saturnian and the Sirian proceeded to wear themselves out in speculating; but after a lot of very ingenious and very doubtful imaginative extrapolation, they were compelled to return to cold hard facts.

'How long are your lifespans?' asked the Sirian.

'Ah! We only live for a very short time,' replied the small man from Saturn.

'Same with us,' said the Sirian. 'We always complain about it. It must be a universal law of nature.'

'Alas! We only live through 500 revolutions of our world around the sun,' said the Saturnian. (This translates to roughly 15,000 earthly years.) 'You can see yourself that this is to die almost at the moment one is born. Our existence is a mere point, our lifespan an instant, our planet an atom. Hardly do we begin to learn a little when death arrives, cutting us off before we have accumulated any experience. As for me, I don't dare make any plans. I see myself as a drop of water in an immense ocean. I am ashamed, especially when I meet someone as impressive as you, to consider what a ridiculous figure I make in this world.'

Micromégas replied, 'If you were not a philosopher, I would fear burdening you by telling you that our lifespan is 700 times longer than yours. Still, you know, of course, that when it is necessary to return your body to the elements, to reanimate nature in that alteration of form which we call death – when that moment of metamorphosis comes, to have lived an eternity and to have lived a day amounts to precisely the same thing. I have been to worlds where folk live a thousand times longer than we do. But they still die. And people everywhere have the good sense to know their role and give thanks to the Author of Nature. He has scattered across this universe a profusion of varieties of life, and done so with truly admirable uniformity. What I mean is: all the universe's thinking beings are different, yet all resemble one another in all possessing the gift of thought and desire. Matter is universal, but it has different properties on each planet. How many diverse properties do you count in yours?'

'If you mean those properties,' said the Saturnian, 'without which we believe that the planet could not subsist, we count 300 of them: things like extension, impenetrability, mobility, gravity, divisibility, and so on.'

'Apparently,' replied the voyager, 'this small number suffices for what the Creator planned for your dwelling place. I admire his wisdom in everything. I see difference everywhere, but also proportion. Your planet is small; your inhabitants are as well. You have few sensations; your matter has few properties; all this is the work of Providence. What colour is your sun?'

'A rather yellowish white,' said the Saturnian. 'When we apply a prism to its rays, we find that they contain seven colours.'

'Our sun burns red,' said the Sirian, 'and we have a spectrum of thirty-nine primary colours. There is no one sun, among those that I have visited, that resembles it, just as there is no one face among you that is identical to the others.'

After numerous questions of this nature, Micromégas discovered how many essentially different substances are found on Saturn. He learned there were only thirty or so: things like *God*, *space*, *matter*, the beings with extension that merely sense, the beings with extension that sense and think, the thinking beings that have no extension; those that are penetrable, those that are not – all these kinds of things. The Sirian, whose home contained 300 and who had discovered 3,000 more on his voyages, prodigiously surprised the philosopher of Saturn by telling him so. Finally, after having exchanged knowledge, a little of what they knew and a lot of what they did not know, and after having debated and discussed during the course of a complete revolution around the sun, they resolved to go on a small philosophical voyage together.

CHAPTER III

VOYAGE OF THE TWO INHABITANTS OF SIRIUS AND SATURN

Our two philosophers were just ready to launch themselves into Saturn's atmosphere, by means of a very nicely calibrated mathematical instrument, when the ruler of Saturn, who had heard news of the departure, came weepingly to remonstrate. She was a pretty, petite, brown-haired girl, a mere 660 fathoms tall, though she compensated for her small stature with many other charms.

'Cruelty!' she cried. 'After resisting you for 1,500 years, just when I was beginning to come around, when I'd spent hardly a hundred years in the embrace of your arms, you abandon me to go on a voyage with a giant from another world. Go on then! You're only curious. You've never been in love. If you were a *true* Saturnian, you'd be faithful. Where are you running off to anyway? What do you even want? Oh, our five moons are less wayward than you, our ring less inconstant. It's over, I will never love anyone ever again.'

The philosopher embraced her, and wept with her (he was a philosopher, after all). The woman, after striking dramatic attitudes, went off to console herself with the help of one of the dandies of the country.

So our two explorers departed. They alighted first on Saturn's ring, which they found to be fairly flat, as conjectured by an illustrious inhabitant of our little sphere.* From there they moved easily from moon to moon. When a comet passed by the last of these they grabbed onto it and flew on it, along with their servants and their scientific instruments. After they had travelled approximately one hundred and fifty million leagues, they rendezvoused with the satellites of Jupiter. They stopped at Jupiter and stayed for a week, during which time they learned some very wonderful secrets that I would furnish here, in print, if it were not for the Inquisition, which found some of the propositions to be a little harsh. But I have read the manuscript in the library of the illustrious Archbishop of [*redacted*], who with a generosity and goodness that is impossible to over-praise allowed me to consult his books. I promised him a long article in the first edition of Moréri,** and I will not forget his children, who give such a great hope of perpetuating the race of their illustrious father.

But let us now return to our travellers. Upon

* Dutch astronomer Christiaan Huygens' 1659 book *Systema Saturnium* describes the ring of Saturn as 'a thin, flat ring, nowhere touching, and inclined to the ecliptic'.

** The reference is to *Le Grand Dictionnaire historique*, an encyclopedia originally compiled by the Catholic priest and theologian Louis Moréri (1643–80).

leaving Jupiter they traversed a distance of some one hundred million leagues and so approached the planet Mars, which, as we know, is five times smaller than our own. They swung by the two moons that attend upon this world, but which have escaped the notice of our astronomers. I know very well that Father Castel* will write, perhaps even politely, against the existence of these two moons. Still, I rely on those who reason by analogy. These good philosophers know how unlikely it would be for Mars, so far from the sun, to have gotten by with fewer than two moons. Whatever the case may be, our explorers found this world so small that they feared they would not be able to land upon it, and so they passed it by like two travellers disdainful of a bad village inn, pressing on instead towards a neighbouring city. But the Sirian and his companion soon regretted it. They travelled a long time without finding anything, until, finally, they perceived a tiny candle. It was the Earth. But what a pitiful sight it was to those who had so recently left Jupiter! Nevertheless, from fear of further regret, they resolved to touch down. Carried by the tail of a comet, and transferring to a convenient aurora borealis, they

* Louis Bertrand Castel (1688–1757), French mathematician and Jesuit priest.

started towards it, and landed upon the Earth, on the northern coast of the Baltic Sea, on 5 July 1737 (new style).

CHAPTER IV

WHAT HAPPENED ON PLANET EARTH

After resting for a while, they ate two mountains for lunch, which their servants prepared pretty nicely for them. Then they decided to familiarize themselves with the small land into which they had arrived. They travelled first north to south. The usual stride of the Sirian and his attendants was approximately 30,000 feet. The dwarf from Saturn, with his mere thousand fathoms of height, trailed behind, gasping heavily. He had to make twelve steps to each of the other's strides. Imagine (if such a comparison is not too impertinent) a very small lapdog following a captain of the guards of the Prussian king.

The speed at which our strangers moved meant that they circumnavigated the globe in thirty-six hours. The sun, of course (or, rather, the Earth), makes a similar voyage in a day; but you have to imagine that the going is much easier when one turns on one's axis instead of walking on one's feet. So there they were, back where they started, after having seen the barely noticeable pond we call *the*

Mediterranean, and another little pool that, under the name *ocean* encircles the molehill. The dwarf never got wet over his knees, and the other hardly splashed his heels. On their way they took pains to try and determine whether the planet was inhabited or not. They crouched, lay down, felt around everywhere; but their eyes and their hands were not proportionate to the little beings that crawl in this place. They could not feel in the least any sensation that might lead them to suspect that we and our fellows – the other inhabitants of this planet – have the honour of existing.

The dwarf, who was a little prone to hastiness, decided immediately that the planet was uninhabited. He reasoned that he had not seen anyone. Micromégas politely suggested to him that this logic was rather flawed: 'For,' said he, 'you do not see with your little eyes certain stars of the fiftieth magnitude that I can perceive very distinctly. Do you conclude that these stars do not exist?'

'But,' said the dwarf, 'I had a pretty good feel, too.'

'But,' answered the other, 'you have pretty feeble senses.'

'But,' replied the dwarf, 'this planet is poorly constructed! It is so irregular and has such a ridiculous shape! Everything here seems to be in chaos. You see these little rivulets, none of which runs in a straight line, these pools of water that are neither round, nor square, nor oval, nor regular by any measure. All these little pointy specks scattered across the earth that grate on my feet? (He was referring to mountains.) Look at its shape again, how it is flattened at the poles, how it clumsily revolves around the sun, how its trajectory necessarily eliminates the climates of the poles? To tell the truth, what really makes me think it is uninhabited is that it seems that no one of good sense would want to live here.'

'Well,' said Micromégas, 'maybe the inhabitants of this planet are not possessed of good sense! The thing is, perhaps all this is the way it is for a reason. Everything *appears* irregular to you here, you say, because everything on Saturn and Jupiter is drawn in straight lines. This might be why you are so puzzled. Have I not told you that I have continually noticed variety in my travels?'

The Saturnian argued each of these points, and the dispute might never have finished if it were not for Micromégas, who, growing increasingly agitated, had the good fortune to snap the thread of his diamond necklace. The diamonds fell: pretty little carats of fairly irregular size, of which the largest weighed four hundred pounds and the smallest fifty. The dwarf recovered some of them, and in doing so, bending down for a better look, he decided to examine how these diamonds were cut with the help of his excellent microscope. So he took out a small microscope of 160 feet in diameter and put it up to his eye; and Micromégas took out another of 2,005 feet in diameter. They were fine instruments; but neither one of them could see anything right away and had to be adjusted. At last the Saturnian saw something elusive that moved in the shallow waters of the Baltic sea. It was a whale. He carefully picked it up with his little finger and, resting it on the nail of his thumb, showed it to the Sirian, who began laughing once again at the ludicrously small scale of the things on our planet. The Saturnian, realizing that our world was indeed inhabited, decided without hesitation that it was inhabited only by whales; and as he prided himself on his deductive reasoning, he was determined to infer the origin and evolution of such a small atom; whether it was possessed of intelligence, will, freedom and so on. Micromégas was confused. He examined the animal very patiently and found no reason to believe that a soul was lodged in it. The two voyagers were therefore inclined to believe that our home planet was a soulless place. Then, with the help of the microscope, they perceived something as large as a whale floating on top of the Baltic sea.

We know that a flock of philosophers was at this

time returning from the Arctic Circle, where they had made some observations which no one had dared make until then. The gazettes claimed that their vessel ran aground off the coast of Bothnia, and that they were having great difficulty setting things straight; but the world never reveals its secrets. I am going to tell how it really happened, straightforwardly and without bias; which is no small thing for a historian.

CHAPTER V

EXPERIMENTS AND REASONINGS OF THE TWO VOYAGERS

Micromégas slowly reached his hand towards the place where the object had appeared, extended two fingers, and withdrew them for fear of being mistaken, then opened and closed them, and skilfully lifted the vessel that carried these fellows, putting it on his fingernail without pressing it too hard for fear of crushing it.

'Here is a very different animal from the first,' said the dwarf from Saturn.

The Sirian put the so-called animal in the palm of his hand. The passengers and the crew, who believed themselves to have been lifted up by a hurricane, and who thought they were on some sort of boulder, scurried around. The sailors took the barrels of wine, threw them overboard onto Micromégas's hand, and then jumped after them. The geometers measured with their quadrants and sextants, assisted by two Lapland girls. They descended onto the Sirian's fingers, where they made so much fuss that he finally felt something move, tickling his fingers. It was a steel-tipped baton being pressed into his index finger. He judged by this tickling that it had been spat out by some small animal that he was holding – he did not suspect anything else at first. The microscope, which could barely distinguish a whale from a boat, could not capture anything as elusive as a man. I am not attempting to insult anyone's vanity, but I am obliged to ask that important men make a simple observation. Taking the size of a man to be about five feet, the figure we make upon Earth is comparable to that made by an animal of about six hundred thousandths the height of a flea on a ball five feet in diameter. Imagine a being that could hold the Earth in its hands, and which has organs in proportion to ours – and it may very well be that there are such things – conceive, I ask you, what such a being would think of the battles that allow a victor to capture a village only to lose it later.

I do not doubt that if ever some captain of some troop of imposing grenadiers reads this work he will increase the size of the hats of his troops by at least two feet – imposing, no question! But I warn him that such action will have been undertaken in vain; that he and his will never grow any larger than infinitely small.

What marvellous skill it must have taken for our philosopher from Sirius merely to perceive the atoms of which I have just spoken! Even Leeuwenhoek and Hartsoëker,* tinkering with the first microscopes and observing the cells that make us up, did not make so astonishing a discovery. What pleasure Micromégas felt at seeing these little machines move, examining all their scurrying, following them in their enterprises! He cried out with joy, and passed one of his microscopes over to his traveling companion.

'I see them,' they said at the same time. 'Look how they are carrying loads, stooping, getting up again.' So they talked, hands trembling from the pleasure of seeing such new objects, and also from fear of losing them. The Saturnian, moving from excessive incredulity to excessive credulity, even thought he saw them mating.

'Ah!' he said. 'I have caught nature in the act.' But he was fooled by appearances, which happens

* Two Dutch microscopists. Antonie Philips van Leeuwenhoek (1632–1723) is known as the father of microbiology and invented the first microscope capable of observing microbes. Nicolaas Hartsoëker (1656–1725) invented the screw-barrel simple microscope *c.* 1694.

only too often, whether one is using a microscope or not.

CHAPTER VI

WHAT HAPPENED TO THEM AMONG MEN

Micromégas, a much better observer than the dwarf, clearly saw that the atoms were speaking to each other, and pointed this out to his companion, who, ashamed of being mistaken about them reproducing, did not want to believe that such a creature could communicate. He had the same facility with languages as did the Sirian and, unable to hear the atoms talk, supposed therefore that they did not speak. After all, how could these impossibly small beings have vocal organs? And even if they did, what could they possibly have to talk about? To speak, one must think, more or less; but if they think, they must therefore have the equivalent of a soul. But to attribute the equivalent of a soul to this species struck him as manifestly absurd.

'But,' said the Sirian, 'you believed right away that they engaged in the act of love. Do you believe that one can make love without thinking – without speaking a single word, or at least without making oneself heard? And do you suppose that it's harder to produce an argument than an infant? Both appear to be great mysteries to me.'

'I do not dare believe or deny it,' said the dwarf. 'I have no more opinions. We must endeavour first to examine these insects, and to rationalize only after that.'

'That is very well said,' echoed Micromégas, and he briskly took out a pair of cuticle scissors he had about his person, and from the parings of his thumbnail he improvized a kind of speaking-trumpet, like a vast funnel. He put the end up to his ear. The circumference of the funnel enveloped the vessel and the entire crew. The weakest voice entered into the circular fibres of the nails in such a way that, thanks to the care with which he had constructed it, the philosopher above could hear the buzz of our insect-voices perfectly well. In only a few hours he was able to distinguish words, and soon enough to understand French. The dwarf managed to do the same, though with more difficulty.

The voyagers' amazement increased second by second, for they heard these mites speak moderately intelligently – though such a performance seemed inexplicable to them. You may well believe that the Sirian and the dwarf burned with impatience to converse with the atoms. The dwarf feared that his thunderous voice – to say nothing of Micromégas's boom – would deafen the mites without being understood. They had to diminish its force, and so placed toothpicks in their mouths, whose tapered ends fell around the ship. The Sirian put the dwarf on his knees and the ship with its crew on a fingernail. He lowered his head and spoke softly. Finally, deploying these precautions and various others, he began to speak:

'Invisible insects that the hand of the Creator has caused to spring up in the abyss of the infinitely small, I thank Him for allowing me to uncover such seemingly impenetrable secrets. Perhaps those at my court would not deign to give you audience, but I mistrust no one, and I offer you my protection.'

If anyone has ever been surprised, it was the people who heard these words. They could not figure out where the speech was coming from. The chaplain of the vessel recited a prayer for the exorcism of devils, the sailors swore, and the philosophers of the vessel constructed systems. But no matter what systems they came up with, they could not figure out who was talking. The dwarf from Saturn, who had a softer voice than Micromégas, told them in a few words what species they were dealing with. He told them all about the voyage from Saturn, brought them up to speed on what Mr Micromégas was, and after lamenting how small they were, asked them if they had always been in this miserable state so near nothingness, what they were doing on a globe that appeared to belong to whales, whether they were happy, if they reproduced, if they had a soul, and a hundred other questions of this nature.

A reasoner among the troop, more daring than the others, and shocked that someone might doubt that he possessed a soul, observed the interlocutor with sight-vanes pointed at a quarter circle from two different stations, and spoke thusly: 'You believe then, sir, that because you are a thousand fathoms tall from head to toe, that you are a—'

'A thousand fathoms!' cried the dwarf. 'Good heavens! How could he know my height? A thousand fathoms! You cannot mistake him for a flea. This atom just measured me! He is a surveyor, he knows my size; and I, who can only see him through a microscope, I still do not know his!'

'Yes, I measured you,' said the physician, 'and I will measure your large companion as well.' The proposition was accepted; His Excellency laid down flat (had he stayed upright his head would have disappeared into the clouds). Our philosophers planted a great shaft upon him, in a place that Doctor Swift would have named, but that I will restrain myself from calling by its name, out of respect for the ladies. Next, by a series of triangles linked together, they concluded that what they saw was in effect a young man of 120,000 feet.

Then Micromégas spoke these words: 'I see more than ever that one must not judge anything by its mere size. Oh God! You have given intelligence to substance that appears contemptible. The infinitely small costs you as little as the infinitely large; and if it is possible that there are such small beings as these, there may just as well be a spirit bigger than those of the superb beings that I have met among the stars, whose feet alone would cover this planet.'

One of the philosophers responded that he could certainly imagine that there are intelligent beings much smaller than man. He recounted, not every fabulous thing Virgil says about bees, but what Swammerdam discovered,* and what Réaumur has anatomized.** He explained finally that there are animals that are to bees what bees are to man, what the Sirian himself was for the vast animals he had spoken of, and what these large animals are to other substances before which they looked like atoms. Gradually the conversation became more interesting, and Micromégas spoke as follows:

* Dutch scientist Jan Swammerdam (1637–80) was the first to prove that the various phases during the life of an insect – egg, larva, pupa and adult – are different forms of the same animal.
** René Antoine Ferchault de Réaumur (1683–1757) was a French entomologist.

CHAPTER VII

CONVERSATION WITH THE MEN

'Oh, intelligent atoms, in which the Eternal Being desired to make manifest his skill and his power, you must, no doubt, taste pure joys on your planet; for having so little matter, and appearing to be entirely spirit, you must live out your life thinking and loving, the true life of the mind. Nowhere have I seen true bliss, but it is here, without a doubt.'

At this all the philosophers shook their heads, and one of them, more honest than the others, avowed that, with the exception of a small group of inhabitants held in poor esteem by the others, we are an assembly of mad, vicious, and wretched people. 'We have more matter than we need,' he said, 'to do evil, if evil comes from matter; and are possessed of too much spirit, if evil comes from spirit. Did you know, for example, that as I am speaking with you, there are 100,000 madmen of our species wearing hats, killing 100,000 other animals wearing turbans, or being massacred by them?* And that we have used almost all the surface of the Earth for this purpose since time immemorial?'

The Sirian shuddered, and asked the reason for

* A reference to the Russo-Turkish War of 1735–39, fought in part over possession of the Crimean peninsula (described two paragraphs later as a 'pile of mud').

these horrible quarrels amongst such inconsequential creatures.

'It is a matter,' said the philosopher, 'of some piles of mud as big as your heel. It is not that any of these millions of men that slit each other's throats care about this pile of mud. It is only a matter of determining if it should belong to a certain man whom we call "Sultan" or to another whom we call, for whatever reason, "Czar". Neither one has ever seen nor will ever see the little piece of Earth, and almost none of these animals that mutually kill themselves have ever seen the animal for which they kill.'

'Oh! How cruel a fate!' cried the Sirian with indignation. 'Who could conceive of such an excess of insane rage? It makes me want to take three steps and crush this whole anthill of ridiculous murderers.'

'Don't waste your time,' one of the humans replied. 'They are working their own ruin quickly enough. Believe me: in another ten years only one-hundredth of these scoundrels will even be here. Know that even if they have not drawn swords, hunger, fatigue, or intemperance will overtake them. More to the point: they're not the ones who deserve punishment. It is those sedentary barbarians who from the depths of their offices order, while they are digesting their last meal, the massacre of a million men, and who subsequently give solemn thanks to God.'

The voyager was moved with pity for the small human race, where he was discovering such surprising contrasts.

'Since you are amongst the small number of wise men,' he told these gentlemen, 'and since apparently you do not kill anyone for money, tell me, I beg of you, what occupies your time.'

'We dissect flies,' said the philosopher, 'we measure lines, we gather figures. We agree with each other on two or three points that we do not understand.'

The Sirian and the Saturnian were both immediately interested to know what it was they agreed upon.

'What do you measure,' said the Saturnian, 'from the Dog Star to the great star of the Gemini?'

They responded all at once, 'Thirty-two and a half degrees.'

'What do you measure from here to the moon?'

'Sixty radii of the Earth even.'

'How much does your air weigh?'

He thought he had caught them, but they all told him that air weighed around 900 times less than an identical volume of the purest water, and 19,000 times less than a gold ducat. The little dwarf from Saturn, surprised at their responses, was tempted to accuse of witchcraft the same people he had refused a soul a mere quarter of an hour earlier.

Finally, Micromégas said to them, 'Since you know the exterior world so well, you must know what is *interior* even better. Tell me what your soul is, and how you form ideas.' The philosophers all broke out speaking, everyone clamouring at once, all with different views. The oldest cited Aristotle, another pronounced the name of Descartes; this one here, Malebranche; another Leibnitz; another Locke.

An old peripatetic spoke up with confidence: 'The soul is an entelechy, and a reason gives it the power to be what it is.' This is what Aristotle expressly declares on page 633 of the Louvre edition. He cited the passage.*

'I do not understand Greek very well,' said the giant.

'Neither do I,' said the philosophical insect.

'Why then,' the Sirian retorted, 'are you citing some man named Aristotle in the Greek?'

'Because,' replied the savant, 'one should always cite what one does not understand at all in the language one understands the least.'

A Cartesian took the floor and said: 'The soul is

* See Aristotle's *De Anima*, 412a27.

a pure spirit that has received in the belly of its mother all metaphysical ideas, and which, leaving that place, is obliged to go to school, and to learn all over again what it already knew, and will not know again.'

'It is not worth the trouble,' responded the eight-league-tall individual, 'for your soul to be so knowledgeable in its mother's stomach, only to be so ignorant when you have hair on your chin. But what do you understand by the mind?'

'You are asking me?' said the reasoner. 'I have no idea. We say that it is not matter—'

'But do you at least know what matter is?'

'Certainly,' replied the man. 'For example, this stone is grey, has such and such a form, has three dimensions, is heavy and divisible.'

'Well!' said the Sirian. 'This thing that appears to you to be divisible, heavy, and grey—please tell me what it is? You see some *attributes*, but what about that which is behind those? Can you tell me about that?'

'No,' said the other.

'So you do not know what matter is.'

So Micromégas, addressing another sage that was balanced on his thumb, asked what his soul was, and what it did.

'Nothing at all,' said the Malebranchist philosopher. 'God does everything for me. I see everything in him, I do everything in him; it is he who does everything that I get mixed up in.'

'It would be just as well not to exist,' retorted the sage of Sirius. 'And you, my friend,' he said to a Leibnitzian who was there, 'what is your soul?'

'It is,' answered the Leibnitzian, 'the hand of a clock that tells the time while my body chimes out. Or, if you like, it is my soul that chimes out while my body tells the time, or my soul is the mirror of the universe, and my body is the border of the mirror. That's all clear.'

A miniature follower of Locke was nearby, and when he was finally given the floor, he said: 'I do not know,' said he, '*how* I think, but I know that I have only ever thought through my senses. That there are immaterial and intelligent substances I do not doubt, and that it is impossible for God to communicate thought to matter I doubt very much. I revere the eternal power. It is not my place to limit it. I affirm nothing, and content myself with believing that many more things are possible than one would think.'

The being from Sirius smiled. He did not find this the least bit sage, while the dwarf from Saturn would have kissed the follower of Locke were it not for the extreme disproportion of their respective sizes. But there was, alas, a little animalcule in a square hat who interrupted all the other animalcule philosophers. He said that he knew the true secret, and that everything would be found in the *Summa* of Saint Thomas Aquinas. He looked the two celestial inhabitants up and down. He argued that their people, their worlds, their suns, their stars, had all been made uniquely for mankind. At this speech, our two voyagers nearly fell over with that inextinguishable laughter which, according to Homer, is shared with the gods. Their shoulders and their stomachs heaved up and down, and in these convulsions the vessel that the Sirian had on his thumbnail fell into one of the Saturnian's trouser pockets. These two good men searched for it a long time, found it finally, and tidied it up neatly. The Sirian resumed his discussion with the little mites. He spoke to them with great kindness, although in the depths of his heart he was a little angry that the infinitely small had, it seemed, an almost infinitely large pride. He promised to make them a beautiful philosophical book, written very small for their convenience, and said that in this book they would see the point of everything. And indeed, he gave them this book before leaving. It was taken to the Academy of Sciences in Paris, but when the ancient secretary opened it, he saw nothing but blank pages. 'Ah!' he said. 'I suspected as much.'

Mary Shelley

Famous today for one book, *Frankenstein* (1818), Mary Shelley (1797–1851) had a long and varied career as a writer. This story was commissioned in 1833 by *The Keepsake*, a literary annual which paired high-quality engravings with poetry and short stories. On this occasion Shelley was given an engraving entitled 'Bertha', from a painting by Henry P. Briggs, of a young man and young woman attending an elderly lady. She decided to write a story premised on a man, rendered immortal by a potion, who sees his wife both as a beautiful young woman and as the old woman she becomes. As with *Frankenstein*, the story ends in the sublime wilderness of the (at that time) unexplored polar wastes.

The Mortal Immortal

JULY 16, 1833

This is a memorable anniversary for me; on it I complete my three hundred and twenty-third year!

The Wandering Jew? – certainly not. More than eighteen centuries have passed over his head. In comparison with him, I am a very young Immortal.

Am I, then, immortal? This is a question which I have asked myself, by day and night, for now three hundred and three years, and yet cannot answer it. I detected a gray hair amidst my brown locks this very day – that surely signifies decay. Yet it may have remained concealed there for three hundred years – for some persons have become entirely white-headed before twenty years of age.

I will tell my story, and my reader shall judge for me. I will tell my story, and so contrive to pass some few hours of a long eternity, become so wearisome to me. For ever! Can it be? to live for ever! I have heard of enchantments, in which the victims were plunged into a deep sleep, to wake, after a hundred years, as fresh as ever: I have heard of the Seven Sleepers – thus to be immortal would not be so burthensome: but, oh! the weight of never-ending time – the tedious passage of the still-succeeding hours! How happy was the fabled Nourjahad! – But to my task.

All the world has heard of Cornelius Agrippa. His memory is as immortal as his arts have made me. All the world has also heard of his scholar, who, unawares, raised the foul fiend during his master's absence, and was destroyed by him. The report, true or false, of this accident, was attended with many inconveniences to the renowned philosopher. All his scholars at once deserted him – his servants disappeared. He had no one near him to put coals on his ever-burning fires while he slept, or to attend to the changeful colours of his medicines while he studied. Experiment after experiment failed, because one pair of hands was insufficient to complete them: the dark spirits laughed at him for not being able to retain a single mortal in his service.

I was then very young – very poor – and very much in love. I had been for about a year the pupil of Cornelius, though I was absent when this accident took place. On my return, my friends implored me not to return to the alchymist's abode. I trembled as I listened to the dire tale they told; I required no second warning; and when Cornelius came and offered me a purse of gold if I would remain under his roof, I felt as if Satan himself tempted me. My teeth chattered – my hair stood on end: – I ran off as fast as my trembling knees would permit.

My failing steps were directed whither for two years they had every evening been attracted, – a gently bubbling spring of pure living waters, beside which lingered a dark-haired girl, whose beaming eyes were fixed on the path I was accustomed each night to tread. I cannot remember the hour when I did not love Bertha; we had been neighbours and playmates from infancy – her parents, like mine, were of humble life, yet respectable – our attachment had been a source of pleasure to them. In an evil hour, a malignant fever carried off both her father and mother, and Bertha became an orphan. She would have found a home beneath my paternal roof, but, unfortunately, the old lady of the near castle, rich, childless, and solitary, declared her intention to adopt her. Henceforth Bertha was clad in silk – inhabited a marble palace – and was looked on as being highly favoured by fortune. But in her new situation among her new associates, Bertha remained true to the friend of her humbler days; she often visited the cottage of my father, and when forbidden to go thither, she would stray towards the neighbouring wood, and meet me beside its shady fountain.

She often declared that she owed no duty to her

new protectress equal in sanctity to that which bound us. Yet still I was too poor to marry, and she grew weary of being tormented on my account. She had a haughty but an impatient spirit, and grew angry at the obstacles that prevented our union. We met now after an absence, and she had been sorely beset while I was away; she complained bitterly, and almost reproached me for being poor. I replied hastily, –

"I am honest, if I am poor! – were I not, I might soon become rich!"

This exclamation produced a thousand questions. I feared to shock her by owning the truth, but she drew it from me; and then, casting a look of disdain on me, she said –

"You pretend to love, and you fear to face the Devil for my sake!"

I protested that I had only dreaded to offend her; – while she dwelt on the magnitude of the reward that I should receive. Thus encouraged – shamed by her – led on by love and hope, laughing at my late fears, with quick steps and a light heart, I returned to accept the offers of the alchymist, and was instantly installed in my office.

A year passed away. I became possessed of no insignificant sum of money. Custom had banished my fears. In spite of the most painful vigilance, I had never detected the trace of a cloven foot; nor was the studious silence of our abode ever disturbed by demoniac howls. I still continued my stolen interviews with Bertha, and Hope dawned on me – Hope – but not perfect joy; for Bertha fancied that love and security were enemies, and her pleasure was to divide them in my bosom. Though true of heart, she was somewhat of a coquette in manner; and I was jealous as a Turk. She slighted me in a thousand ways, yet would never acknowledge herself to be in the wrong. She would drive me mad with anger, and then force me to beg her pardon. Sometimes she fancied that I was not sufficiently submissive, and then she had some story of a rival, favoured by her protectress. She was surrounded by silk-clad youths – the rich and gay – What chance had the sad-robed scholar of Cornelius compared with these?

On one occasion, the philosopher made such large demands upon my time, that I was unable to meet her as I was wont. He was engaged in some mighty work, and I was forced to remain, day and night, feeding his furnaces and watching his chemical preparations. Bertha waited for me in vain at the fountain. Her haughty spirit fired at this neglect; and when at last I stole out during the few short minutes allotted to me for slumber, and hoped to be consoled by her, she received me with disdain, dismissed me in scorn, and vowed that any man should possess her hand rather than he who could not be in two places at once for her sake. She would be revenged! – And truly she was. In my dingy retreat I heard that she had been hunting, attended by Albert Hoffer. Albert Hoffer was favoured by her protectress, and the three passed in cavalcade before my smoky window. Methought that they mentioned my name – it was followed by a laugh of derision, as her dark eyes glanced contemptuously towards my abode.

Jealousy, with all its venom, and all its misery, entered my breast. Now I shed a torrent of tears, to think that I should never call her mine; and, anon, I imprecated a thousand curses on her inconstancy. Yet, still I must stir the fires of the alchymist, still attend on the changes of his unintelligible medicines.

Cornelius had watched for three days and nights, nor closed his eyes. The progress of his alembics was slower than he expected: in spite of his anxiety, sleep weighed upon his eyelids. Again and again he threw off drowsiness with more than human energy; again and again it stole away his senses. He eyed his crucibles wistfully. "Not ready yet," he murmured; "will another night pass before the work is accomplished? Winzy, you are vigilant – you are faithful – you have slept, my boy – you slept last night. Look at that glass vessel. The liquid it contains is of a soft rose-colour: the moment it begins to change its hue, awaken me – till then I may close my eyes. First, it will turn white, and then emit golden flashes; but wait not till then; when the rose-colour fades, rouse me." I scarcely heard the last words, muttered, as they were, in sleep. Even then he did not quite yield to nature. "Winzy, my boy," he again said, "do not touch the vessel – do not put it to your lips; it is a philter – a philter to cure love; you would not cease to love your Bertha – beware to drink!"

And he slept. His venerable head sunk on his breast, and I scarce heard his regular breathing. For a few minutes I watched the vessel – the rosy hue of the liquid remained unchanged. Then my thoughts wandered – they visited the fountain, and dwelt on a thousand charming scenes never to be renewed – never! Serpents and adders were in my heart as the word "Never!" half formed itself on my lips. False girl! – false and cruel! Never more would she smile on me as that evening she smiled on Albert. Worthless, detested woman! I would not remain unrevenged – she should see Albert expire at her feet – she should die beneath my vengeance. She had smiled in disdain and triumph – she knew my wretchedness and her power. Yet what power had she? – the power of exciting my hate – my utter scorn – my – oh, all but indifference! Could I attain that – could I regard her with careless eyes, transferring my rejected love to one fairer and more true, that were indeed a victory!

A bright flash darted before my eyes. I had forgotten the medicine of the adept; I gazed on it with wonder: flashes of admirable beauty, more bright than those which the diamond emits when the sun's rays are on it, glanced from the surface of the liquid; an odour the most fragrant and grateful stole over my sense; the vessel seemed one globe of living radiance, lovely to the eye, and most inviting to the taste. The first thought, instinctively inspired by the grosser sense, was, I will – I must drink. I raised the vessel to my lips. "It will cure me of love – of torture!" Already I had quaffed half of the most delicious liquor ever tasted by the palate of man, when the philosopher stirred. I started – I dropped the glass – the fluid flamed and glanced along the floor, while I felt Cornelius's gripe at my throat, as he shrieked aloud, "Wretch! you have destroyed the labour of my life!"

The philosopher was totally unaware that I had drunk any portion of his drug. His idea was, and I gave a tacit assent to it, that I had raised the vessel from curiosity, and that, frighted at its brightness, and the flashes of intense light it gave forth, I had let it fall. I never undeceived him. The fire of the medicine was quenched – the fragrance died away – he grew calm, as a philosopher should under the heaviest trials, and dismissed me to rest.

I will not attempt to describe the sleep of glory and bliss which bathed my soul in paradise during the remaining hours of that memorable night. Words would be faint and shallow types of my enjoyment, or of the gladness that possessed my bosom when I woke. I trod air – my thoughts were in heaven. Earth appeared heaven, and my inheritance upon it was to be one trance of delight. "This it is to be cured of love," I thought; "I will see Bertha this day, and she will find her lover cold and regardless; too happy to be disdainful, yet how utterly indifferent to her!"

The hours danced away. The philosopher, secure that he had once succeeded, and believing that he might again, began to concoct the same medicine once more. He was shut up with his books and drugs, and I had a holiday. I dressed myself with care; I looked in an old but polished shield, which served me for a mirror; methought my good looks had wonderfully improved. I hurried beyond the precincts of the town, joy in my soul, the beauty of heaven and earth around me. I turned my steps towards the castle – I could look on its lofty turrets with lightness of heart, for I was cured of love. My Bertha saw me afar off, as I came up the avenue. I know not what sudden impulse animated her bosom, but at the sight, she sprung with a light fawn-like bound down the marble steps, and was hastening towards me. But I had been perceived by another person. The old high-born hag, who called herself her protectress, and was her tyrant, had seen me, also; she hobbled, panting, up the terrace; a page, as ugly as herself, held up her train, and fanned her as she hurried along, and stopped my fair girl with a "How, now, my bold mistress? whither so fast? Back to your cage – hawks are abroad!"

Bertha clasped her hands – her eyes were still bent on my approaching figure. I saw the contest. How I abhorred the old crone who checked the kind impulses of my Bertha's softening heart. Hitherto, respect for her rank had caused me to avoid the lady of the castle; now I disdained such trivial considerations. I was cured of love, and lifted above all human fears; I hastened forwards, and soon reached the terrace. How lovely Bertha looked! her eyes flashing fire, her cheeks glowing with impatience and anger, she was a thousand times more graceful and charming than ever – I no longer loved – Oh! no, I adored – worshipped – idolized her!

She had that morning been persecuted, with more than usual vehemence, to consent to an immediate marriage with my rival. She was reproached with the encouragement that she had shown him – she was threatened with being turned out of doors with disgrace and shame. Her proud spirit rose in arms at the threat; but when she remembered the scorn that she had heaped upon me, and how, perhaps, she had thus lost one whom she now regarded as her only friend, she wept with remorse and rage. At that moment I appeared. "O, Winzy!" she exclaimed, "take me to your mother's cot; swiftly let me leave the detested luxuries and wretchedness of this noble dwelling – take me to poverty and happiness."

I clasped her in my arms with transport. The old lady was speechless with fury, and broke forth into invective only when we were far on our road to my natal cottage. My mother received the fair fugitive, escaped from a gilt cage to nature and liberty, with tenderness and joy; my father, who loved her, welcomed her heartily; it was a day of rejoicing, which did not need the addition of the celestial potion of the alchymist to steep me in delight.

Soon after this eventful day, I became the husband of Bertha. I ceased to be the scholar of Cornelius, but I continued his friend. I always felt grateful to him for having, unawares, procured me that delicious draught of a divine elixir, which, instead of curing me of love (sad cure! solitary and joyless remedy for evils which seem blessings to the memory), had inspired me with courage and resolution, thus winning for me an inestimable treasure in my Bertha.

I often called to mind that period of trance-like inebriation with wonder. The drink of Cornelius had not fulfilled the task for which he affirmed that it had been prepared, but its effects were more potent and blissful than words can express. They had faded by degrees, yet they lingered long – and painted life in hues of splendour. Bertha often wondered at my lightness of heart and unaccustomed gaiety; for, before, I had been rather serious, or even sad, in my disposition. She loved me the better for my cheerful temper, and our days were winged by joy.

Five years afterwards I was suddenly summoned to the bedside of the dying Cornelius. He had sent for me in haste, conjuring my instant presence, I found him stretched on his pallet, enfeebled even to death; all of life that yet remained animated his piercing eyes, and they were fixed on a glass vessel, full of a roseate liquid.

"Behold," he said, in a broken and inward voice, "the vanity of human wishes! a second time my hopes are about to be crowned, a second time they are destroyed. Look at that liquor – you remember five years ago I had prepared the same, with the same success; – then, as now, my thirsting lips expected to taste the immortal elixir – you dashed it from me! and at present it is too late."

He spoke with difficulty, and fell back on his pillow. I could not help saying, –

"How, revered master, can a cure for love restore you to life?"

A faint smile gleamed across his face as I listened earnestly to his scarcely intelligible answer.

"A cure for love and for all things – the Elixir of Immortality. Ah! if now I might drink, I should live for ever!"

As he spoke, a golden flash gleamed from the fluid; a well-remembered fragrance stole over the air; he raised himself, all weak as he was – strength seemed miraculously to re-enter his frame – he stretched forth his hand – a loud explosion startled me – a ray of fire shot up from the elixir, and the glass vessel which contained it was shivered to atoms! I turned my eyes towards the philosopher; he had fallen back – his eyes were glassy – his features rigid – he was dead!

But I lived, and was to live for ever! So said the unfortunate alchymist, and for a few days I believed his words. I remembered the glorious drunkenness that had followed my stolen draught. I reflected on the change I had felt in my frame – in my soul. The bounding elasticity of the one – the buoyant lightness of the other. I surveyed myself in a mirror, and could perceive no change in my features during the space of the five years which had elapsed. I remembered the radiant hues and grateful scent of that delicious beverage – worthy the gift it was capable of bestowing – I was, then, IMMORTAL!

A few days after I laughed at my credulity. The old proverb, that "a prophet is least regarded in his own country," was true with respect to me and my defunct master. I loved him as a man – I respected him as a sage – but I derided the notion that he could command the powers of darkness, and laughed at the superstitious fears with which he was regarded by the vulgar. He was a wise philosopher, but had no acquaintance with any spirits but those clad in flesh and blood. His science was simply human; and human science, I soon persuaded myself, could never conquer nature's laws so far as to imprison the soul for ever within its carnal habitation. Cornelius had brewed a soul-refreshing drink – more inebriating than wine – sweeter and more fragrant than any fruit: it possessed probably strong medicinal powers, imparting gladness to the heart and vigor to the limbs; but its effects would wear out; already were they diminished in my frame. I was a lucky fellow to have quaffed health and joyous spirits, and perhaps long life, at my master's hands; but my good fortune ended there: longevity was far different from immortality.

I continued to entertain this belief for many years. Sometimes a thought stole across me – Was the alchymist indeed deceived? But my habitual credence was that I should meet the fate of all the children of Adam at my appointed time – a little late, but still at a natural age. Yet it was certain that I retained a wonderfully youthful look. I was laughed at for my vanity in consulting the mirror so often, but consulted it in vain – my brow was untrenched – my cheeks – my eyes – my whole person continued as untarnished as in my twentieth year.

I was troubled. I looked at the faded beauty of Bertha – I seemed more like her son. By degrees our neighbours began to make similar observations, and I found at last that I went by the name of the Scholar bewitched. Bertha herself grew uneasy. She became jealous and peevish, and at length she began to question me. We had no children; we were all in all to each other; and though, as she grew older, her vivacious spirit became a little allied to ill-temper, and her beauty sadly diminished, I cherished her in my heart as the mistress I had idolized, the wife I had sought and won with such perfect love.

At last our situation became intolerable: Bertha was fifty – I twenty years of age. I had, in very shame, in some measure adopted the habits of a more advanced age; I no longer mingled in the dance among the young and gay, but my heart bounded along with them while I restrained my feet; and a sorry figure I cut among the Nestors of our village. But before the time I mention, things were altered – we were universally shunned; we were – at least, I was – reported to have kept up an iniquitous acquaintance with some of my former master's supposed friends. Poor Bertha was pitied, but deserted. I was regarded with horror and detestation.

What was to be done? We sat by our winter fire – poverty had made itself felt, for none would buy the produce of my farm; and often I had been forced to journey twenty miles, to some place where I was not known, to dispose of our property. It is true we had saved something for an evil day – that day was come.

We sat by our lone fireside – the old-hearted youth and his antiquated wife. Again Bertha insisted on knowing the truth; she recapitulated all she had ever heard said about me, and added her own observations. She conjured me to cast off the spell; she described how much more comely gray hairs were than my chestnut locks; she descanted on the reverence and respect due to age – how preferable to the slight regard paid to mere children: could I imagine that the despicable gifts of youth and good looks outweighed disgrace, hatred, and scorn? Nay, in the end I should be burnt as a dealer in the black art, while she, to whom I had not deigned to communicate any portion of my good fortune, might be stoned as my accomplice. At length she insinuated that I must share my secret with her, and bestow on her like benefits to those I myself enjoyed, or she would denounce me – and then she burst into tears.

Thus beset, methought it was the best way to tell the truth. I revealed it as tenderly as I could, and spoke only of a *very long life*, not of immortality – which representation, indeed, coincided best with my own ideas. When I ended, I rose and said,

"And now, my Bertha, will you denounce the lover of your youth? – You will not, I know. But it is too hard, my poor wife, that you should suffer from my ill-luck and the accursed arts of Cornelius. I will leave you – you have wealth enough, and friends will return in my absence. I will go; young as I seem, and strong as I am, I can work and gain my bread among strangers, unsuspected and unknown. I loved you in youth; God is my witness that I would not desert you in age, but that your safety and happiness require it."

I took my cap and moved towards the door; in a

moment Bertha's arms were round my neck, and her lips were pressed to mine. "No, my husband, my Winzy," she said, "you shall not go alone – take me with you; we will remove from this place, and, as you say, among strangers we shall be unsuspected and safe. I am not so very old as quite to shame you, my Winzy; and I dare say the charm will soon wear off, and, with the blessing of God, you will become more elderly-looking, as is fitting; you shall not leave me."

I returned the good soul's embrace heartily. "I will not, my Bertha; but for your sake I had not thought of such a thing. I will be your true, faithful husband while you are spared to me, and do my duty by you to the last."

The next day we prepared secretly for our emigration. We were obliged to make great pecuniary sacrifices – it could not be helped. We realised a sum sufficient, at least, to maintain us while Bertha lived; and, without saying adieu to any one, quitted our native country to take refuge in a remote part of western France.

It was a cruel thing to transport poor Bertha from her native village, and the friends of her youth, to a new country, new language, new customs. The strange secret of my destiny rendered this removal immaterial to me; but I compassionated her deeply, and was glad to perceive that she found compensation for her misfortunes in a variety of little ridiculous circumstances. Away from all tell-tale chroniclers, she sought to decrease the apparent disparity of our ages by a thousand feminine arts – rouge, youthful dress, and assumed juvenility of manner. I could not be angry – Did not I myself wear a mask? Why quarrel with hers, because it was less successful? I grieved deeply when I remembered that this was my Bertha, whom I had loved so fondly, and won with such transport – the dark-eyed, dark-haired girl, with smiles of enchanting archness and a step like a fawn – this mincing, simpering, jealous old woman. I should have revered her gray locks and withered cheeks: but thus! – It was my work, I knew; but I did not the less deplore this type of human weakness.

Her jealousy never slept. Her chief occupation was to discover that, in spite of outward appearances, I was myself growing old. I verily believe that the poor soul loved me truly in her heart, but never had woman so tormenting a mode of displaying fondness. She would discern wrinkles in my face and decrepitude in my walk, while I bounded along in youthful vigour, the youngest looking of twenty youths. I never dared address another woman: on one occasion, fancying that the belle of the village regarded me with favouring eyes, she bought me a gray wig. Her constant discourse among her acquaintances was, that though I looked so young, there was ruin at work within my frame; and she affirmed that the worst symptom about me was my apparent health. My youth was a disease, she said, and I ought at all times to prepare, if not for a sudden and awful death, at least to awake some morning white-headed, and bowed down with all the marks of advanced years. I let her talk – I often joined in her conjectures. Her warnings chimed in with my never-ceasing speculations concerning my state, and I took an earnest, though painful, interest in listening to all that her quick wit and excited imagination could say on the subject.

Why dwell on these minute circumstances? We lived on for many long years. Bertha became bed-rid and paralytic: I nursed her as a mother might a child. She grew peevish, and still harped upon one string – of how long I should survive her. It has ever been a source of consolation to me, that I performed my duty scrupulously towards her. She had been mine in youth, she was mine in age, and at last, when I heaped the sod over her corpse, I wept to feel that I had lost all that really bound me to humanity.

Since then how many have been my cares and woes, how few and empty my enjoyments! I pause here in my history – I will pursue it no further. A sailor without rudder or compass, tossed on a stormy sea – a traveller lost on a wide-spread heath, without landmark or star to guide him – such have I been: more lost, more hopeless than either. A nearing ship, a gleam from some far cot, may save them; but I have no beacon except the hope of death.

Death! mysterious, ill-visaged friend of weak humanity! Why alone of all mortals have you cast me from your sheltering fold? O, for the peace of the grave! the deep silence of the iron-bound tomb! that thought would cease to work in my brain, and my heart beat no more with emotions varied only by new forms of sadness!

Am I immortal? I return to my first question. In the first place, is it not more probable that the beverage of the alchymist was fraught rather with longevity than eternal life? Such is my hope. And then be it remembered, that I only drank *half* of the potion prepared by him. Was not the whole necessary to complete the charm? To have drained half the Elixir of Immortality is but to be half immortal – my For-ever is thus truncated and null.

But again, who shall number the years of the half of eternity? I often try to imagine by what rule the infinite may be divided. Sometimes I fancy age advancing upon me. One gray hair I have found. Fool! do I lament? Yes, the fear of age and death often creeps coldly into my heart; and the more I live, the more I dread death, even while I abhor life. Such an enigma is man – born to perish – when he wars, as I do, against the established laws of his nature.

But for this anomaly of feeling surely I might die: the medicine of the alchymist would not be proof against fire – sword – and the strangling waters. I have gazed upon the blue depths of many a placid lake, and the tumultuous rushing of many a mighty river, and have said, peace inhabits those waters; yet I have turned my steps away, to live yet another day. I have asked myself, whether suicide would be a crime in one to whom thus only the portals of the other world could be opened. I have done all, except presenting myself as a soldier or duellist, an object of destruction to my – no, *not* my fellow-mortals, and therefore I have shrunk away. They are not my fellows. The inextinguishable power of life in my frame, and their ephemeral existence, place us wide as the poles asunder. I could not raise a hand against the meanest or the most powerful among them.

Thus I have lived on for many a year – alone, and weary of myself – desirous of death, yet never dying – a mortal immortal. Neither ambition nor avarice can enter my mind, and the ardent love that gnaws at my heart never to be returned – never to find an equal on which to expend itself – lives there only to torment me.

This very day I conceived a design by which I may end all – without self-slaughter, without making another man a Cain – an expedition, which mortal frame can never survive, even endued with the youth and strength that inhabits mine. Thus I shall put my immortality to the test, and rest for ever – or return, the wonder and benefactor of the human species.

Before I go, a miserable vanity has caused me to pen these pages. I would not die, and leave no name behind. Three centuries have passed since I quaffed the fatal beverage: another year shall not elapse before, encountering gigantic dangers – warring with the powers of frost in their home – beset by famine, toil, and tempest – I yield this body, too tenacious a cage for a soul which thirsts for freedom, to the destructive elements of air and water – or, if I survive, my name shall be recorded as one of the most famous among the sons of men; and, my task achieved, I shall adopt more resolute means, and, by scattering and annihilating the atoms that compose my frame, set at liberty the life imprisoned within, and so cruelly prevented from soaring from this dim earth to a sphere more congenial to its immortal essence.

Edgar Allan Poe

Poe's greatest skill was in evoking a beautifully estranging and unsettling Gothic-ness of mood and effect. His touch was not always sure, and sometimes he slides into pomposity (as in his windily vatic prose poem *Eureka* [1848]) or else into a kind of facetiousness; the moon voyage of 'The Unparalleled Adventure of One Hans Pfaall' (1835) is revealed, jokingly, to be nothing more than a hoax. But often enough he hits his spot exactly. What insinuates 'A Tale of the Ragged Mountain' into the reader's imagination is its very unsettledness: a story perhaps of telepathy, or time travel, or madness, or something else, and I'm not sure I could say what exactly.

During the fall of the year 1827, while residing near Charlottesville, Virginia, I casually made the acquaintance of Mr. Augustus Bedloe. This young gentleman was remarkable in every respect, and excited in me a profound interest and curiosity. I found it impossible to comprehend him either in his moral or his physical relations. Of his family I could obtain no satisfactory account. Whence he came, I never ascertained. Even about his age—although I call him a young gentleman—there was something which perplexed me in no little degree. He certainly *seemed* young—and he made a point of speaking about his youth—yet there were moments when I should have had little trouble in imagining him a hundred years of age. But in no regard was he more peculiar than in his personal appearance. He was singularly tall and thin. He stooped much. His limbs were exceedingly long and emaciated. His forehead was broad and low. His complexion was absolutely bloodless. His mouth was large and flexible, and his teeth were more wildly uneven, although sound, than I had ever before seen teeth in a human head. The expression of his smile, however, was by no means unpleasing, as might be supposed; but it had no variation whatever. It was one of profound melancholy—of a phaseless and unceasing gloom. His eyes were abnormally large, and round like those of a cat. The pupils, too, upon any accession or diminution of light, underwent contraction or dilation, just such as is observed in the feline tribe. In moments of excitement the orbs grew bright to a degree almost inconceivable; seeming to emit luminous rays, not of a reflected but of an intrinsic lustre, as does a candle or the sun; yet their ordinary condition was so totally vapid, filmy, and dull, as to convey the idea of the eyes of a long-interred corpse.

These peculiarities of person appeared to cause him much annoyance, and he was continually alluding to them in a sort of half explanatory, half apologetic strain, which, when I first heard it, impressed me very painfully. I soon, however, grew accustomed to it, and my uneasiness wore off. It seemed to be his design rather to insinuate than directly to assert that, physically, he had not always been what he was—that a long series of neuralgic attacks had reduced him from a condition of more than usual personal beauty, to that which I saw. For many years past he had been attended by a physician, named Templeton—an old gentleman, perhaps seventy years of age—whom he had first encountered at Saratoga, and from whose attention, while there, he either received, or fancied that he received, great benefit. The result was that Bedloe, who was wealthy, had made an arrangement with Dr. Templeton, by which the latter, in consideration of a liberal annual allowance, had consented to devote his time and medical experience exclusively to the care of the invalid.

Doctor Templeton had been a traveller in his younger days, and at Paris had become a convert, in great measure, to the doctrine of Mesmer. It was altogether by means of magnetic remedies that he had succeeded in alleviating the acute pains of his patient; and this success had very naturally inspired the latter with a certain degree of confidence in the opinions from which the remedies had been educed. The doctor, however, like all enthusiasts, had struggled hard to make a thorough convert of his pupil, and finally so far gained his point as to induce the sufferer to submit to numerous experiments. By a frequent repetition of these, a result had arisen, which of late days has become so common as to attract little or no attention, but which, at the period of which I write, had very rarely been known in America. I mean to say, that between Doctor Templeton and Bedloe there had grown up, little by little, a very distinct and strongly marked *rapport,* or magnetic relation. I am not prepared to assert, however, that this *rapport* extended beyond the limits of the simple sleep-producing power; but this power itself had attained great intensity. At the first attempt to induce the magnetic somnolency, the mesmerist entirely failed. In the fifth or sixth he succeeded very partially, and after long-continued effort. Only at the twelfth was the triumph complete. After this the will of the patient succumbed rapidly to that of the physician, so that, when I first became acquainted with the two, sleep was brought about almost instantaneously by the mere volition of the operator, even when the invalid was unaware of his presence. It is only now, in the year 1845, when similar miracles are witnessed daily by thousands, that I dare venture to record this apparent impossibility as a matter of serious fact.

The temperature of Bedloe was, in the highest degree sensitive, excitable, enthusiastic. His imagination was singularly vigorous and creative; and no doubt it derived additional force from the habitual use of morphine, which he swallowed in great quantity, and without which he would have found it impossible to exist. It was his practice to take a very large dose of it immediately after breakfast each morning,—or, rather, immediately after a cup of strong coffee, for he ate nothing in the forenoon,—and then set forth alone, or attended only by a dog, upon a long ramble among the chain of wild and dreary hills that lie westward and southward of Charlottesville, and are there dignified by the title of the Ragged Mountains.

Upon a dim, warm, misty day, toward the close of November, and during the strange *interregnum* of the seasons which in America is termed the Indian summer, Mr. Bedloe departed as usual for the hills. The day passed, and still he did not return.

About eight o'clock at night, having become seriously alarmed at his protracted absence, we were about setting out in search of him, when he unexpectedly made his appearance, in health no worse than usual, and in rather more than ordinary spirits. The account which he gave of his expedition, and of the events which had detained him, was a singular one indeed.

"You will remember," said he, "that it was about nine in the morning when I left Charlottesville. I bent my steps immediately to the mountains, and, about ten, entered a gorge which was entirely new to me. I followed the windings of this pass with much interest. The scenery which presented itself on all sides, although scarcely entitled to be called grand, had about it an indescribable and to me a delicious aspect of dreary desolation. The solitude seemed absolutely virgin. I could not help believing that the green sods and the gray rocks upon which I trod had been trodden never before by the foot of a human being. So entirely secluded, and in fact inaccessible, except through a series of accidents, is the entrance of the ravine, that it is by no means impossible that I was indeed the first adventurer—the very first and sole adventurer who had ever penetrated its recesses.

"The thick and peculiar mist, or smoke, which distinguishes the Indian summer, and which now hung heavily over all objects, served, no doubt, to deepen the vague impressions which these objects created. So dense was this pleasant fog that I could at no time see more than a dozen yards of the path before me. This path was excessively sinuous, and as the sun could not be seen, I soon lost all idea of the direction in which I journeyed. In the meantime the morphine had its customary effect—that of enduing all the external world with an intensity of interest. In the quivering of a leaf—in the hue of a blade of grass—in the shape of a trefoil—in the humming of a bee—in the gleaming of a dew-drop—in the breathing of the wind—in the faint odors that came from the forest—there came a whole universe of suggestion—a gay and motley train of rhapsodical and immethodical thought.

"Busied in this, I walked on for several hours, during which the mist deepened around me to so great an extent that at length I was reduced to an absolute groping of the way. And now an indescribable uneasiness possessed me—a species of nervous hesitation and tremor. I feared to tread, lest I should be precipitated into some abyss. I remembered, too, strange stories told about these Ragged Hills, and of the uncouth and fierce races of men who tenanted their groves and caverns. A thousand vague fancies oppressed and disconcerted me—fancies the more distressing because vague. Very suddenly my attention was arrested by the loud beating of a drum.

"My amazement was, of course, extreme. A drum in these hills was a thing unknown. I could not have been more surprised at the sound of the trump of the Archangel. But a new and still more astounding source of interest and perplexity arose. There came a wild rattling or jingling sound, as if of a bunch of large keys, and upon the instant a dusky-visaged and half-naked man rushed past me with a shriek. He came so close to my person that I felt his hot breath upon my face. He bore in one hand an instrument composed of an assemblage of steel rings, and shook them vigorously as he ran. Scarcely had he disappeared in the mist, before, panting after him, with open mouth and glaring eyes, there darted a huge beast. I could not be mistaken in its character. It was a hyena.

"The sight of this monster rather relieved than heightened my terrors—for I now made sure that I dreamed, and endeavored to arouse myself to waking consciousness. I stepped boldly and briskly forward. I rubbed my eyes. I called aloud. I pinched my limbs. A small spring of water presented itself to my view, and here, stooping, I bathed my hands and my head and neck. This seemed to dissipate the equivocal sensations which had hitherto annoyed me. I arose, as I thought, a new man, and proceeded steadily and complacently on my unknown way.

"At length, quite overcome by exertion, and by a certain oppressive closeness of the atmosphere, I seated myself beneath a tree. Presently there came a feeble gleam of sunshine, and the shadow of the leaves of the tree fell faintly but definitely upon the grass. At this shadow I gazed wonderingly for many minutes. Its character stupefied me with astonishment. I looked upward. The tree was a palm.

"I now arose hurriedly, and in a state of fearful agitation—for the fancy that I dreamed would serve me no longer. I saw—I felt that I had perfect command of my senses—and these senses now brought to my soul a world of novel and singular sensation. The heat became all at once intolerable. A strange odor loaded the breeze. A low, continuous murmur, like that arising from a full, but gently flowing river, came to my ears, intermingled with the peculiar hum of multitudinous human voices.

"While I listened in an extremity of astonishment which I need not attempt to describe, a strong and brief gust of wind bore off the incumbent fog as if by the wand of an enchanter.

"I found myself at the foot of a high mountain, and looking down into a vast plain, through which wound a majestic river. On the margin of this river stood an Eastern-looking city, such as we read of in the Arabian Tales, but of a character even more singular than any there described. From my position, which was far above the level of the town, I could perceive its every nook and corner, as if delineated on a map. The streets seemed innumerable, and crossed each other irregularly in all directions, but were rather long winding alleys than streets, and absolutely swarmed with inhabitants. The houses were wildly picturesque. On every hand was a wilderness of balconies, of verandas, of minarets, of shrines, and fantastically carved oriels. Bazaars abounded; and there were displayed rich wares in infinite variety and profusion—silks, muslins, the most dazzling cutlery, the most magnificent jewels and gems. Besides these things, were seen, on all sides, banners and palanquins, litters with stately dames close-veiled, elephants gorgeously caparisoned, idols grotesquely hewn, drums, banners, and gongs, spears, silver and gilded maces. And amid the crowd, and the clamor, and the general intricacy and confusion—amid the million of black and yellow men, turbaned and robed, and of flowing beard, there roamed a countless multitude of holy filleted bulls, while vast legions of the filthy but sacred ape clambered, chattering and shrieking, about the cornices of the mosques, or clung to the minarets and oriels. From the swarming streets to the banks of the river, there descended innumerable flights of steps leading to bathing places, while the river itself seemed to force a passage with difficulty through the vast fleets of deeply burdened ships that far and wide encountered its surface. Beyond the limits of the city arose, in frequent majestic groups, the palm and the cocoa, with other gigantic and weird trees of vast age; and here and there might be seen a field of rice, the thatched hut of a peasant, a tank, a stray temple, a gypsy camp, or a solitary graceful maiden taking her way, with a pitcher upon her head, to the banks of the magnificent river.

"You will say now, of course, that I dreamed; but not so. What I saw—what I heard—what I felt—what I thought—had about it nothing of the unmistakable idiosyncrasy of the dream. All was rigorously self-consistent. At first, doubting that I was really awake, I entered into a series of tests, which soon convinced me that I really was. Now, when one dreams, and, in the dream, suspects that he dreams, the suspicion *never fails to confirm itself*, and the sleeper is almost immediately aroused. Thus Novalis errs not in saying that 'we are near waking when we dream that we dream.' Had the vision occurred to me as I describe it, without my suspecting it as a dream, then a dream it might absolutely have been, but, occurring as it did, and suspected and tested as it was, I am forced to class it among other phenomena."

"In this I am not sure that you are wrong," observed Dr. Templeton, "but proceed. You arose and descended into the city."

"I arose," continued Bedloe, regarding the doctor with an air of profound astonishment, "I arose, as you say, and descended into the city. On my way I fell in with an immense populace, crowding through every avenue, all in the same direction, and exhibiting in every action the wildest excitement. Very suddenly, and by some inconceivable impulse, I became intensely imbued with personal interest in what was going on. I seemed to feel that I had an important part to play, without exactly understanding what it was. Against the crowd which environed me, however, I experienced a deep sentiment of animosity. I shrank from amid them, and, swiftly, by a circuitous path, reached and entered the city. Here all was the wildest tumult and contention. A small party of men, clad in garments half Indian, half European, and officered by gentlemen in a uniform partly British, were engaged, at great odds, with the swarming rabble of the alleys. I joined the weaker party, arming myself with the weapons of a fallen officer, and fighting I knew not whom with the nervous ferocity of despair. We were soon overpowered by numbers, and driven to seek refuge in a species of kiosk. Here we barricaded ourselves, and, for the present, were secure. From a loop-hole near the summit of the kiosk, I perceived a vast crowd, in furious agitation, surrounding and assaulting a gay palace that overhung the river. Presently, from an upper window of this palace, there descended an effeminate-looking person, by means of a string made of the turbans of his attendants. A boat was at hand, in which he escaped to the opposite bank of the river.

"And now a new object took possession of my soul. I spoke a few hurried but energetic words to my companions, and, having succeeded in gaining over a few of them to my purpose, made a frantic sally from the kiosk. We rushed amid the crowd that surrounded it. They retreated, at first, before us. They rallied, fought madly, and retreated again. In the meantime we were borne far from the kiosk, and became bewildered and entangled among the narrow streets of tall, overhanging houses, into the recesses of which the sun had never been able to shine. The rabble pressed impetuously upon us, harassing us with their spears, and overwhelming us with flights of arrows. These latter were very remarkable, and resembled in some respects the writhing creese of the Malay. They were made to imitate the body of a creeping serpent, and were long and black, with a poisoned barb. One of them struck me upon the right temple. I reeled and fell. An instantaneous and dreadful sickness seized me. I struggled—I gasped—I died."

"You will hardly persist *now*," said I, smiling, "that the whole of your adventure was not a dream. You are not prepared to maintain that you are dead?"

When I said these words, I of course expected some lively sally from Bedloe in reply; but, to my astonishment, he hesitated, trembled, became fearfully pallid, and remained silent. I looked toward Templeton. He sat erect and rigid in his chair—his teeth chattered, and his eyes were starting from their sockets. "Proceed!" he at length said hoarsely to Bedloe.

"For many minutes," continued the latter, "my sole sentiment—my sole feeling—was that of darkness and nonentity, with the consciousness of death. At length there seemed to pass a violent and sudden shock through my soul, as if of electricity. With it came the sense of elasticity and of light. This latter I felt—not saw. In an instant I seemed to rise from the ground. But I had no bodily, no visible, audible, or palpable presence. The crowd had departed. The tumult had ceased. The city was in comparative repose. Beneath me lay my corpse, with the arrow in my temple, the whole head greatly swollen and disfigured. But all these things I felt—not saw. I took interest in nothing. Even the corpse seemed a matter in which I had no concern. Volition I had none, but appeared to be impelled into motion, and flitted buoyantly out of the city, retracing the circuitous path by which I had entered it. When I had attained that point of the ravine in the mountains at which I had encountered the hyena, I again experienced a shock as of a galvanic battery; the sense of weight, of volition, of substance, returned. I became my original self, and bent my steps eagerly homeward—but the past had not lost the vividness of the real—and not now, even for an instant, can I compel my understanding to regard it as a dream."

"Nor was it," said Templeton, with an air of deep solemnity, "yet it would be difficult to say how otherwise it should be termed. Let us suppose only, that the soul of the man of to-day is upon the verge of some stupendous psychal discoveries. Let us content ourselves with this supposition. For the rest I have some explanation to make. Here is a water-color drawing, which I should have shown you before, but which an unaccountable sentiment of horror has hitherto prevented me from showing."

We looked at the picture which he presented. I saw nothing in it of an extraordinary character; but its effect upon Bedloe was prodigious. He nearly fainted as he gazed. And yet it was but a miniature portrait—a miraculously accurate one, to be sure—of his own very remarkable features. At least this was my thought as I regarded it.

"You will perceive," said Templeton, "the date of this picture—it is here, scarcely visible, in this corner—1780. In this year was the portrait taken. It is the likeness of a dead friend—a Mr. Oldeb—to whom I became much attached at Calcutta, during the administration of Warren Hastings. I was then only twenty years old. When I first saw you, Mr. Bedloe, at Saratoga, it was the miraculous similarity which existed between yourself and the painting which induced me to accost you, to seek your friendship, and to bring about those arrangements which resulted in my becoming your constant companion. In accomplishing this point, I was urged partly, and perhaps principally, by a regretful memory of the deceased, but also, in part, by an uneasy, and not altogether horrorless curiosity respecting yourself.

"In your detail of the vision which presented itself to you amid the hills, you have described, with the minutest accuracy, the Indian city of Benares, upon the Holy River. The riots, the combat, the massacre, were the actual events of the insurrection of Cheyte Sing, which took place in 1780, when Hastings was put in imminent peril of his life. The man escaping by the string of turbans was Cheyte Sing himself. The party in the kiosk were sepoys and British officers, headed by Hastings. Of this party I was one, and did all I could to prevent the rash and fatal sally of the officer who fell, in the crowded alleys, by the poisoned arrow of a Bengalee. That officer was my dearest friend. It was Oldeb. You will perceive by these manuscripts," (here the speaker produced a note-book in which several pages appeared to have been freshly written) "that at the very period in which you fancied these things amid the hills, I was engaged in detailing them upon paper here at home."

In about a week after this conversation, the following paragraphs appeared in a Charlottesville paper:

"We have the painful duty of announcing the

death of MR. AUGUSTUS BEDLO, a gentleman whose amiable manners and many virtues have long endeared him to the citizens of Charlottesville.

"Mr. B., for some years past, has been subject to neuralgia, which has often threatened to terminate fatally; but this can be regarded only as the mediate cause of his decease. The proximate cause was one of especial singularity. In an excursion to the Ragged Mountains, a few days since, a slight cold and fever were contracted, attended with great determination of blood to the head. To relieve this, Dr. Templeton resorted to topical bleeding. Leeches were applied to the temples. In a fearfully brief period the patient died, when it appeared that, in the jar containing the leeches, had been introduced, by accident, one of the venomous vermicular sangsues which are now and then found in the neighboring ponds. This creature fastened itself upon a small artery in the right temple. Its close resemblance to the medicinal leech caused the mistake to be overlooked until too late.

"N.B.—The poisonous sangsue of Charlottesville may always be distinguished from the medicinal leech by its blackness, and especially by its writhing or vermicular motions, which very nearly resemble those of a snake."

I was speaking with the editor of the paper in question, upon the topic of this remarkable accident, when it occurred to me to ask how it happened that the name of the deceased had been given as Bedlo.

"I presume," said I, "you have authority for this spelling, but I have always supposed the name to be written with an *e* at the end."

"Authority?—no," he replied. "It is a mere typographical error. The name is Bedlo with an *e*, all the world over, and I never knew it to be spelt otherwise in my life."

"Then," said I mutteringly, as I turned upon my heel, "then indeed has it come to pass that one truth is stranger than any fiction—for Bedlo, without the *e*, what is it but Oldeb conversed! And this man tells me it is a typographical error."

Florence McLandburgh

American writer Florence McLandburgh was born in Ohio in 1850. She wrote a good deal of mediocre poetry, much of it militaristically patriotic, under the pseudonym McLandburgh Wilson, but wrote her intriguing science-fiction short stories, published in 1876 under the title *The Automaton Ear, and Other Sketches*, under her own name. The title story first appeared in the magazine *Scribner's Monthly* in May 1873, and is premised on a machine that is capable of recovering all the sounds that ever existed, a striking variant of the notion of time travel that unlocks the past.

The day was hardly different from many another day, though I will likely recall it even when the mist of years has shrouded the past in an undefined hueless cloud. The sunshine came in at my open window. Out of doors it flooded all the land in its warm summer light—the spires of the town and the bare college campus; farther, the tall bearded barley and rustling oats; farther still, the wild grass and the forest, where the river ran and the blue haze dipped from the sky.

The temptation was greater than I could stand, and taking my book I shut up the "study," as the students called my small apartment, leaving it for one bounded by no walls or ceiling.

The woods rang with the hum and chirp of insects and birds. I threw myself down beneath a tall, broad-spreading tree. Against its moss-covered trunk I could hear the loud tap of the woodpecker secreted high up among its leaves, and off at the end of a tender young twig a robin trilled, swinging himself to and fro through the checkered sunlight. I never grew weary listening to the changeful voice of the forest and the river, and was hardly conscious of reading until I came upon this paragraph:—

"As a particle of the atmosphere is never lost, so sound is never lost. A strain of music or a simple tone will vibrate in the air forever and ever, decreasing according to a fixed ratio. The diffusion of the agitation extends in all directions, like the waves in a pool, but the ear is unable to detect it beyond a certain point. It is well known that some individuals can distinguish sounds which to others under precisely similar circumstances are wholly lost. Thus the fault is not in the sound itself, but in our organ of hearing, and a tone once in existence is always in existence."

This was nothing new to me. I had read it before, though I had never thought of it particularly; but while I listened to the robin, it seemed singular to know that all the sounds ever uttered, ever born, were floating in the air *now*—all music, every tone, every bird-song—and we, alas! could not hear them.

Suddenly a strange idea shot through my brain—Why not? Ay, *why not hear?* Men had constructed instruments which could magnify to the eye and—was it possible?—Why not?

I looked up and down the river, but saw neither it, nor the sky, nor the moss that I touched. Did the woodpecker still tap secreted among the leaves, and the robin sing, and the hum of insects run along the bank as before? I can not recollect, I can not recollect anything, only Mother Flinse, the deaf and dumb old crone that occasionally came to beg, and sell nuts to the students, was standing in the gateway. I nodded to her as I passed, and walked up her long, slim shadow that lay on the path. It was a strange idea that had come so suddenly into my head and startled me. I hardly dared to think of it, but I could think of nothing else. It could not be possible, and yet—why not?

Over and over in the restless hours of the night I asked myself, I said aloud, Why not? Then I laughed at my folly, and wondered what I was thinking of and tried to sleep—but if it *could* be done?

The idea clung to me. It forced itself up in class hours and made confusion in the lessons. Some said the professor was ill those two or three days before the vacation; perhaps I was. I scarcely slept; only the one thought grew stronger—Men had done more wonderful things; it certainly was possible, and I would accomplish this grand invention. I would construct the king of all instruments—I would construct an instrument which could catch these faint tones vibrating in the air and render them audible. Yes, and I would labor quietly until it was perfected, or the world might laugh.

The session closed and the college was deserted, save by the few musty students whom, even in imagination, one could hardly separate or distinguish from the old books on the library shelves. I could wish for no better opportunity to begin my great work. The first thing would be to prepare for it by a careful study of acoustics, and I buried myself among volumes on the philosophy of sound.

I went down to London and purchased a common ear-trumpet. My own ear was exceedingly acute, and to my great delight I found that, with the aid of the trumpet just as it was, I could distinguish sounds at a much greater distance, and those nearer were magnified in power. I had only to improve upon this instrument; careful study, careful work, careful experiment, and my hopes would undoubtedly be realized.

Back to my old room in the college I went with a complete set of tools. So days and weeks I shut myself in, and every day and every week brought nothing but disappointment. The instrument seemed only to diminish sound rather than increase it, yet still I worked on and vowed I would not grow discouraged.

Hour after hour I sat, looking out of my narrow window. The fields of barley and waving oats had been reaped, the wheat too had ripened and gone, but I did not notice. I sprang up with a joyful exclamation—Strange never to have thought of it before! Perhaps I had not spent my time in vain, after all. How could I expect to test my instrument in this close room with only that little window? It should be removed from immediate noises, high up in the open air, where there would be no obstructions. I would never succeed here—but where should I go? It must be some place in which I would never be liable to interruption, for my first object was to be shielded and work in secret.

I scoured the neighborhood for an appropriate spot without success, when it occurred to me that I had heard some one say the old gray church was shut up. This church was situated just beyond the suburbs of the town. It was built of rough stone, mottled and stained by unknown years. The high, square tower, covered by thick vines that clung and crept round its base, was the most venerable monument among all the slabs and tombs where it stood sentinel. Only graves deserted and uncared for by the living kept it company. People said the place was too damp for use, and talked of rebuilding, but it had never been done. Now if I could gain access to the tower, that was the very place for my purpose.

I found the door securely fastened, and walked round and round without discovering any way of entrance; but I made up my mind, if it were possible to get inside of that church I would do it, and without the help of keys. The high windows were not to be thought of; but in the rear of the building, lower down, where the fuel had probably been kept, there was a narrow opening which was boarded across. With very little difficulty I knocked out the planks and crept through. It was a cellar, and, as I had anticipated, the coal receptacle. After feeling about, I found a few rough steps which led to a door that was unlocked and communicated with the passage back of the vestry-room.

The tower I wished to explore was situated in the remote corner of the building. I passed on to the church. Its walls were discolored by green mould, and blackened where the water had dripped through. The sun, low down in the sky, lit the tall arched windows on the west, and made yellow strips across the long aisles, over the faded pews with their stiff, straight backs, over the chancel rail, over the altar with its somber wood-work; but there was no warmth; only the cheerless glare seemed to penetrate the cold, dead atmosphere,—only the cheerless glare without sparkle, without life, came into that voiceless sanctuary where the organ slept. At the right of the vestibule a staircase led to the tower; it ascended to a platform laid on a level with the four windows and a little above the point of the church roof. These four windows were situated one on each side of the tower, running high up, and the lower casement folding inward.

Here was my place. Above the tree-tops, in the free open air, with no obstacle to obstruct the wind, I could work unmolested by people or noise. The fresh breeze that fanned my face was cool and pleasant. An hour ago I had been tired, disappointed, and depressed; but now, buoyant with hope, I was ready to begin work again—work that I was determined to accomplish.

The sun had gone. I did not see the broken slabs and urns in the shadow down below; I did not see the sunken graves and the rank grass and the briers. I looked over them and saw the gorgeous fringes along the horizon, scarlet and gold and pearl; saw them quiver and brighten to flame, and the white wings of pigeons whirl and circle in the deepening glow.

I closed the windows, and when I had crawled out of the narrow hole, carefully reset the boards just as I had found them. In another day all the tools and books that I considered necessary were safely deposited in the tower. I only intended to make this my workshop, still, of course, occupying my old room in the college.

Here I matured plan after plan. I studied, read, worked, knowing, *feeling* that at last I must succeed;

but failure followed failure, and I sank into despondency only to begin again with a kind of desperation. When I went down to London and wandered about, hunting up different metals and hard woods, I never entered a concert-room or an opera-house. Was there not music in store for me, such as no mortal ear had ever heard? *All* the music, every strain that had sounded in the past ages? Ah, I could wait; I would work patiently and wait.

I was laboring now upon a theory that I had not tried heretofore. It was my last resource; if this failed, then—but it would not fail! I resolved not to make any test, not to put it near my ear until it was completed. I discarded all woods and used only the metals which best transmitted sound. Finally it was finished, even to the ivory ear-piece. I held the instrument all ready—I held it and looked eastward and westward and back again. Suddenly all control over the muscles of my hand was gone, it felt like stone; then the strange sensation passed away. I stood up and lifted the trumpet to my ear—What! Silence? No, no—I was faint, my brain was confused, whirling. I would not believe it; I would wait a moment until this dizziness was gone, and then—then I would be able to hear. I was deaf now. I still held the instrument; in my agitation the ivory tip shook off and rolled down rattling on the floor. I gazed at it mechanically, as if it had been a pebble; I never thought of replacing it, and, mechanically, I raised the trumpet a second time to my ear. A crash of discordant sounds, a confused jarring noise broke upon me and I drew back trembling, dismayed.

Fool! O fool of fools never to have thought of this, which a child, a dunce would not have overlooked! My great invention was nothing, was worse than nothing, was worse than a failure. I might have known that my instrument would magnify present sounds in the air to such a degree as to make them utterly drown all others, and, clashing together, produce this noise like the heavy rumble of thunder.

The college reopened, and I took up my old line of duties, or at least attempted them, for the school had grown distasteful to me. I was restless, moody, and discontented. I tried to forget my disappointment, but the effort was vain.

The spires of the town and the college campus glittered white, the fields of barley and oats were fields of snow, the forest leaves had withered and fallen, and the river slumbered, wrapped in a sheeting of ice. Still I brooded over my failure, and when again the wild grass turned green I no longer cared. I was not the same man that had looked out at the waving grain and the blue haze only a year before. A gloomy despondency had settled upon me, and I grew to hate the students, to hate the college, to hate society. In the first shock of discovered failure I had given up all hope, and the Winter passed I knew not how. I never wondered if the trouble could be remedied. Now it suddenly occurred to me, perhaps it was no failure after all. The instrument might be made adjustable, so as to be sensible to faint or severe vibrations at pleasure of the operator, and thus separate the sounds. I remembered how but for the accidental removal of the ivory my instrument perhaps would not have reflected any sound. I would work again and persevere.

I would have resigned my professorship, only it might create suspicion. I knew not that already they viewed me with curious eyes and sober faces. When the session finally closed, they tried to persuade me to leave the college during vacation and travel on the continent. I would feel much fresher, they told me, in the Autumn. In the Autumn? Ay, perhaps I might, perhaps I might, and I would not go abroad.

Once more the reapers came unnoticed. My work progressed slowly. Day by day I toiled up in the old church tower, and night by night I dreamed. In my sleep it often seemed that the instrument was suddenly completed, but before I could raise it to my ear I would always waken with a nervous start. So the feverish time went by, and at last I held it ready for a second trial. Now the instrument was adjustable, and I had also improved it so far as to be able to set it very accurately for any particular period, thus rendering it sensible only to sounds of that time, all heavier and fainter vibrations being excluded.

I drew it out almost to its limits.

All the maddening doubts that had haunted me like grinning specters died. I felt no tremor, my hand was steady, my pulse-beat regular.

The soft breeze had fallen away. No leaf stirred in the quiet that seemed to await my triumph. Again the crimson splendor of sunset illumined the western sky and made a glory overhead—and the dusk was thickening down below among the mouldering slabs. But that mattered not.

I raised the trumpet to my ear.

Hark!—The hum of mighty hosts! It rose and fell, fainter and more faint; then the murmur of water was heard and lost again, as it swelled and gathered and burst in one grand volume of sound like a hallelujah from myriad lips. Out of the resounding echo, out of the dying cadence a single female voice arose. Clear, pure, rich, it soared above the tumult of the host that hushed itself, a living thing. Higher, sweeter, it seemed to break the fetters of mortality and tremble in sublime adoration before the Infinite. My breath stilled with awe. Was it a spirit-voice—one of the glittering host in the jasper city "that had no need of the sun, neither of the moon to shine in it"? And the water, was it the river clear as crystal flowing from the great white throne? But no! The tone now floated out soft, sad, human. There was no sorrowful strain in that nightless land where the leaves of the trees were for the healing of the nations. The beautiful voice was of the earth and sin-stricken. From the sobbing that mingled with the faint ripple of water it went up once more, ringing gladly, joyfully; it went up inspired with praise to the sky, and—hark! the Hebrew tongue:—

"The horse and his rider hath he thrown into the sea."

Then the noise of the multitude swelled again, and a crash of music broke forth from innumerable timbrels. I raised my head quickly—it was the song of Miriam after the passage of the Red Sea.

I knew not whether I lived.

I bent my ear eagerly to the instrument again and heard—the soft rustle, the breathing as of a sleeping forest. A plaintive note stole gently out, more solemn and quiet than the chant of the leaves. The mournful lay, forlorn, frightened, trembled on the air like the piteous wail of some wounded creature. Then it grew stronger. Clear, brilliant, it burst in a shower of silver sounds like a whole choir of birds in the glitter of the tropical sunlight. But the mournful wail crept back, and the lonely heartbroken strain was lost, while the leaves still whispered to one another in the midnight.

Like the light of a distant star came to me this song of some nightingale, thousands of years after the bird had mouldered to nothing.

At last my labor had been rewarded. As sound travels in waves, and these waves are continually advancing as they go round and round the world, therefore I would never hear the same sound over again at the same time, but it passed beyond and another came in its stead.

All night I listened with my ear pressed to the instrument. I heard the polished, well-studied compliments, the rustle of silks, and the quick music of the dance at some banquet. I could almost see the brilliant robes and glittering jewels of the waltzers, and the sheen of light, and the mirrors. But hush! a cry, a stifled moan. Was that at the—No, the music and the rustle of silk were gone.

"Mother, put your hand here,—I am tired, and my head feels hot and strange. Is it night, already, that it has grown so dark? I am resting now, for my book is almost done, and then, mother, we can go back to the dear old home where the sun shines so bright and the honeysuckles are heavy with perfume. And, mother, we will never be poor any more. I know you are weary, for your cheeks are pale and your fingers are thin; but they shall not touch a needle then, and you will grow better, mother, and we will forget these long, long, bitter years. I will not write in the evenings then, but sit with you and watch the twilight fade as we used to do, and listen to the murmur of the frogs. I described the little stream, our little stream, mother, in my book.—Hark! I hear the splash of its waves now. Hold me by the hand tight, mother. I am tired, but we are almost there. See! the house glimmers white through the trees, and the red bird has built its nest again in the cedar. Put your arm around me, mother, mother—"

Then single, echoless, the mother's piercing cry went up— "O my God!"

Great Heaven! It would not always be music that I should hear. Into this ear, where all the world poured its tales, sorrow and suffering and death would come in turn with mirth and gladness.

I listened again. The long-drawn ahoy!—ahoy!—of the sailor rang out in slumbrous musical monotone, now free, now muffled—gone. The gleeful laugh of children at play, then the drunken boisterous shout of the midnight reveler—What was that? A chime of bells, strange, sublime, swimming in the air they made a cold, solemn harmony. But even over them dashed the storm-blast of passion that sweeps continually up and down the earth, and the harmony that bound them in peace broke up in a wild, angry clamor, that set loose shrill screams which were swallowed up in a savage tumult of discord, like a mad carnival of yelling demons. Then, as if terrified by their own fiendish rage, they retreated shivering, remorseful, and hushed themselves in hoarse whispers about the gray belfry. It was the Carillonneur, Matthias Vander Gheyn, playing at Louvain on the first of July, 1745.

Yes, my invention had proved a grand success. I had worked and worked in order to give this instrument to the world; but now when it was finished, strange to say, all my ambition, all my desire for fame left me, and I was anxious only to guard it from discovery, to keep it secret, to keep it more jealously than a miser hoards his gold. An undefinable delight filled my soul that I alone out of all humanity possessed this treasure, this great Ear of the World, for which kings might have given up their thrones. Ah! they dreamed not of the wonders I could relate. It was a keen, intense pleasure to see the public for which I had toiled live on, deaf forever save to the few transient sounds of the moment, while I, their slave, reveled in another world above, beyond theirs. But they should never have this instrument; no, not for kingdoms would I give it up, not for life itself.

It exerted a strange fascination over me, and in my eager desire to preserve my secret a tormenting fear suddenly took possession of me that some one might track me to the tower and discover all. It seemed as if the people looked after me with curious faces as I passed. I went no longer on the main road that led to the church, but, when I left my room, took an opposite direction until out of sight, and then made a circuit across the fields. I lived in a continual fear of betraying myself, so that at night I closed my window and door lest I might talk aloud in my sleep. I could never again bear the irksome duties of my office, and when the college re-opened I gave up my situation and took lodgings in town. Still the dread of detection haunted me. Every day I varied my route to the church, and every day the people seemed to stare at me with a more curious gaze. Occasionally some of my old pupils came to visit me, but they appeared constrained in my presence and were soon gone. However, no one seemed to suspect my secret; perhaps all this was merely the work of my imagination, for I had grown watchful and reticent.

I hardly ate or slept. I lived perpetually in the

past listening to the echoing song of the Alpine shepherd; the rich, uncultivated soprano of the Southern slave making strange wild melody. I heard grand organ fugues rolling, sweeping over multitudes that kneeled in awe, while a choir of voices broke into a gloria that seemed to sway the great cathedral. The thrilling artistic voices of the far past rang again, making my listening soul tremble in their magnificent harmony. It was music of which we could not dream.

Then suddenly I determined to try the opera once more; perhaps I was prejudiced: I had not been inside of a concert-room for more than a year.

I went down to London. It was just at the opening of the season. I could hardly wait that evening until the curtain rose; the orchestra was harsh and discordant, the house hot and disagreeable, the gas painfully bright. My restlessness had acquired a feverish pitch before the prima donna made her appearance. Surely that voice was not the one before which the world bowed! Malibran's song stood out in my memory clearly defined and complete, like a magnificent cathedral of pure marble, with faultless arches and skillfully chiseled carvings, where the minarets rose from wreaths of lilies and vine-leaves cut in bas-relief, and the slender spire shot high, glittering yellow in the upper sunlight, its golden arrow, burning like flame, pointing towards the East. But this prima donna built only a flat, clumsy structure of wood ornamented by gaudily painted lattice. I left the opera amid the deafening applause of the audience with a smile of scorn upon my lips. Poor deluded creatures! they knew nothing of music, they knew not what they were doing.

I went to St. Paul's on the Sabbath. There was no worship in the operatic voluntary sung by hired voices; it did not stir my soul, and their cold hymns did not warm with praise to the Divine Creator, or sway the vast pulseless congregation that came and went without one quickened breath.

All this time I felt a singular, inexpressible pleasure in the consciousness of my great secret, and I hurried back with eager haste. In London I had accidentally met two or three of my old acquaintances. I was not over glad to see them myself: as I have said, I had grown utterly indifferent to society; but I almost felt ashamed when they offered me every attention within their power, for I had not anticipated it, nor was it deserved on my part. Now, when I returned, every body in the street stopped to shake hands with me and inquire for my health. At first, although I was surprised at the interest they manifested, I took it merely as the common civility on meeting, but when the question was repeated so particularly by each one, I thought it appeared strange, and asked if they had ever heard to the contrary; no, oh no, they said, but still I was astonished at the unusual care with which they all made the same inquiry.

I went up to my room and walked directly to the glass. It was the first time I had consciously looked into a mirror for many weeks. Good Heavens! The mystery was explained now. *I could hardly recognize myself.* At first the shock was so great that I stood gazing, almost petrified. The demon of typhus fever could not have wrought a more terrific change in my face if he had held it in his clutches for months. My hair hung in long straggling locks around my neck. I was thin and fearfully haggard. My eyes sunken far back in my head, looked out from dark, deep hollows; my heavy black eyebrows were knit together by wrinkles that made seams over my forehead: my fleshless cheeks clung tight to the bone, and a bright red spot on either one was half covered by thick beard. I had thought so little about my personal appearance lately that I had utterly neglected my hair, and I wondered now that it had given me no annoyance. I smiled while I still looked at myself. This was the effect of the severe study and loss of sleep, and the excitement under which I had labored for months, yes, for more than a year. I had not been conscious of fatigue, but my work was done now and I would soon regain my usual weight. I submitted myself immediately to the hands of a barber, dressed with considerable care, and took another look in the glass. My face appeared pinched and small since it had been freed from beard. The caverns around my eyes seemed even larger, and the bright color in my cheeks contrasted strangely with the extremely sallow tint of my complexion. I turned away with an uncomfortable feeling, and started on a circuitous route to the church, for I never trusted my instrument in any other place.

It was a sober autumn day. Every thing looked dreary with that cold, gray, sunless sky stretched overhead. The half-naked trees shivered a little in their seared garments of ragged leaves. Occasionally a cat walked along the fence-top, or stood trembling on three legs. Sometimes a depressed bird suddenly tried to cheer its drooping spirits and uttered a few sharp, discontented chirps. Just in front of me two boys were playing ball on the road-side. As I passed I accidentally caught this sentence:

"They say the professor ain't just right in his head."

For a moment I stood rooted to the ground; then wheeled round and cried out fiercely,

"What did you say?"

"Sir?"

"What was that you said just now?" I repeated still more fiercely.

The terrified boys looked at me an instant, then without answering turned and ran as fast as fright could carry them.

So the mystery now was really explained! It was not sick the people thought me, but crazy. I walked on with a queer feeling and began vaguely to wonder why I had been so savage to those boys. The fact which I had learned so suddenly certainly gave me a shock, but it was nothing to me. What did I care, even if the people did think me crazy? Ah! perhaps if I told my secret they would consider it a desperate case of insanity. But the child's words kept ringing in my ears until an idea flashed upon me more terrifying than death itself. How did I know that I was *not* insane? How did I know that my great invention might be only an hallucination of my brain?

Instantly a whole army of thoughts crowded up like ghostly witnesses to affright me. I had studied myself to a shadow; my pallid face, with the red spots on the cheeks and the blue hollows around the eyes, came before my mental vision afresh. The fever in my veins told me I was unnaturally excited. I had not slept a sound, dreamless sleep for weeks. Perhaps in the long, long days and nights my brain, like my body, had been over-wrought; perhaps in my eager desire to succeed, in my desperate determination, the power of my will had disordered my mind, and it was all deception: the sounds, the music I had heard, merely the creation of my diseased fancy, and the instrument I had handled useless metal. The very idea was inexpressible torture to me. I could not bear that a single doubt of its reality should exist; but, after once entering my head, how would I ever be able to free myself from distrust? I could not do it; I would be obliged to live always in uncertainty. It was maddening: now I felt as if I might have struck the child in my rage if I could have found him. Then suddenly it occurred to me, for the first time, that my invention could easily be tested by some other person. Almost instantly I rejected the thought, for it would compel me to betray my secret, and in my strange infatuation I would rather have destroyed the instrument. But the doubts of my sanity on this subject returned upon me with tenfold strength, and again I thought in despair of the only method left me by which they could ever be settled.

In the first shock, when the unlucky sentence fell upon my ear, I had turned after the boys, and then walked on mechanically towards the town. Now, when I looked up I found myself almost at the college gate. No one was to be seen, only Mother Flinse with her basket on her arm was just raising the latch. Half bewildered I turned hastily round and bent my steps in the direction of my lodgings, while I absently wondered whether that old woman had stood there ever since, since—when? I did not recollect, but her shadow was long and slim—no, there were no shadows this afternoon; it was sunless.

As I reached the stairs leading to my room, my trouble, which I had forgotten for the moment, broke upon me anew. I dragged myself up and sat down utterly overwhelmed. As I have said, I would sooner destroy the instrument than give it to a thankless world; but to endure the torturing doubt of its reality was impossible. Suddenly it occurred to me that Mother Flinse was mute. I might get her to test my invention without fear of betrayal, for she could neither speak nor write, and her signs on this subject, if she attempted to explain, would be altogether unintelligible to others. I sprang up in wild delight, then immediately fell back in my chair with a hoarse laugh—Mother Flinse was *deaf* as well as dumb. I had not remembered that. I sat quietly a moment trying to calm myself and think. Why need this make any difference? The instrument ought to, at least it was possible that it might, remedy loss of hearing. I too was deaf to these sounds in the air that it made audible. They would have to be magnified to a greater degree for her. I might set it for the present and use the full power of the instrument: there certainly would be no harm in trying, at any rate, and if it failed it would prove nothing, if it did not fail it would prove every thing. Then a new difficulty presented itself. How could I entice the old woman into the church?

I went back towards the college expecting to find her, but she was nowhere to be seen, and I smiled that only a few moments ago I had wondered if she did not always stand in the gateway. Once, I could not exactly recall the time, I had passed her hut. I remembered distinctly that there was a line full of old ragged clothes stretched across from the fence to a decayed tree, and a bright red flannel petticoat blew and flapped among the blackened branches. It was a miserable frame cabin, set back from the Spring road, about half a mile out of town. There I went in search of her.

The blasted tree stood out in bold relief against the drab sky. There appeared no living thing about the dirty, besmoked hovel except one lean rat, that squatted with quivering nose and stared a moment, then retreated under the loose plank before the door, leaving its smellers visible until I stepped upon the board. I knocked loudly without receiving any reply; then, smiling at the useless ceremony I had performed, pushed it open. The old woman, dressed in her red petticoat and a torn calico frock, with a faded shawl drawn over her head, was standing with her back towards me, picking over a pile of rags. She did not move. I hesitated an instant, then walked in. The moment I put my foot upon the floor she sprang quickly round. At first she remained motionless, with her small, piercing gray eyes fixed upon me, holding a piece of orange-and-black spotted muslin; evidently she recognized me, for, suddenly dropping it, she began a series of wild gestures, grinning until all the wrinkles of her skinny face converged in the region of her mouth, where a few scattered teeth, long and sharp, gleamed strangely white. A rim of grizzled hair stood out round the edge of the turbaned shawl and set off the withered and watchful countenance of the speechless old crone. The yellow, shriveled skin hung loosely about her slim neck like leather, and her knotted hands were brown and dry as the claws of an eagle.

I went through the motion of sweeping and pointed over my shoulder, making her understand that I wished her to do some cleaning. She drew the seams of her face into a new grimace by way of assent, and, putting the piece of orange-and-black spotted muslin around her shoulders in lieu of a cloak, preceded me out of the door. She started immediately in the direction of the college, and I was obliged to take hold of her before I could attract her attention; then, when I shook my head, she regarded me in surprise, and fell once more into a series of frantic gesticulations. With considerable trouble I made her comprehend that she was merely to follow me. The old woman was by no means dull, and her small, steel-gray eyes had a singular sharpness about them that is only found in the deaf-mute, where they perform the part of the ear and tongue. As soon as we came in sight of the church she was perfectly satisfied. I walked up to the main entrance, turned the knob and shook it, then suddenly felt in all my pockets, shook the door over, and felt through all my pockets again. This hypocritical pantomime had the desired effect. The old beldam slapped her hands together and poked her lean finger at the hole of the lock, apparently amused that I had forgotten the key. Then of her own accord she went round and tried the other doors, but without success. As we passed the narrow window in the rear I made a violent effort in knocking out the loose boards. The old woman seemed greatly delighted, and when I crawled through willingly followed. I gave her a brush, which fortunately one day I had discovered lying in the vestibule, and left her in the church to dust, while I went up in the tower to prepare and remove from sight all the tools which were scattered about. I put them in a recess and screened it from view by a map of the Holy Land. Then I took my instrument and carefully adjusted it, putting on its utmost power.

In about an hour I went down and motioned to Mother Flinse that I wanted her up stairs. She came directly after me without hesitation, and I felt greatly relieved, for I saw that I would likely have no trouble with the old woman. When we got into the tower she pointed down to the trees and then upward, meaning, I presume, that it was high. I nodded, and taking the instrument placed my ear to it for a moment. A loud blast of music, like a dozen bands playing in concert, almost stunned me. She watched me very attentively, but when I made signs for her to come and try she drew back. I held up the instrument and went through all manner of motions indicating that it would not hurt her, but she only shook her head. I persevered in my endeavor to coax her until she seemed to gain courage and walked up within a few feet of me, then suddenly stopped and stretched out her hands for the instrument. As she did not seem afraid, provided she had it herself, I saw that she took firm hold.

In my impatience to know the result of this

experiment, I was obliged to repeat my signs again and again before I could prevail upon her to raise it to her ear. Then breathlessly I watched her face, a face I thought which looked as if it might belong to some mummy that had been withering for a thousand years. Suddenly it was convulsed as if by a galvanic shock, then the shriveled features seemed to dilate, and a great light flashed through them, transforming them almost into the radiance of youth; a strange light as of some seraph had taken possession of the wrinkled old frame and looked out at the gray eyes, making them shine with unnatural beauty. No wonder the dumb countenance reflected a brightness inexpressible, for the Spirit of Sound had just alighted with silvery wings upon a silence of seventy years.

A heavy weight fell unconsciously from my breast while I stood almost awed before this face, which was transfigured, as if it might have caught a glimmer of that mystical morn when, in a moment, in the twinkling of an eye, we shall all be changed.

My instrument had stood the test; it was proved forever. I could no longer cherish any doubts of its reality, and an indescribable peace came into my soul, like a sudden awakening from some frightful dream. I had not noticed the flight of time. A pale shadow hung already over the trees—yes, and under them on the slime-covered stones. Ay! and a heavier shadow than the coming night was even then gathering unseen its rayless folds. The drab sky had blanched and broken, and the sinking sun poured a fading light through its ragged fissures.

The old woman, as if wrapped in an enchantment, had hardly moved. I tried vainly to catch her attention; she did not even appear conscious of my presence. I walked up and shook her gently by the shoulder, and, pointing to the setting sun, held out my hand for the instrument. She looked at me a moment, with the singular unearthly beauty shining through every feature; then suddenly clutching the trumpet tight between her skinny claws, sprang backward towards the stairs, uttering a sound that was neither human nor animal, that was not a wail or a scream, but it fell upon my ears like some palpable horror. Merciful Heaven! Was that thing yonder a woman? The shriveled, fleshless lips gaped apart, and a small pointed tongue lurked behind five glittering, fang-like teeth. The wild beast had suddenly been developed in the hag. Like a hungry tigress defending its prey, she stood hugging the trumpet to her, glaring at me with stretched neck and green eyes.

A savage fierceness roused within me when I found she would not give up the instrument, and I rushed at her with hands ready to snatch back the prize I valued more than my life—*or hers*; but, quicker than a hunted animal, she turned and fled with it down the stairs, making the tower ring with the hideous cries of her wordless voice. Swiftly—it seemed as if the danger of losing the trumpet gave me wings to fly in pursuit—I crossed the vestibule. She was not there. Every thing was silent, and I darted with fleet steps down the dusky aisle of the church, when suddenly the jarring idiotic sounds broke loose again, echoing up in the organ-pipes and rattling along the galleries. The fiend sprang from behind the altar, faced about an instant with flashing eyes and gleaming teeth, then fled through the vestry-room into the passage. The sight of her was fresh fuel to my rage, and it flamed into a frenzy that seemed to burn the human element out of my soul. When I gained the steps leading into the coal-room she was already in the window, but I cleared the distance at a single bound and caught hold of her clothes as she leaped down. I crawled through, but she clutched the instrument tighter. I could not prize it out of her grasp; and in her ineffectual efforts to free herself from my hold she made loud, grating cries, that seemed to me to ring and reverberate all through the forest; but presently they grew smothered, gurgled, then ceased. Her clasp relaxed in a convulsive struggle, and the trumpet was in my possession. It was easily done, for her neck was small and lean, and my hands made a circle strong as a steel band.

The tremor died out of her frame and left it perfectly still. Through the silence I could hear the hiss of a snake in the nettle-weeds, and the flapping wings of some night bird fanned my face as it rushed swiftly through the air in its low flight. The gray twilight had deepened to gloom and the graves seemed to have given up their tenants. The pale monuments stood out like shrouded specters. But all the dead in that church-yard were not under ground, for on the wet grass at my feet there was something stark and stiff, more frightful than any phantom of imagination—something that the daylight would not rob of its ghastly features. It must be put out of sight, yes, it must be hid, to save my invention from discovery. The old hag might be missed, and if she was found here it would ruin me and expose my secret. I placed the trumpet on the window-ledge, and, carrying the grim burden in my arms, plunged into the damp tangle of weeds and grass.

In a lonesome corner far back from the church, in the dense shade of thorn-trees, among the wild brambles where poisonous vines grew, slippery with the mould of forgotten years, unsought, uncared for by any human hand, was a tomb. Its sides were half buried in the tall under-brush, and the long slab had been broken once, for a black fissure ran zigzag across the middle. In my muscles that night there was the strength of two men. I lifted off one-half of the stone and heard the lizards dart startled from their haunt, and felt the spiders crawl. When the stone was replaced it covered more than the lizards or the spiders in the dark space between the narrow walls.

As I have said, the instrument possessed a singular fascination over me. I had grown to love it, not alone as a piece of mechanism for the transmission of sound, but like a *living* thing, and I replaced it in the tower with the same pleasure one feels who has rescued a friend from death. My listening ear never grew weary, but now I drew quickly away. It was not music I heard, or the ripple of water, or the prattle of merry tongues, but the harsh grating cries that had echoed in the church, that had rattled and died out in the forest—that voice which was not a voice. I shivered while I readjusted the instrument; perhaps it was the night wind which chilled me, but the rasping sounds were louder than before. *I could not exclude them*. There was no element of superstition in my nature, and I tried it over again: still I heard them—sometimes sharp, sometimes only a faint rumbling. Had the soul of the deaf-mute come in retribution to haunt me and cry eternally in my instrument? Perhaps on the morrow it would not disturb me, but there was no difference. I could hear only it, though I drew out the trumpet for vibrations hundreds of years old. I had rid myself of the withered hag who would have stolen my treasure, but now I could not rid myself of her invisible ghost. She had conquered, even through death, and come from the spirit world to gain possession of the prize for which she had given up her life. The instrument was no longer of any value to me, though cherishing a vague hope I compelled myself to listen, even with chattering teeth; for it was a terrible thing to hear these hoarse, haunting cries of the dumb soul—of the soul I had strangled from its body, a soul which I would have killed itself if it were possible. But my hope was vain, and the trumpet had become not only worthless to me, but an absolute horror.

Suddenly I determined to destroy it. I turned it over ready to dash it in pieces, but it cost me a struggle to crush this work of my life, and while I stood irresolute a small green-and-gold beetle crawled out of it and dropped like a stone to the floor. The insect was an electric flash to me, that dispelled the black gloom through which I had been battling. It had likely fallen into the instrument down in the church-yard, or when I laid it upon the window-sill, and the rasping of its wings, magnified, had produced the sounds which resembled the strange grating noise uttered by the deafmute.

Instantly I put the trumpet to my ear. Once more the music of the past surged in. Voices, leaves, water, all murmured to me their changeful melody; every zephyr wafting by was filled with broken but melodious whispers.

Relieved from doubts, relieved from fears and threatening dangers, I slept peacefully, dreamlessly as a child. With a feeling of rest to which I had long been unused, I walked out in the soft clear morning. Every thing seemed to have put on new life, for the sky was not gray or sober, and the leaves, if they were brown, trimmed their edges in scarlet, and if many had fallen, the squirrels played among them on the ground. But suddenly the sky and the leaves and the squirrels might have been blotted from existence. I did not see them, but I saw—*I saw Mother Flinse come through the college gateway and walk slowly down the road!*

The large faded shawl pinned across her shoulders nearly covered the red flannel petticoat, and the orange-and-black spotted muslin was wrapped into a turban on her head. Without breathing, almost without feeling, I watched the figure until at the corner it turned out of sight, and a long dark outline on the grass behind it ran into the fence. The shadow! Then it was not a ghost. Had the grave given up its dead? I would see.

At the churchyard the briers tore my face and clothes, but I plunged deeper where the shade thickened under the thorn-trees. There in the corner I stooped to lift the broken slab of a tomb, but all my strength would not avail to move it. As I leaned over, bruising my hands in a vain endeavor to raise it, my eyes fell for an instant on the stone, and with a start I turned quickly and ran to the church; then I stopped—the narrow fissure that cut zigzag across the slab on the tomb was filled with green moss, and this window was nailed up, and hung full of heavy cobwebs.

And my instrument?

Suddenly, while I stood there, some substance in my brain seemed to break up—it was the fetters of monomania which had bound me since that evening long ago, when, by the river in the oak-forest, I had heard the robin trill.

No murder stained my soul: and there, beside the black waves of insanity through which I had passed unharmed, I gave praise to the great Creator—praise silent, but intense as Miriam's song by the sea.

Edward Page Mitchell

American writer Edward Page Mitchell published many short stories in *The New York Sun*, a daily newspaper, all anonymously, a fact which inhibited his larger reputation. He died in 1927, but it was not until US editor Sam Moskowitz identified and republished a collection of his stories in 1973 that he achieved his due as a writer. Moskowitz called him 'the lost giant of American science fiction', and his stories covered such topics as invisibility, time travel, robots, computers and mutants.

In 1872 the twenty-year-old Mitchell was on a train to Bath, Maine, when a scalding smut from the locomotive's smokestack flew through the open window and burnt his left eye, blinding it. During medical treatment for this injury, Mitchell's physically sound right eye experienced sympathetic blindness, leaving him completely sightless. Strangely, his left eye eventually healed and regained its sight, but his uninjured right eye stayed blind and indeed was eventually surgically removed and replaced with a glass eyeball. It was while recovering from this surgery that Mitchell wrote what is today his most famous story, 'The Tachypomp'.

The Tachypomp

A MATHEMATICAL DEMONSTRATION

There was nothing mysterious about Professor Surd's dislike for me. I was the only poor mathematician in an exceptionally mathematical class. The old gentleman sought the lecture-room every morning with eagerness, and left it reluctantly. For was it not a thing of joy to find seventy young men who, individually and collectively, preferred *x* to XX; who had rather differentiate than dissipate; and for whom the limbs of the heavenly bodies had more attractions than those of earthly stars upon the spectacular stage?

So affairs went on swimmingly between the Professor of Mathematics and the Junior Class at Polyp University. In every man of the seventy the sage saw the logarithm of a possible La Place, of a Sturm, or of a Newton. It was a delightful task for him to lead them through the pleasant valleys of conic sections, and beside the still waters of the integral calculus. Figuratively speaking, his problem was not a hard one. He had only to manipulate, and eliminate, and to raise to a higher power, and the triumphant result of examination day was assured.

But I was a disturbing element, a perplexing unknown quantity, which had somehow crept into the work, and which seriously threatened to impair the accuracy of his calculations. It was a touching sight to behold the venerable mathematician as he pleaded with me not so utterly to disregard precedent in the use of cotangents; or as he urged, with eyes almost tearful, that ordinates were dangerous things to trifle with. All in vain. More theorems went on to my cuff than into my head. Never did chalk do so much work to so little purpose. And, therefore, it came that Furnace Second was reduced to zero in Professor Surd's estimation. He looked upon me with all the horror which an un-algebraic nature could inspire. I have seen the Professor walk around an entire square rather than meet the man who had no mathematics in his soul.

For Furnace Second were no invitations to Professor Surd's house. Seventy of the class supped in delegations around the periphery of the Professor's tea-table. The seventy-first knew nothing of the charms of that perfect ellipse, with its twin bunches of fuchsias and geraniums in gorgeous precision at the two foci.

This, unfortunately enough, was no trifling deprivation. Not that I longed especially for segments of Mrs. Surd's justly celebrated lemon pies; not that the spheroidal damsons of her excellent preserving had any marked allurements; not even that I yearned to hear the Professor's jocose table-talk about binomials, and chatty illustrations of abstruse paradoxes. The explanation is far different. Professor Surd had a daughter. Twenty years before, he made a proposition of marriage to the present Mrs. S. He added a little Corollary to his proposition not long after. The Corollary was a girl.

Abscissa Surd was as perfectly symmetrical as Giotto's circle, and as pure, withal, as the mathematics her father taught. It was just when spring was coming to extract the roots of frozen-up vegetation that I fell in love with the Corollary. That she herself was not indifferent I soon had reason to regard as a self-evident truth.

The sagacious reader will already recognize nearly all the elements necessary to a well-ordered plot. We have introduced a heroine, inferred a hero, and constructed a hostile parent after the most approved model. A movement for the story, a *Deus ex machina*, is alone lacking. With considerable satisfaction I can promise a perfect novelty in this line, a *Deus ex machina* never before offered to the public.

It would be discounting ordinary intelligence to say that I sought with unwearying assiduity to figure my way into the stern father's good-will; that never did dullard apply himself to mathematics more patiently than I; that never did faithfulness achieve such meagre reward. Then I engaged a private tutor. His instructions met with no better success.

My tutor's name was Jean Marie Rivarol. He was a unique Alsatian—though Gallic in name, thoroughly Teuton in nature; by birth a Frenchman, by education a German. His age was thirty; his profession, omniscience; the wolf at his door, poverty; the skeleton in his closet, a consuming but unrequited passion. The most recondite principles of practical science were his toys; the deepest intricacies of abstract science his diversions. Problems which were foreordained mysteries to me were to him as clear as Tahoe water. Perhaps this very fact will explain our lack of success in the relation of tutor and pupil; perhaps the failure is alone due to my own unmitigated stupidity. Rivarol had hung about the skirts of the University for several years; supplying his few wants by writing for scientific journals, or by giving assistance to students who, like myself, were characterized by a plethora of purse and a paucity of ideas; cooking, studying and sleeping in his attic lodgings; and prosecuting queer experiments all by himself.

We were not long discovering that even this eccentric genius could not transplant brains into my deficient skull. I gave over the struggle in despair. An unhappy year dragged its slow length around. A gloomy year it was, brightened only by occasional interviews with Abscissa, the Abbie of my thoughts and dreams.

Commencement day was coming on apace. I was soon to go forth, with the rest of my class, to astonish and delight a waiting world. The Professor seemed to avoid me more than ever. Nothing but the conventionalities, I think, kept him from shaping his treatment of me on the basis of unconcealed disgust.

At last, in the very recklessness of despair, I resolved to see him, plead with him, threaten him if need be, and risk all my fortunes on one desperate chance. I wrote him a somewhat defiant letter, stating my aspirations, and, as I flattered myself, shrewdly giving him a week to get over the first shock of horrified surprise. Then I was to call and learn my fate.

During the week of suspense I nearly worried myself into a fever. It was first crazy hope, and then saner despair. On Friday evening, when I presented myself at the Professor's door, I was such a haggard, sleepy, dragged-out spectre, that even Miss Jocasta, the harsh-favored maiden sister of the Surds, admitted me with commiserate regard, and suggested pennyroyal tea.

Professor Surd was at a faculty meeting. Would I wait?

Yes, till all was blue, if need be. Miss Abbie?

Abscissa had gone to Wheelborough to visit a school-friend. The aged maiden hoped I would make myself comfortable, and departed to the unknown haunts which knew Jocasta's daily walk.

Comfortable! But I settled myself in a great uneasy chair and waited, with the contradictory spirit common to such junctures, dreading every step lest it should herald the man whom, of all men, I wished to see.

I had been there at least an hour, and was growing right drowsy.

At length Professor Surd came in. He sat down in the dusk opposite me, and I thought his eyes glinted with malignant pleasure as he said, abruptly:

"So, young man, you think you are a fit husband for my girl?"

I stammered some inanity about making up in affection what I lacked in merit; about my expectations, family and the like. He quickly interrupted me.

"You misapprehend me, sir. Your nature is destitute of those mathematical perceptions and acquirements which are the only sure foundations of character. You have no mathematics in you. You are fit for treason, stratagems, and spoils.—Shakespeare. Your narrow intellect cannot understand and appreciate a generous mind. There is all the difference between you and a Surd, if I may say it, which intervenes between an infinitesimal and an infinite. Why, I will even venture to say that you do not comprehend the Problem of the Couriers!"

I admitted that the Problem of the Couriers should be classed rather without my list of accomplishments than within it. I regretted this fault very deeply, and suggested amendment. I faintly hoped that my fortune would be such—

"Money!" he impatiently exclaimed. "Do you seek to bribe a Roman Senator with a penny whistle? Why, boy, do you parade your paltry wealth, which, expressed in mills, will not cover ten decimal places, before the eyes of a man who measures the planets in their orbits, and close crowds infinity itself?"

I hastily disclaimed any intention of obtruding my foolish dollars, and he went on:

"Your letter surprised me not a little. I thought *you* would be the last person in the world to presume to an alliance here. But having a regard for you personally"—and again I saw malice twinkle in his small eyes—"and still more regard for Abscissa's happiness, I have decided that you shall have her—upon conditions. Upon conditions," he repeated, with a half-smothered sneer.

"What are they?" cried I, eagerly enough. "Only name them."

"Well, sir," he continued, and the deliberation of his speech seemed the very refinement of cruelty, "you have only to prove yourself worthy of an alliance with a mathematical family. You have only to accomplish a task which I shall presently give you. Your eyes ask me what it is. I will tell you. Distinguish yourself in that noble branch of abstract science in which, you cannot but acknowledge, you are at present sadly deficient. I will place Abscissa's hand in yours whenever you shall come before me and square the circle to my satisfaction. No! That is too easy a condition. I should cheat myself. Say perpetual motion. How do you like that? Do you think it lies within the range of your mental capabilities? You don't smile. Perhaps your talents don't run in the way of perpetual motion. Several people have found that theirs didn't. I'll give you another chance. We were speaking of the Problem of the Couriers, and I think you expressed a desire to know more of that ingenious question. You shall have the opportunity. Sit down some day, when you have nothing else to do, and discover the principle of infinite speed. I mean the law of motion which shall accomplish an infinitely great distance in an infinitely short time. You may mix in a little practical mechanics, if you choose. Invent some method of taking the tardy Courier over his road at the rate of sixty miles a minute. Demonstrate me this discovery (when you have made it!) mathematically, and approximate it practically, and Abscissa is yours. Until you can, I will thank you to trouble neither myself nor her."

I could stand his mocking no longer. I stumbled mechanically out of the room, and out of the house. I even forgot my hat and gloves. For an hour I walked in the moonlight. Gradually I succeeded to a more hopeful frame of mind. This was due to my ignorance of mathematics. Had I understood the real meaning of what he asked, I should have been utterly despondent.

Perhaps this problem of sixty miles a minute was not so impossible after all. At any rate I could attempt, though I might not succeed. And Rivarol came to my mind. I would ask him. I would enlist his knowledge to accompany my own devoted perseverance. I sought his lodgings at once.

The man of science lived in the fourth story, back. I had never been in his room before. When I entered, he was in the act of filling a beer mug from a carboy labelled *Aqua fortis*.

"Seat you," he said. "No, not in that chair. That is my Petty Cash Adjuster." But he was a second too late. I had carelessly thrown myself into a chair of seductive appearance. To my utter amazement it reached out two skeleton arms and clutched me with a grasp against which I struggled in vain. Then a skull stretched itself over my shoulder and grinned with ghastly familiarity close to my face.

Rivarol came to my aid with many apologies. He touched a spring somewhere and the Petty Cash Adjuster relaxed its horrid hold. I placed myself gingerly in a plain cane-bottomed rocking-chair, which Rivarol assured me was a safe location.

"That seat," he said, "is an arrangement upon which I much felicitate myself. I made it at Heidelberg. It has saved me a vast deal of small annoyance. I consign to its embraces the friends who bore, and the visitors who exasperate, me. But it is never so useful as when terrifying some tradesman with an insignificant account. Hence the pet name which I have facetiously given it. They are invariably too glad to purchase release at the price of a bill receipted. Do you well apprehend the idea?"

While the Alsatian diluted his glass of *Aqua fortis*, shook into it an infusion of bitters, and tossed off the bumper with apparent relish, I had time to look around the strange apartment.

The four corners of the room were occupied respectively by a turning-lathe, a Ruhmkorff Coil, a small steam-engine and an orrery in stately motion. Tables, shelves, chairs and floor supported an odd aggregation of tools, retorts, chemicals, gas-receivers, philosophical instruments, boots, flasks, paper-collar boxes, books diminutive and books of preposterous size. There were plaster busts of Aristotle, Archimedes, and Comte, while a great drowsy owl was blinking away, perched on the benign brow of Martin Farquhar Tupper. "He always roosts there when he proposes to slumber," explained my tutor. "You are a bird of no ordinary mind. *Schlafen sie wohl.*"

Through a closet door, half open, I could see a human-like form covered with a sheet. Rivarol caught my glance.

"That," said he, "will be my masterpiece. It is a Microcosm, an Android, as yet only partially complete. And why not? Albertus Magnus constructed an image perfect to talk metaphysics and confute the schools. So did Sylvester II; so did Robertus Greathead. Roger Bacon made a brazen head that held discourses. But the first named of these came to destruction. Thomas Aquinas got wrathful at some of its syllogisms and smashed its head. The idea is reasonable enough. Mental action will yet be reduced to laws as definite as those which govern the physical. Why should not I accomplish a manikin which shall preach as original discourses as the Rev. Dr. Allchin, or talk poetry as mechanically as Paul Anapest? My Android can already work problems in vulgar fractions and compose sonnets. I hope to teach it the Positive Philosophy."

Out of the bewildering confusion of his effects Rivarol produced two pipes and filled them. He handed one to me.

"And here," he said, "I live and am tolerably comfortable. When my coat wears out at the elbows I seek the tailor and am measured for another. When I am hungry I promenade myself to the butcher's and bring home a pound or so of steak, which I cook very nicely in three seconds by this oxy-hydrogen flame. Thirsty, perhaps, I send for a carboy of *Aqua fortis*. But I have it charged, all charged. My spirit is above any small pecuniary transaction. I loathe your dirty greenbacks, and never handle what they call scrip."

"But are you never pestered with bills?" I asked. "Don't the creditors worry your life out?"

"Creditors!" gasped Rivarol. "I have learned no such word in your very admirable language. He who will allow his soul to be vexed by creditors is a relic of an imperfect civilization. Of what use is science if it cannot avail a man who has accounts current? Listen. The moment you or any one else enters the outside door this little electric bell sounds me warning. Every successive step on Mrs. Grimler's staircase is a spy and informer vigilant for my benefit.

The first step is trod upon. That trusty first step immediately telegraphs your weight. Nothing could be simpler. It is exactly like any platform scale. The weight is registered up here upon this dial. The second step records the size of my visitor's feet. The third his height, the fourth his complexion, and so on. By the time he reaches the top of the first flight I have a pretty accurate description of him right here at my elbow, and quite a margin of time for deliberation and action. Do you follow me? It is plain enough. Only the A B C of my science."

"I see all that," I said, "but I don't see how it helps you any. The knowledge that a creditor is coming won't pay his bill. You can't escape unless you jump out of the window."

Rivarol laughed softly. "I will tell you. You shall see what becomes of any poor devil who goes to demand money of me—of a man of science. Ha! ha! It pleases me. I was seven weeks perfecting my Dun Suppressor. Did you know"—he whispered exultingly—"did you know that there is a hole through the earth's centre? Physicists have long suspected it; I was the first to find it. You have read how Rhuyghens, the Dutch navigator, discovered in Kerguellen's Land an abysmal pit which fourteen hundred fathoms of plumb-line failed to sound. Herr Tom, that hole has no bottom! It runs from one surface of the earth to the antipodal surface. It is diametric. But where is the antipodal spot? You stand upon it. I learned this by the merest chance. I was deep-digging in Mrs. Grimler's cellar, to bury a poor cat I had sacrificed in a galvanic experiment, when the earth under my spade crumbled, caved in, and wonder-stricken I stood upon the brink of a yawning shaft. I dropped a coal-hod in. It went down, down down, bounding and rebounding. In two hours and a quarter that coal-hod came up again. I caught it and restored it to the angry Grimler. Just think a minute. The coal-hod went down, faster and faster, till it reached the centre of the earth. There it would stop, were it not for acquired momentum. Beyond the centre its journey was relatively upward, toward the opposite surface of the globe. So, losing velocity, it went slower and slower till it reached that surface. Here it came to rest for a second and then fell back again, eight thousand odd miles, into my hands. Had I not interfered with it, it would have repeated its journey, time after time, each trip of shorter extent, like the diminishing oscillations of a pendulum, till it finally came to eternal rest at the centre of the sphere. I am not slow to give a practical application to any such grand discovery. My Dun Suppressor was born of it. A trap, just outside my chamber door: a spring in here: a creditor on the trap:—need I say more?"

"But isn't it a trifle inhuman?" I mildly suggested. "Plunging an unhappy being into a perpetual journey to and from Kerguellen's Land, without a moment's warning."

"I give them a chance. When they come up the first time I wait at the mouth of the shaft with a rope in hand. If they are reasonable and will come to terms, I fling them the line. If they perish, 'tis their own fault. Only," he added, with a melancholy smile, "the centre is getting so plugged up with creditors that I am afraid there soon will be no choice whatever for 'em."

By this time I had conceived a high opinion of my tutor's ability. If anybody could send me waltzing through space at an infinite speed, Rivarol could do it. I filled my pipe and told him the story. He heard with grave and patient attention. Then, for full half an hour, he whiffed away in silence. Finally he spoke.

"The ancient cipher has overreached himself. He has given you a choice of two problems, both of which he deems insoluble. Neither of them is insoluble. The only gleam of intelligence Old Cotangent showed was when he said that squaring the circle was too easy. He was right. It would have given you your *Liebchen* in five minutes. I squared the circle before I discarded pantalets. I will show you the work—but it would be a digression, and you are in no mood for digressions. Our first chance, therefore, lies in perpetual motion. Now, my good friend, I will frankly tell you that, although I have compassed this interesting problem, I do not choose to use it on your behalf. I too, Herr Tom, have a heart. The loveliest of her sex frowns upon me. Her somewhat mature charms are not for Jean Marie Rivarol. She has cruelly said that her years demand of me filial rather than connubial regard. Is love a matter of years or of eternity? This question did I put to the cold, yet lovely Jocasta."

"Jocasta Surd!" I remarked in surprise. "Abscissa's aunt!"

"The same," he said, sadly. "I will not attempt to conceal that upon the maiden Jocasta my maiden heart has been bestowed. Give me your hand, my nephew, in affliction as in affection!"

Rivarol dashed away a not discreditable tear, and resumed:

"My only hope lies in this discovery of perpetual motion. It will give me the fame, the wealth. Can Jocasta refuse these? If she can, there is only the trap-door and—Kerguellen's Land!"

I bashfully asked to see the perpetual-motion machine. My uncle in affliction shook his head.

"At another time." he said. "Suffice it at present to say, that it is something upon the principle of a woman's tongue. But you see now why we must turn in your case to the alternative condition—infinite speed. There are several ways in which this may be accomplished, theoretically. By the lever, for instance. Imagine a lever with a very long and a very short arm. Apply power to the shorter arm which will move it with great velocity. The end of the long arm will move much faster. Now keep shortening the short arm and lengthening the long one, and as you approach infinity in their difference of length, you approach infinity in the speed of the long arm. It would be difficult to demonstrate this practically to the Professor. We must seek another solution. Jean Marie will meditate. Come to me in a fortnight. Good-night. But stop! Have you the money—*das Geld?*"

"Much more than I need."

"Good! Let us strike hands. Gold and Knowledge; Science and Love. What may not such a partnership achieve? We go to conquer thee, Abscissa. *Vorwärts!*"

When, at the end of a fortnight, I sought Rivarol's chamber, I passed with some little trepidation over the terminus of the Air Line to Kerguellen's Land, and evaded the extended arms of the Petty Cash Adjuster. Rivarol drew a mug of ale for me, and filled himself a retort of his own peculiar beverage.

"Come," he said at length. "Let us drink success to the TACHYPOMP."

"The TACHYPOMP?"

"Yes. Why not? *Tachy*, quickly, and *pempo, pepompa,* to send. May it send you quickly to your wedding-day. Abscissa is yours. It is done. When shall we start for the prairies?"

"Where is it?" I asked, looking in vain around the room for any contrivance which might seem calculated to advance matrimonial prospects.

"It is here," and he gave his forehead a significant tap. Then he held forth didactically.

"There is force enough in existence to yield us a speed of sixty miles a minute, or even more. All we need is the knowledge how to combine and apply it. The wise man will not attempt to make some great force yield some great speed. He will keep adding the little force to the little force, making each little force yield its little speed, until an aggregate of little forces shall be a great force, yielding an aggregate of little speeds, a great speed. The difficulty is not in aggregating the forces; it lies in the corresponding aggregation of the speeds. One musket-ball will go, say, a mile. It is not hard to increase the force of muskets to a thousand, yet the thousand musket-balls will go no farther, and no faster, than the one. You see, then, where our trouble lies. We cannot readily add speed to speed, as we add force to force. My discovery is simply the utilization of a principle which extorts an increment of speed from each increment of power. But this is the metaphysics of physics. Let us be practical or nothing.

"When you have walked forward, on a moving train, from the rear car, toward the engine, did you ever think what you were really doing?"

"Why, yes, I have generally been going to the smoking-car to have a cigar."

"Tut, tut—not that! I mean, did it ever occur to you on such an occasion, that absolutely you were moving faster than the train? The train passes the telegraph poles at the rate of thirty miles an hour, say. You walk toward the smoking-car at the rate of four miles an hour. Then *you* pass the telegraph poles at the rate of thirty-four miles. Your absolute speed is the speed of the engine, plus the speed of your own locomotion. Do you follow me?"

I began to get an inkling of his meaning, and told him so.

"Very well. Let us advance a step. Your addition to the speed of the engine is trivial, and the space in which you can exercise it, limited. Now suppose two stations, A and B, two miles distant by the track. Imagine a train of platform cars, the last car resting at station A. The train is a mile long, say. The engine is therefore within a mile of station B. Say the train can move a mile in ten minutes. The last car, having two miles to go, would reach B in twenty minutes, but the engine, a mile ahead, would get there in ten. You jump on the last car, at A, in a prodigious hurry to reach Abscissa, who is at B. If you stay on the last car it will be twenty long minutes before you see her. But the engine reaches B and the fair lady in ten. You will be a stupid reasoner, and an indifferent lover, if you don't put for the engine over those platform cars, as fast as your legs will carry you. You can run a mile, the length of the train, in ten minutes. Therefore, you reach Abscissa when the engine does, or in ten minutes—ten minutes sooner than if you had lazily sat down upon the rear car and talked politics with the brakeman. You have diminished the time by one half. You have added your speed to that of the locomotive to some purpose. *Nicht wahr?*"

I saw it perfectly; much plainer, perhaps, for his putting in the clause about Abscissa.

He continued:

"This illustration, though a slow one, leads up to a principle which may be carried to any extent. Our first anxiety will be to spare your legs and wind. Let us suppose that the two miles of track are perfectly straight, and make our train one platform car, a mile long, with parallel rails laid upon its top. Put a little dummy engine on these rails, and let it run to and fro along the platform car, while the platform car is pulled along the ground track. Catch the idea? The dummy takes your place. But it can run its mile much faster. Fancy that our locomotive is strong enough to pull the platform car over the two miles in two minutes. The dummy can attain the same speed. When the engine reaches B in one minute, the dummy, having gone a mile a-top the platform car, reaches B also. We have so combined the speeds of those two engines as to accomplish two miles in one minute. Is this all we can do? Prepare to exercise your imagination."

I lit my pipe.

"Still two miles of straight track, between A and B. On the track a long platform car, reaching from A to within a quarter of a mile of B. We will now discard ordinary locomotives and adopt as our motive power a series of compact magnetic engines, distributed underneath the platform car, all along its length."

"I don't understand those magnetic engines."

"Well, each of them consists of a great iron

horseshoe, rendered alternately a magnet and not a magnet by an intermittent current of electricity from a battery, this current in its turn regulated by clock-work. When the horseshoe is in the circuit, it is a magnet, and it pulls its clapper toward it with enormous power. When it is out of the circuit, the next second, it is not a magnet, and it lets the clapper go. The clapper, oscillating to and fro, imparts a rotatory motion to a fly-wheel, which transmits it to the drivers on the rails. Such are our motors. They are no novelty, for trial has proved them practicable.

"With a magnetic engine for every truck of wheels, we can reasonably expect to move our immense car, and to drive it along at a speed, say, of a mile a minute.

"The forward end, having but a quarter of a mile to go, will reach B in fifteen seconds. We will call this platform car number 1. On top of number 1 are laid rails on which another platform car, number 2, a quarter of a mile shorter than number 1, is moved in precisely the same way. Number 2, in its turn, is surmounted by number 3, moving independently of the tiers beneath, and a quarter of a mile shorter than number 2. Number 2 is a mile and a half long; number 3 a mile and a quarter. Above, on successive levels, are number 4, a mile long; number 5, three quarters of a mile; number 6, half a mile; number 7, a quarter of a mile, and number 8, a short passenger car, on top of all.

"Each car moves upon the car beneath it, independently of all the others, at the rate of a mile a minute. Each car has its own magnetic engines. Well, the train being drawn up with the latter end of each car resting against a lofty bumping-post at A, Tom Furnace, the gentlemanly conductor, and Jean Marie Rivarol, engineer, mount by a long ladder to the exalted number 8. The complicated mechanism is set in motion. What happens?

"Number 8 runs a quarter of a mile in fifteen seconds and reaches the end of number 7. Meanwhile number 7 has run a quarter of a mile in the same time and reached the end of number 6; number 6, a quarter of a mile in fifteen seconds, and reached the end of number 5; number 5, the end of number 4; number 4, of number 3; number 3, of number 2; number 2, of number 1. And number 1, in fifteen seconds, has gone its quarter of a mile along the ground track, and has reached station B. All this has been done in fifteen seconds. Wherefore, numbers 1, 2, 3, 4, 5, 6, 7, and 8 come to rest against the bumping-post at B, at precisely the same second. We, in number 8, reach B just when number 1 reaches it. In other words, we accomplish two miles in fifteen seconds. Each of the eight cars, moving at the rate of a mile a minute, has contributed a quarter of a mile to our journey, and has done its work in fifteen seconds. All the eight did their work at once, during the same fifteen seconds. Consequently we have been whizzed through the air at the somewhat startling speed of seven and a half seconds to the mile. This is the Tachypomp. Does it justify the name?"

Although a little bewildered by the complexity of cars, I apprehended the general principle of the machine. I made a diagram, and understood it much better. "You have merely improved on the idea of my moving faster than the train when I was going to the smoking car?"

"Precisely. So far we have kept within the bounds of the practicable. To satisfy the Professor, you can theorize in something after this fashion: If we double the number of cars, thus decreasing by one half the distance which each has to go, we shall attain twice the speed. Each of the sixteen cars will have but one eighth of a mile to go. At the uniform rate we have adopted, the two miles can be done in seven and a half instead of fifteen seconds. With thirty-two cars, and a sixteenth of a mile, or twenty rods difference in their length, we arrive at the speed of a mile in less than two seconds; with sixty-four cars, each travelling but ten rods, a mile under the second.

More than sixty miles a minute! If this isn't rapid enough for the Professor, tell him to go on, increasing the number of his cars and diminishing the distance each one has to run. If sixty-four cars yield a speed of a mile inside the second, let him fancy a Tachypomp of six hundred and forty cars, and amuse himself calculating the rate of car number 640. Just whisper to him that when he has an infinite number of cars with an infinitesimal difference in their lengths, he will have obtained that infinite speed for which he seems to yearn. Then demand Abscissa."

I wrung my friend's hand in silent and grateful admiration. I could say nothing.

"You have listened to the man of theory," he said proudly. "You shall now behold the practical engineer. We will go to the west of the Mississippi and find some suitably level locality. We will erect thereon a model Tachypomp. We will summon thereunto the professor, his daughter, and why not his fair sister Jocasta, as well? We will take them on a journey which shall much astonish the venerable Surd. He shall place Abscissa's digits in yours and bless you both with an algebraic formula. Jocasta shall contemplate with wonder the genius of Rivarol. But we have much to do. We must ship to St. Joseph the vast amount of material to be employed in the construction of the Tachypomp. We must engage a small army of workmen to effect that construction, for we are to annihilate time and space. Perhaps you had better see your bankers."

I rushed impetuously to the door. There should be no delay.

"Stop! stop! *Um Gottes willen*, stop!" shrieked Rivarol. "I launched my butcher this morning and I haven't bolted the—"

But it was too late. I was upon the trap. It swung open with a crash, and I was plunged down, down, down! I felt as if I were falling through illimitable space. I remember wondering, as I rushed through the darkness, whether I should reach Kerguellen's Land or stop at the center. It seemed an eternity. Then my course was suddenly and painfully arrested.

I opened my eyes. Around me were the walls of Professor Surd's study. Under me was a hard, unyielding plane which I knew too well was Professor Surd's study floor. Behind me was the black, slippery, hair-cloth chair which had belched me forth, much as the whale served Jonah. In front of me stood Professor Surd himself, looking down with a not unpleasant smile.

"Good-evening, Mr. Furnace. Let me help you up. You look tired, sir. No wonder you fell asleep when I kept you so long waiting. Shall I get you a glass of wine? No? By the way, since receiving your letter I find that you are a son of my old friend, Judge Furnace. I have made inquiries, and see no reason why you should not make Abscissa a good husband."

Still I can see no reason why the Tachypomp should not have succeeded. Can you?

H. P. Lovecraft

Howard Phillips Lovecraft (1890–1937) has had, arguably, a greater influence upon weird fiction than any other writer. He was not prolific – sixty-five stories constitute his whole oeuvre – but he was a master at evoking a particular kind of unsettling, existentially unnerving atmosphere, a dark cosmic horror that generates its powerful effect by being hinted at rather than spelled out. In this, perhaps his most famous story, something extra-terrestrial and deeply alien has invaded the New England landscape. Though an American, Lovecraft preferred British-English spellings, as with the 'u'-spelled *colour* of the title here. But that seems to me only fitting: 'u' are, as it were, added to the American-set *color*. You feel the horror; the colour touches you.

West of Arkham the hills rise wild, and there are valleys with deep woods that no axe has ever cut. There are dark narrow glens where the trees slope fantastically, and where thin brooklets trickle without ever having caught the glint of sunlight. On the gentler slopes there are farms, ancient and rocky, with squat, moss-coated cottages brooding eternally over old New England secrets in the lee of great ledges; but these are all vacant now, the wide chimneys crumbling and the shingled sides bulging perilously beneath low gambrel roofs.

The old folk have gone away, and foreigners do not like to live there. French-Canadians have tried it, Italians have tried it, and the Poles have come and departed. It is not because of anything that can be seen or heard or handled, but because of something that is imagined. The place is not good for the imagination, and does not bring restful dreams at night. It must be this which keeps the foreigners away, for old Ammi Pierce has never told them of anything he recalls from the strange days. Ammi, whose head has been a little queer for years, is the only one who still remains, or who ever talks of the strange days; and he dares to do this because his house is so near the open fields and the travelled roads around Arkham.

There was once a road over the hills and through the valleys, that ran straight where the blasted heath is now; but people ceased to use it and a new road was laid curving far toward the south. Traces of the old one can still be found amidst the weeds of a returning wilderness, and some of them will doubtless linger even when half the hollows are flooded for the new reservoir. Then the dark woods will be cut down and the blasted heath will slumber far below blue waters whose surface will mirror the sky and ripple in the sun. And the secrets of the strange days will be one with the deep's secrets; one with the hidden lore of old ocean, and all the mystery of primal earth.

When I went into the hills and vales to survey for the new reservoir they told me the place was evil. They told me this in Arkham, and because that is a very old town full of witch legends I thought the evil must be something which grandams had whispered to children through centuries. The name "blasted heath" seemed to me very odd and theatrical, and I wondered how it had come into the folklore of a Puritan people. Then I saw that dark westward tangle of glens and slopes for myself, and ceased to wonder at anything beside its own elder mystery. It was morning when I saw it, but shadow lurked always there. The trees grew too thickly, and their trunks were too big for any healthy New England wood. There was too much silence in the dim alleys between them, and the floor was too soft with the dank moss and mattings of infinite years of decay.

In the open spaces, mostly along the line of the old road, there were little hillside farms; sometimes with all the buildings standing, sometimes with only one or two, and sometimes with only a lone chimney or fast-filling cellar. Weeds and briers reigned, and furtive wild things rustled in the undergrowth. Upon everything was a haze of restlessness and oppression; a touch of the unreal and the grotesque, as if some vital element of perspective or chiaroscuro were awry. I did not wonder that the foreigners would not stay, for this was no region to sleep in. It was too much like a landscape of Salvator Rosa; too much like some forbidden woodcut in a tale of terror.

But even all this was not so bad as the blasted heath. I knew it the moment I came upon it at the bottom of a spacious valley; for no other name could fit such a thing, or any other thing fit such a name. It was as if the poet had coined the phrase from having seen this one particular region. It must, I thought as I viewed it, be the outcome of a fire; but why had nothing new ever grown over those five acres of grey desolation that sprawled open to the sky like a great spot eaten by acid in the woods and fields? It lay largely to the north of the ancient road line, but encroached a little on the other side. I felt an odd reluctance about approaching, and did so at last only because my business took me through and past it. There was no vegetation of any kind on that broad expanse, but only a fine grey dust or ash which no wind seemed ever to blow about. The trees near it were sickly and stunted, and many dead trunks stood or lay rotting at the rim. As I walked hurriedly by I saw the tumbled bricks and stones of an old chimney and cellar on my right, and the yawning black maw of an abandoned well whose stagnant vapours played strange tricks with the hues of the sunlight. Even the long, dark woodland climb beyond seemed welcome in contrast, and I marvelled no more at the frightened whispers of Arkham people. There had been no house or ruin near; even in the old days the place must have been lonely and remote. And at twilight, dreading to re-pass that ominous spot, I walked circuitously back to the town by the curving road on the south. I vaguely wished some clouds would gather, for an odd timidity about the deep skyey voids above had crept into my soul.

In the evening I asked old people in Arkham about the blasted heath, and what was meant by that phrase "strange days" which so many evasively muttered. I could not, however, get any good answers, except that all the mystery was much more recent than I had dreamed. It was not a matter of old legendry at all, but something within the lifetime of those who spoke. It had happened in the 'eighties, and a family had disappeared or was killed. Speakers would not be exact; and because they all told me to pay no attention to old Ammi Pierce's crazy tales, I sought him out the next morning, having heard that he lived alone in the ancient tottering cottage where the trees first begin to get very thick. It was a fearsomely archaic place, and had begun to exude the faint miasmal odour which clings about houses that have stood too long. Only with persistent knocking could I rouse the aged man, and when he shuffled timidly to the door I could tell he was not glad to see me. He was not so feeble as I had expected; but his eyes drooped in a curious way, and his unkempt clothing and white beard made him seem very worn and dismal. Not knowing just how he could best be launched on his tales, I feigned a matter of business; told him of my surveying, and asked vague questions about the district. He was far brighter and more educated than I had been led to think, and before I knew it had grasped quite as much of the subject as any man I had talked with in Arkham. He was not like other rustics I had known in the sections where reservoirs were to be. From him there were no protests at the miles of old wood and farmland to be blotted out, though perhaps there would have been had not his home lain outside the bounds of the future lake. Relief was all that he shewed; relief at the doom of the dark ancient valleys through which he had roamed all his life. They were better under water now—better under water since the strange days. And with this opening his husky voice sank low, while his body leaned forward and his right forefinger began to point shakily and impressively.

It was then that I heard the story, and as the rambling voice scraped and whispered on I shivered again and again despite the summer day. Often I had to recall the speaker from ramblings, piece out scientific points which he knew only by a fading parrot memory of professors' talk, or bridge over gaps where his sense of logic and continuity broke down. When he was done I did not wonder that his mind had snapped a trifle, or that the folk of Arkham would not speak much of the blasted heath. I hurried back before sunset to my hotel, unwilling to have the stars come out above me in the open; and the next day returned to Boston to give up my position. I could not go into that dim chaos of old forest and slope again, or face another time that grey blasted heath where the black well yawned deep beside the tumbled bricks and stones. The reservoir will soon be built now, and all those elder secrets will lie safe for ever under watery fathoms. But even then I do not believe I would like to visit that country by night—at least, not when the sinister stars are out; and nothing could bribe me to drink the new city water of Arkham.

It all began, old Ammi said, with the meteorite. Before that time there had been no wild legends at all since the witch trials, and even then these western woods were not feared half so much as the small island in the Miskatonic where the devil held court beside a curious stone altar older than the Indians. These were not haunted woods, and their fantastic dusk was never terrible till the strange days. Then there had come that white noontide cloud, that string of explosions in the air, and that pillar of smoke from the valley far in the wood. And by night all Arkham had heard of the great rock that fell out of the sky and bedded itself in the ground beside the well at the Nahum Gardner place. That was the house which had stood where the blasted heath was to come—the trim white Nahum Gardner house amidst its fertile gardens and orchards.

Nahum had come to town to tell people about the stone, and had dropped in at Ammi Pierce's on the way. Ammi was forty then, and all the queer things were fixed very strongly in his mind. He and his wife had gone with the three professors from Miskatonic University who hastened out the next morning to see the weird visitor from unknown stellar space, and had wondered why Nahum had called it so large the day before. It had shrunk, Nahum said as he pointed out the big brownish mound above the ripped earth and charred grass near the archaic well-sweep in his front yard; but the wise men answered that stones do not shrink. Its heat lingered persistently, and Nahum declared it had glowed faintly in the night. The professors tried it with a geologist's hammer and found it was oddly soft. It was, in truth, so soft as to be almost plastic; and they gouged rather than chipped a specimen to take back to the college for testing. They took it in an old pail borrowed from Nahum's kitchen, for even the small piece refused to grow cool. On the trip back they stopped at Ammi's to rest, and seemed thoughtful when Mrs. Pierce remarked that the fragment was growing smaller and burning the bottom of the pail. Truly, it was not large, but perhaps they had taken less than they thought.

The day after that—all this was in June of '82—the professors had trooped out again in a great excitement. As they passed Ammi's they told him what queer things the specimen had done, and how it had faded wholly away when they put it in a glass beaker. The beaker had gone, too, and the wise men talked of the strange stone's affinity for silicon. It had acted quite unbelievably in that well-ordered laboratory; doing nothing at all and shewing no occluded gases when heated on charcoal, being wholly negative in the borax bead, and soon proving itself absolutely non-volatile at any producible temperature, including that of the oxy-hydrogen blowpipe. On an anvil it appeared highly malleable, and in the dark its luminosity was very marked. Stubbornly refusing to grow cool, it soon had the college in a state of real excitement; and when upon heating before the spectroscope it displayed shining bands unlike any known colours of the normal spectrum there was much breathless talk of new elements, bizarre optical properties, and other things which puzzled men of science are wont to say when faced by the unknown.

Hot as it was, they tested it in a crucible with all the proper reagents. Water did nothing. Hydrochloric acid was the same. Nitric acid and even aqua regia merely hissed and spattered against its torrid invulnerability. Ammi had difficulty in recalling all these things, but recognised some solvents as I mentioned them in the usual order of use. There were ammonia and caustic soda, alcohol and ether, nauseous carbon disulphide and a dozen others; but although the weight grew steadily less as time passed, and the fragment seemed to be slightly cooling, there was no change in the solvents to shew that they had attacked the substance at all. It was a metal, though, beyond a doubt. It was magnetic, for one thing; and after its immersion in the acid solvents there seemed to be faint traces of the Widmanstätten figures found on meteoric iron. When the cooling had grown very considerable, the testing was carried on in glass; and it was in a glass beaker that they left all the chips made of the original fragment during the work. The next morning both chips and beaker were gone without trace, and only a charred spot marked the place on the wooden shelf where they had been.

All this the professors told Ammi as they paused at his door, and once more he went with them to see the stony messenger from the stars, though this time his wife did not accompany him. It had now most certainly shrunk, and even the sober professors could not doubt the truth of what they saw. All around the dwindling brown lump near the well was a vacant space, except where the earth had caved in; and whereas it had been a good seven feet across the day before, it was now scarcely five. It was still hot, and the sages studied its surface curiously as they detached another and larger piece with hammer and chisel. They gouged deeply this time, and as they pried away the smaller mass they saw that the core of the thing was not quite homogeneous.

They had uncovered what seemed to be the side of a large coloured globule imbedded in the substance. The colour, which resembled some of the bands in the meteor's strange spectrum, was almost impossible to describe; and it was only by analogy that they called it colour at all. Its texture was glossy, and upon tapping it appeared to promise both brittleness and hollowness. One of the professors gave it a smart blow with a hammer, and it burst with a nervous little pop. Nothing was emitted, and all trace of the thing vanished with the puncturing. It left behind a hollow spherical space about three inches across, and all thought it probable that others would be discovered as the enclosing substance wasted away.

Conjecture was vain; so after a futile attempt to find additional globules by drilling, the seekers left again with their new specimen—which proved, however, as baffling in the laboratory as its predecessor had been. Aside from being almost plastic, having heat, magnetism, and slight luminosity, cooling slightly in powerful acids, possessing an unknown spectrum, wasting away in air, and attacking silicon compounds with mutual destruction as a result, it presented no identifying features whatsoever; and at the end of the tests the college scientists were forced to own that they could not place it. It was nothing of this earth, but a piece of the great outside; and as such dowered with outside properties and obedient to outside laws.

That night there was a thunderstorm, and when the professors went out to Nahum's the next day they met with a bitter disappointment. The stone, magnetic as it had been, must have had some peculiar electrical property; for it had "drawn the lightning", as Nahum said, with a singular persistence. Six times within an hour the farmer saw the lightning strike the furrow in the front yard, and when the storm was over nothing remained but a ragged pit by the ancient well-sweep, half-choked with caved-in earth. Digging had borne no fruit, and the scientists verified the fact of the utter vanishment. The failure was total; so that nothing was left to do but go back to the laboratory and test again the disappearing fragment left carefully cased in lead. That fragment lasted a week, at the end of which nothing of value had been learned of it. When it had gone, no residue was left behind, and in time the professors felt scarcely sure they had indeed seen with waking eyes that cryptic vestige of the fathomless gulfs outside; that lone, weird message from other universes and other realms of matter, force, and entity.

As was natural, the Arkham papers made much of the incident with its collegiate sponsoring, and sent reporters to talk with Nahum Gardner and his family. At least one Boston daily also sent a scribe, and Nahum quickly became a kind of local celebrity. He was a lean, genial person of about fifty, living with his wife and three sons on the pleasant farmstead in the valley. He and Ammi exchanged visits frequently, as did their wives; and Ammi had nothing but praise for him after all these years. He seemed slightly proud of the notice his place had attracted, and talked often of the meteorite in the succeeding weeks. That July and August were hot, and Nahum worked hard at his haying in the ten-acre pasture across Chapman's Brook; his rattling wain wearing deep ruts in the shadowy lanes between. The labour tired him more than it had in other years, and he felt that age was beginning to tell on him.

Then fell the time of fruit and harvest. The pears and apples slowly ripened, and Nahum vowed that his orchards were prospering as never before. The fruit was growing to phenomenal size and unwonted gloss, and in such abundance that extra barrels were ordered to handle the future crop. But with the ripening came sore disappointment, for of all that gorgeous array of specious lusciousness not one single jot was fit to eat. Into the fine flavour of the pears and apples had crept a stealthy bitterness and sickishness, so that even the smallest of bites induced a lasting disgust. It was the same with the melons and tomatoes, and Nahum sadly saw that his entire crop was lost. Quick to connect events, he declared that the meteorite had poisoned the soil, and thanked heaven that most of the other crops were in the upland lot along the road.

Winter came early, and was very cold. Ammi saw Nahum less often than usual, and observed that he had begun to look worried. The rest of his family, too, seemed to have grown taciturn; and were far from steady in their churchgoing or their attendance at the various social events of the countryside. For this reserve or melancholy no cause could be found, though all the household confessed now and then to poorer health and a feeling of vague disquiet. Nahum himself gave the most definite statement of anyone when he said he was disturbed about certain footprints in the snow. They were the usual winter prints of red squirrels, white rabbits, and foxes, but the brooding farmer professed to see something not quite right about their nature and arrangement. He was never specific, but appeared to think that they were not as characteristic of the anatomy and habits of squirrels and rabbits and foxes as they ought to be. Ammi listened without interest to this talk until one night when he drove past Nahum's house in his sleigh on the way back from Clark's Corners. There had been a moon, and a rabbit had run across the road; and the leaps of that rabbit were longer than either Ammi or his horse liked. The latter, indeed, had almost run away when brought up by a firm rein. Thereafter Ammi gave Nahum's tales more respect, and wondered why the Gardner dogs seemed so cowed and quivering every morning. They had, it developed, nearly lost the spirit to bark.

In February the McGregor boys from Meadow Hill were out shooting woodchucks, and not far from the Gardner place bagged a very peculiar specimen. The proportions of its body seemed slightly altered in a queer way impossible to describe, while its face had taken on an expression which no one ever saw in a woodchuck before. The boys were genuinely frightened, and threw the thing away at once, so that only their grotesque tales of it ever reached the people of the countryside. But the shying of the horses near Nahum's house had now become an acknowledged thing, and all the basis for a cycle of whispered legend was fast taking form.

People vowed that the snow melted faster around Nahum's than it did anywhere else, and early in March there was an awed discussion in Potter's general store at Clark's Corners. Stephen Rice had driven past Gardner's in the morning, and had noticed the skunk-cabbages coming up through the mud by the woods across the road. Never were things of such size seen before, and they held strange colours that could not be put into any words. Their shapes were monstrous, and the horse had snorted at an odour which struck Stephen as wholly unprecedented. That afternoon several persons drove past to see the abnormal growth, and all agreed that plants of that kind ought never to sprout in a healthy world. The bad fruit of the fall before was freely mentioned, and it went from mouth to mouth that there was poison in Nahum's ground. Of course it was the meteorite; and remembering how strange the men from the college had found that stone to be, several farmers spoke about the matter to them.

One day they paid Nahum a visit; but having no love of wild tales and folklore were very conservative in what they inferred. The plants were certainly odd, but all skunk-cabbages are more or less odd in shape and odour and hue. Perhaps some mineral element from the stone had entered the soil, but it would soon be washed away. And as for the footprints and frightened horses—of course this was mere country talk which such a phenomenon as the aërolite would be certain to start. There was really nothing for serious men to do in cases of wild gossip, for superstitious rustics will say and believe anything. And so all through the strange days the professors stayed away in contempt. Only one of them, when given two phials of dust for analysis in a police job over a year and a half later, recalled that the queer colour of that skunk-cabbage had been very like one of the anomalous bands of light shewn by the meteor fragment in the college spectroscope, and like the brittle globule found imbedded in the stone from the abyss. The samples in this analysis case gave the same odd bands at first, though later they lost the property.

The trees budded prematurely around Nahum's, and at night they swayed ominously in the wind. Nahum's second son, Thaddeus, a lad of fifteen, swore that they swayed also when there was no wind; but even the gossips would not credit this. Certainly, however, restlessness was in the air. The entire Gardner family developed the habit of stealthy listening, though not for any sound which they could consciously name. The listening was, indeed, rather a product of moments when consciousness seemed half to slip away. Unfortunately such moments increased week by week, till it became common speech that "something was wrong with all Nahum's folks". When the early saxifrage came out it had another strange colour; not quite like that of the skunk-cabbage, but plainly related and equally unknown to anyone who saw it. Nahum took some blossoms to Arkham and shewed them to the editor of the *Gazette,* but that dignitary did no more than write a humorous article about them, in which the dark fears of rustics were held up to polite ridicule. It was a mistake of Nahum's to tell a stolid city man about the way the great, overgrown mourning-cloak butterflies behaved in connexion with these saxifrages.

April brought a kind of madness to the country folk, and began that disuse of the road past Nahum's which led to its ultimate abandonment. It was the vegetation. All the orchard trees blossomed forth in strange colours, and through the stony soil of the yard and adjacent pasturage there sprang up a bizarre growth which only a botanist could connect with the proper flora of the region. No sane wholesome colours were anywhere to be seen except in the green grass and leafage; but everywhere those hectic and prismatic variants of some diseased, underlying primary tone without a place among the known tints of earth. The Dutchman's breeches became a thing of sinister menace, and the bloodroots grew insolent in their chromatic perversion. Ammi and the

Gardners thought that most of the colours had a sort of haunting familiarity, and decided that they reminded one of the brittle globule in the meteor. Nahum ploughed and sowed the ten-acre pasture and the upland lot, but did nothing with the land around the house. He knew it would be of no use, and hoped that the summer's strange growths would draw all the poison from the soil. He was prepared for almost anything now, and had grown used to the sense of something near him waiting to be heard. The shunning of his house by neighbours told on him, of course; but it told on his wife more. The boys were better off, being at school each day; but they could not help being frightened by the gossip. Thaddeus, an especially sensitive youth, suffered the most.

In May the insects came, and Nahum's place became a nightmare of buzzing and crawling. Most of the creatures seemed not quite usual in their aspects and motions, and their nocturnal habits contradicted all former experience. The Gardners took to watching at night—watching in all directions at random for something . . . they could not tell what. It was then that they all owned that Thaddeus had been right about the trees. Mrs. Gardner was the next to see it from the window as she watched the swollen boughs of a maple against a moonlit sky. The boughs surely moved, and there was no wind. It must be the sap. Strangeness had come into everything growing now. Yet it was none of Nahum's family at all who made the next discovery. Familiarity had dulled them, and what they could not see was glimpsed by a timid windmill salesman from Bolton who drove by one night in ignorance of the country legends. What he told in Arkham was given a short paragraph in the *Gazette*; and it was there that all the farmers, Nahum included, saw it first. The night had been dark and the buggy-lamps faint, but around a farm in the valley which everyone knew from the account must be Nahum's the darkness had been less thick. A dim though distinct luminosity seemed to inhere in all the vegetation, grass, leaves, and blossoms alike, while at one moment a detached piece of the phosphorescence appeared to stir furtively in the yard near the barn.

The grass had so far seemed untouched, and the cows were freely pastured in the lot near the house, but toward the end of May the milk began to be bad. Then Nahum had the cows driven to the uplands, after which the trouble ceased. Not long after this the change in grass and leaves became apparent to the eye. All the verdure was going grey, and was developing a highly singular quality of brittleness. Ammi was now the only person who ever visited the place, and his visits were becoming fewer and fewer.

When school closed the Gardners were virtually cut off from the world, and sometimes let Ammi do their errands in town. They were failing curiously both physically and mentally, and no one was surprised when the news of Mrs. Gardner's madness stole around.

It happened in June, about the anniversary of the meteor's fall, and the poor woman screamed about things in the air which she could not describe. In her raving there was not a single specific noun, but only verbs and pronouns. Things moved and changed and fluttered, and ears tingled to impulses which were not wholly sounds. Something was taken away—she was being drained of something—something was fastening itself on her that ought not to be—someone must make it keep off—nothing was ever still in the night—the walls and windows shifted. Nahum did not send her to the county asylum, but let her wander about the house as long as she was harmless to herself and others. Even when her expression changed he did nothing. But when the boys grew afraid of her, and Thaddeus nearly fainted at the way she made faces at him, he decided to keep her locked in the attic. By July she had ceased to speak and crawled on all fours, and before that month was over Nahum got the mad notion that she was slightly luminous in the dark, as he now clearly saw was the case with the nearby vegetation.

It was a little before this that the horses had stampeded. Something had aroused them in the night, and their neighing and kicking in their stalls had been terrible. There seemed virtually nothing to do to calm them, and when Nahum opened the stable door they all bolted out like frightened woodland deer. It took a week to track all four, and when found they were seen to be quite useless and unmanageable. Something had snapped in their brains, and each one had to be shot for its own good. Nahum borrowed a horse from Ammi for his haying, but found it would not approach the barn. It shied, balked, and whinnied, and in the end he could do nothing but drive it into the yard while the men used their own strength to get the heavy wagon near enough the hayloft for convenient pitching. And all the while the vegetation was turning grey and brittle. Even the flowers whose hues had been so strange were greying now, and the fruit was coming out grey and dwarfed and tasteless. The asters and goldenrod bloomed grey and distorted, and the roses and zinneas and hollyhocks in the front yard were such blasphemous-looking things that Nahum's oldest boy Zenas cut them down. The strangely puffed insects died about that time, even the bees that had left their hives and taken to the woods.

By September all the vegetation was fast crumbling to a greyish powder, and Nahum feared that the trees would die before the poison was out of the soil. His wife now had spells of terrific screaming, and he and the boys were in a constant state of nervous tension. They shunned people now, and when school opened the boys did not go. But it was Ammi, on one of his rare visits, who first realised that the well water was no longer good. It had an evil taste that was not exactly foetid nor exactly salty, and Ammi advised his friend to dig another well on higher ground to use till the soil was good again. Nahum, however, ignored the warning, for he had by that time become calloused to strange and unpleasant things. He and the boys continued to use the tainted supply, drinking it as listlessly and mechanically as they ate their meagre and ill-cooked meals and did their thankless and monotonous chores through the aimless days. There was something of stolid resignation about them all, as if they walked half in another world between lines of nameless guards to a certain and familiar doom.

Thaddeus went mad in September after a visit to the well. He had gone with a pail and had come back empty-handed, shrieking and waving his arms, and sometimes lapsing into an inane titter or a whisper about "the moving colours down there". Two in one family was pretty bad, but Nahum was very brave about it. He let the boy run about for a week until he began stumbling and hurting himself, and then he shut him in an attic room across the hall from his mother's. The way they screamed at each other from behind their locked doors was very terrible, especially to little Merwin, who fancied they talked in some horrible language that was not of earth. Merwin was getting frightfully imaginative, and his restlessness was worse after the shutting away of the brother who had been his greatest playmate.

Almost at the same time the mortality among the livestock commenced. Poultry turned greyish and died very quickly, their meat being found dry and noisome upon cutting. Hogs grew inordinately fat, then suddenly began to undergo loathsome changes which no one could explain. Their meat was of course useless, and Nahum was at his wits' end. No rural veterinary would approach his place, and the city veterinary from Arkham was openly baffled. The swine began growing grey and brittle and falling to pieces before they died, and their eyes and muzzles developed singular alterations. It was very inexplicable, for they had never been fed from the tainted vegetation. Then something struck the cows. Certain areas or sometimes the whole body would be uncannily shrivelled or compressed, and atrocious collapses or disintegrations were common. In the last stages—and death was always the result—there would be a greying and turning brittle like that which beset the hogs. There could be no question of poison, for all the cases occurred in a locked and undisturbed barn. No bites of prowling things could have brought the virus, for what live beast of earth can pass through solid obstacles? It must be only natural disease—yet what disease could wreak such results was beyond any mind's guessing. When the harvest came there was not an animal surviving on the place, for the stock and poultry were dead and the dogs had run away. These dogs, three in number, had all vanished one night and were never heard of again. The five cats had left some time before, but their going was scarcely noticed since there now seemed to be no mice, and only Mrs. Gardner had made pets of the graceful felines.

On the nineteenth of October Nahum staggered into Ammi's house with hideous news. The death had come to poor Thaddeus in his attic room, and it had come in a way which could not be told. Nahum had dug a grave in the railed family plot behind the farm, and had put therein what he found. There could have been nothing from outside, for the small barred window and locked door were intact; but it was much as it had been in the barn. Ammi and his wife consoled the stricken man as best they could, but shuddered as they did so. Stark terror seemed to cling round the Gardners and all they touched, and the very presence of one in the house was a breath from regions unnamed and unnamable. Ammi accompanied Nahum home with the greatest reluctance, and did what he might to calm the hysterical sobbing of little Merwin. Zenas needed no calming. He had come of late to do nothing but stare into space and obey what his father told him; and Ammi thought that his fate was very merciful. Now and then Merwin's screams were answered faintly from the attic, and in response to an inquiring look Nahum said that his wife was getting very feeble. When night approached, Ammi managed to get away; for not even friendship could make him stay in that spot when the faint glow of the vegetation began and the trees may or may not have swayed without wind. It was really lucky for Ammi that he was not more imaginative. Even as things were, his mind was bent ever so slightly; but had he been able to connect and reflect upon all the portents around him he must inevitably have turned a total maniac. In the twilight he hastened home, the screams of the mad woman and the nervous child ringing horribly in his ears.

Three days later Nahum lurched into Ammi's kitchen in the early morning, and in the absence of his host stammered out a desperate tale once more, while Mrs. Pierce listened in a clutching fright. It was little Merwin this time. He was gone. He had gone out late at night with a lantern and pail for water, and had never come back. He'd been going to pieces for days, and hardly knew what he was about. Screamed at everything. There had been a frantic shriek from the yard then, but before the father could get to the door, the boy was gone. There was no glow from the lantern he had taken, and of the child himself no trace. At the time Nahum thought the lantern and pail were gone too; but when dawn came, and the man had plodded back from his all-night search of the woods and fields, he had found some very curious things near the well. There was a crushed and apparently somewhat melted mass of iron which had certainly been the lantern; while a bent handle and twisted iron hoops beside it, both half-fused, seemed to hint at the remnants of the pail. That was all. Nahum was past imagining, Mrs. Pierce was blank, and Ammi, when he had reached home and heard the tale, could give no guess. Merwin was gone, and there would be no use in telling the people around, who shunned all Gardners now. No use, either, in telling the city people at Arkham who laughed at everything. Thad was gone, and now Mernie was gone. Something was creeping and creeping and waiting to be seen and felt and heard. Nahum would go soon, and he wanted Ammi to look after his wife and Zenas if they survived him. It must all be a judgment of some sort; though he could not fancy what for, since he had always walked uprightly in the Lord's ways so far as he knew.

For over two weeks Ammi saw nothing of Nahum; and then, worried about what might have happened, he overcame his fears and paid the Gardner place a visit. There was no smoke from the great chimney, and for a moment the visitor was apprehensive of the worst. The aspect of the whole farm was shocking—greyish withered grass and leaves on the ground, vines falling in brittle wreckage from archaic walls and gables, and great bare trees clawing up at the grey November sky with a studied malevolence which Ammi could not but feel had come from some subtle change in the tilt of the branches. But Nahum was alive, after all. He was weak, and lying on a couch in the low-ceiled kitchen, but perfectly conscious and able to give simple orders to Zenas. The room was deadly cold; and as Ammi visibly shivered, the host shouted huskily to

Zenas for more wood. Wood, indeed, was sorely needed; since the cavernous fireplace was unlit and empty, with a cloud of soot blowing about in the chill wind that came down the chimney. Presently Nahum asked him if the extra wood had made him any more comfortable, and then Ammi saw what had happened. The stoutest cord had broken at last, and the hapless farmer's mind was proof against more sorrow.

Questioning tactfully, Ammi could get no clear data at all about the missing Zenas. "In the well—he lives in the well—" was all that the clouded father would say. Then there flashed across the visitor's mind a sudden thought of the mad wife, and he changed his line of inquiry. "Nabby? Why, here she is!" was the surprised response of poor Nahum, and Ammi soon saw that he must search for himself. Leaving the harmless babbler on the couch, he took the keys from their nail beside the door and climbed the creaking stairs to the attic. It was very close and noisome up there, and no sound could be heard from any direction. Of the four doors in sight, only one was locked, and on this he tried various keys on the ring he had taken. The third key proved the right one, and after some fumbling Ammi threw open the low white door.

It was quite dark inside, for the window was small

and half-obscured by the crude wooden bars; and Ammi could see nothing at all on the wide-planked floor. The stench was beyond enduring, and before proceeding further he had to retreat to another room and return with his lungs filled with breathable air. When he did enter he saw something dark in the corner, and upon seeing it more clearly he screamed outright. While he screamed he thought a momentary cloud eclipsed the window, and a second later he felt himself brushed as if by some hateful current of vapour. Strange colours danced before his eyes; and had not a present horror numbed him he would have thought of the globule in the meteor that the geologist's hammer had shattered, and of the morbid vegetation that had sprouted in the spring. As it was he thought only of the blasphemous monstrosity which confronted him, and which all too clearly had shared the nameless fate of young Thaddeus and the livestock. But the terrible thing about this horror was that it very slowly and perceptibly moved as it continued to crumble.

Ammi would give me no added particulars of this scene, but the shape in the corner does not reappear in his tale as a moving object. There are things which cannot be mentioned, and what is done in common humanity is sometimes cruelly judged by the law. I gathered that no moving thing was left in that attic room, and that to leave anything capable of motion there would have been a deed so monstrous as to damn any accountable being to eternal torment. Anyone but a stolid farmer would have fainted or gone mad, but Ammi walked conscious through that low doorway and locked the accursed secret behind him. There would be Nahum to deal with now; he must be fed and tended, and removed to some place where he could be cared for.

Commencing his descent of the dark stairs, Ammi heard a thud below him. He even thought a scream had been suddenly choked off, and recalled nervously the clammy vapour which had brushed by him in that frightful room above. What presence had his cry and entry started up? Halted by some vague fear, he heard still further sounds below. Indubitably there was a sort of heavy dragging, and a most detestably sticky noise as of some fiendish and unclean species of suction. With an associative sense goaded to feverish heights, he thought unaccountably of what he had seen upstairs. Good God! What eldritch dream-world was this into which he had blundered? He dared move neither backward nor forward, but stood there trembling at the black curve of the boxed-in staircase. Every trifle of the scene burned itself into his brain. The sounds, the sense of dread expectancy, the darkness, the steepness of the narrow steps—and merciful heaven! . . . the faint but unmistakable luminosity of all the woodwork in sight; steps, sides, exposed laths, and beams alike.

Then there burst forth a frantic whinny from Ammi's horse outside, followed at once by a clatter which told of a frenzied runaway. In another moment horse and buggy had gone beyond earshot, leaving the frightened man on the dark stairs to guess what had sent them. But that was not all. There had been another sound out there. A sort of liquid splash—water—it must have been the well. He had left Hero untied near it, and a buggy-wheel must have brushed the coping and knocked in a stone. And still the pale phosphorescence glowed in that detestably ancient woodwork. God! how old the house was! Most of it built before 1670, and the gambrel roof not later than 1730.

A feeble scratching on the floor downstairs now sounded distinctly, and Ammi's grip tightened on a heavy stick he had picked up in the attic for some purpose. Slowly nerving himself, he finished his descent and walked boldly toward the kitchen. But he did not complete the walk, because what he sought was no longer there. It had come to meet him, and it was still alive after a fashion. Whether it had crawled or whether it had been dragged by any external force, Ammi could not say; but the death had been at it. Everything had happened in the last half-hour, but collapse, greying, and disintegration were already far advanced. There was a horrible brittleness, and dry fragments were scaling off. Ammi could not touch it, but looked horrifiedly into the distorted parody that had been a face. "What was it, Nahum—what was it?" he whispered, and the cleft, bulging lips were just able to crackle out a final answer.

"Nothin' . . . nothin' . . . the colour . . . it burns . . . cold an' wet, but it burns . . . it lived in the well . . . I seen it . . . a kind o' smoke . . . jest like the flowers last spring . . . the well shone at night . . . Thad an' Mernie an' Zenas . . . everything alive . . . suckin' the life out of everything . . . in that stone . . . it must a' come in that stone . . . pizened the whole place . . . dun't know what it wants . . . that round thing them men from the college dug outen the stone . . . they smashed it . . . it was that same colour . . . jest the same, like the flowers an' plants . . . must a' ben more of 'em . . . seeds . . . seeds . . . they growed . . . I seen it the fust time this week . . . must a' got strong on Zenas . . . he was a big boy, full o' life . . . it beats down your mind an' then gits ye . . . burns ye up . . . in the well water . . . you was right about that . . . evil water . . . Zenas never come back from the well . . . can't git away . . .

draws ye . . . ye know summ'at's comin', but tain't no use . . . I seen it time an' agin senct Zenas was took . . . whar's Nabby, Ammi? . . . my head's no good . . . dun't know how long senct I fed her . . . it'll git her ef we ain't keerful . . . jest a colour . . . her face is gettin' to hev that colour sometimes towards night . . . an' it burns an' sucks . . . it come from some place whar things ain't as they is here . . . one o' them professors said so . . . he was right . . . look out, Ammi, it'll do suthin' more . . . sucks the life out . . ."

But that was all. That which spoke could speak no more because it had completely caved in. Ammi laid a red checked tablecloth over what was left and reeled out the back door into the fields. He climbed the slope to the ten-acre pasture and stumbled home by the north road and the woods. He could not pass that well from which his horse had run away. He had looked at it through the window, and had seen that no stone was missing from the rim. Then the lurching buggy had not dislodged anything after all—the splash had been something else—something which went into the well after it had done with poor Nahum . . .

When Ammi reached his house the horse and buggy had arrived before him and thrown his wife into fits of anxiety. Reassuring her without explanations, he set out at once for Arkham and notified the authorities that the Gardner family was no more. He indulged in no details, but merely told of the deaths of Nahum and Nabby, that of Thaddeus being already known, and mentioned that the cause seemed to be the same strange ailment which had killed the livestock. He also stated that Merwin and Zenas had disappeared. There was considerable questioning at the police station, and in the end Ammi was compelled to take three officers to the Gardner farm, together with the coroner, the medical examiner, and the veterinary who had treated the diseased animals. He went much against his will, for the afternoon was advancing and he feared the fall of night over that accursed place, but it was some comfort to have so many people with him.

The six men drove out in a democrat-wagon, following Ammi's buggy, and arrived at the pest-ridden farmhouse about four o'clock. Used as the officers were to gruesome experiences, not one remained unmoved at what was found in the attic and under the red checked tablecloth on the floor below. The whole aspect of the farm with its grey desolation was terrible enough, but those two crumbling objects were beyond all bounds. No one could look long at them, and even the medical examiner admitted that there was very little to examine. Specimens could be analysed, of course, so he busied himself in obtaining them—and here it develops that a very puzzling aftermath occurred at the college laboratory where the two phials of dust were finally taken. Under the spectroscope both samples gave off an unknown spectrum, in which many of the baffling bands were precisely like those which the strange meteor had yielded in the previous year. The property of emitting this spectrum vanished in a month, the dust thereafter consisting mainly of alkaline phosphates and carbonates.

Ammi would not have told the men about the well if he had thought they meant to do anything then and there. It was getting toward sunset, and he was anxious to be away. But he could not help glancing nervously at the stony curb by the great sweep, and when a detective questioned him he admitted that Nahum had feared something down there—so much so that he had never even thought of searching it for Merwin or Zenas. After that nothing would do but that they empty and explore the well immediately, so Ammi had to wait trembling while pail after pail of rank water was hauled up and splashed on the soaking ground outside. The men sniffed in disgust at the fluid, and toward the last held their noses against the foetor they were uncovering. It was not so long a job as they had feared it would be, since the water was phenomenally low. There is no need to speak too exactly of what they found. Merwin and Zenas were both there, in part, though the vestiges were mainly skeletal. There were also a small deer and a large dog in about the same state, and a number of bones of smaller animals. The ooze and slime at the bottom seemed inexplicably porous and bubbling, and a man who descended on handholds with a long pole found that he could sink the wooden shaft to any depth in the mud of the floor without meeting any solid obstruction.

Twilight had now fallen, and lanterns were brought from the house. Then, when it was seen that nothing further could be gained from the well, everyone went indoors and conferred in the ancient sitting-room while the intermittent light of a spectral half-moon played wanly on the grey desolation outside. The men were frankly nonplussed by the entire case, and could find no convincing common element to link the strange vegetable conditions, the unknown disease of livestock and humans, and the unaccountable deaths of Merwin and Zenas in the tainted well. They had heard the common country talk, it is true; but could not believe that anything contrary to natural law had occurred. No doubt the meteor had poisoned the soil, but the illness of persons and animals who had eaten nothing grown in that soil was another matter. Was it the well water? Very possibly. It might be a good idea to analyse it. But what peculiar madness could have made both boys jump into the well? Their deeds were so similar—and the fragments shewed that they had both suffered from the grey brittle death. Why was everything so grey and brittle?

It was the coroner, seated near a window overlooking the yard, who first noticed the glow about the well. Night had fully set in, and all the abhorrent grounds seemed faintly luminous with more than the fitful moonbeams; but this new glow was something definite and distinct, and appeared to shoot up from the black pit like a softened ray from a searchlight, giving dull reflections in the little ground pools where the water had been emptied. It had a very queer colour, and as all the men clustered round the window Ammi gave a violent start. For this strange beam of ghastly miasma was to him of no unfamiliar hue. He had seen that colour before, and feared to think what it might mean. He had seen it in the nasty brittle globule in that aërolite two summers ago, had seen it in the crazy vegetation of the springtime, and had thought he had seen it for an instant that very morning against the small barred window of that terrible attic room where nameless things had happened. It had flashed there a second, and a clammy and hateful current of vapour had brushed past him—and then poor Nahum had been taken by something of that colour. He had said so at the last—said it was like the globule and the plants. After that had come the runaway in the yard and the splash in the well—and now that well was belching forth to the night a pale insidious beam of the same daemoniac tint.

It does credit to the alertness of Ammi's mind that he puzzled even at that tense moment over a point which was essentially scientific. He could not but wonder at his gleaning of the same impression from a vapour glimpsed in the daytime, against a window opening on the morning sky, and from a nocturnal exhalation seen as a phosphorescent mist against the black and blasted landscape. It wasn't right—it was against Nature—and he thought of those terrible last words of his stricken friend, "It come from some place whar things ain't as they is here . . . one o' them professors said so . . ."

All three horses outside, tied to a pair of shrivelled saplings by the road, were now neighing and pawing frantically. The wagon driver started for the door to do something, but Ammi laid a shaky hand on his shoulder. "Dun't go out thar," he whispered. "They's more to this nor what we know. Nahum said somethin' lived in the well that sucks your life out.

He said it must be some'at growed from a round ball like one we all seen in the meteor stone that fell a year ago June. Sucks an' burns, he said, an' is jest a cloud of colour like that light out thar now, that ye can hardly see an' can't tell what it is. Nahum thought it feeds on everything livin' an' gits stronger all the time. He said he seen it this last week. It must be somethin' from away off in the sky like the men from the college last year says the meteor stone was. The way it's made an' the way it works ain't like no way o' God's world. It's some'at from beyond."

So the men paused indecisively as the light from the well grew stronger and the hitched horses pawed and whinnied in increasing frenzy. It was truly an awful moment; with terror in that ancient and accursed house itself, four monstrous sets of fragments—two from the house and two from the well—in the woodshed behind, and that shaft of unknown and unholy iridescence from the slimy depths in front. Ammi had restrained the driver on impulse, forgetting how uninjured he himself was after the clammy brushing of that coloured vapour in the attic room, but perhaps it is just as well that he acted as he did. No one will ever know what was abroad that night; and though the blasphemy from beyond had not so far hurt any human of unweakened mind, there is no telling what it might not have done at that last moment, and with its seemingly increased strength and the special signs of purpose it was soon to display beneath the half-clouded moonlit sky.

All at once one of the detectives at the window gave a short, sharp gasp. The others looked at him, and then quickly followed his own gaze upward to the point at which its idle straying had been suddenly arrested. There was no need for words. What had been disputed in country gossip was disputable no longer, and it is because of the thing which every man of that party agreed in whispering later on that the strange days are never talked about in Arkham. It is necessary to premise that there was no wind at that hour of the evening. One did arise not long afterward, but there was absolutely none then. Even the dry tips of the lingering hedge-mustard, grey and blighted, and the fringe on the roof of the standing democrat-wagon were unstirred. And yet amid that tense, godless calm the high bare boughs of all the trees in the yard were moving. They were twitching morbidly and spasmodically, clawing in convulsive and epileptic madness at the moonlit clouds; scratching impotently in the noxious air as if jerked by some alien and bodiless line of linkage with subterrene horrors writhing and struggling below the black roots.

Not a man breathed for several seconds. Then a cloud of darker depth passed over the moon, and the silhouette of clutching branches faded out momentarily. At this there was a general cry; muffled with awe, but husky and almost identical from every throat. For the terror had not faded with the silhouette, and in a fearsome instant of deeper darkness the watchers saw wriggling at that treetop height a thousand tiny points of faint and unhallowed radiance, tipping each bough like the fire of St. Elmo or the flames that came down on the apostles' heads at Pentecost. It was a monstrous constellation of unnatural light, like a glutted swarm of corpse-fed fireflies dancing hellish sarabands over an accursed marsh; and its colour was that same nameless intrusion which Ammi had come to recognise and dread. All the while the shaft of phosphorescence from the well was getting brighter and brighter, bringing to the minds of the huddled men a sense of doom and abnormality which far outraced any image their conscious minds could form. It was no longer *shining* out; it was *pouring* out; and as the shapeless stream of unplaceable colour left the well it seemed to flow directly into the sky.

The veterinary shivered, and walked to the front door to drop the heavy extra bar across it. Ammi shook no less, and had to tug and point for lack of a controllable voice when he wished to draw notice to the growing luminosity of the trees. The neighing and stamping of the horses had become utterly frightful, but not a soul of that group in the old house would have ventured forth for any earthly reward. With the moments the shining of the trees increased, while their restless branches seemed to strain more and more toward verticality. The wood of the well-sweep was shining now, and presently a policeman dumbly pointed to some wooden sheds and bee-hives near the stone wall on the west. They were commencing to shine, too, though the tethered vehicles of the visitors seemed so far unaffected. Then there was a wild commotion and clopping in the road, and as Ammi quenched the lamp for better seeing they realised that the span of frantic greys had broken their sapling and run off with the democrat-wagon.

The shock served to loosen several tongues, and embarrassed whispers were exchanged. "It spreads on everything organic that's been around here," muttered the medical examiner. No one replied, but the man who had been in the well gave a hint that his long pole must have stirred up something intangible. "It was awful," he added. "There was no bottom at all. Just ooze and bubbles and the feeling of something lurking under there." Ammi's horse still pawed and screamed deafeningly in the road outside, and nearly drowned its owner's faint quaver as he mumbled his formless reflections. "It come from that stone . . . it growed down thar . . . it got everything livin' . . . it fed itself on 'em, mind and body . . . Thad an' Mernie, Zenas an' Nabby . . . Nahum was the last . . . they all drunk the water . . . it got strong on 'em . . . it come from beyond, whar things ain't like they be here . . . now it's goin' home . . ."

At this point, as the column of unknown colour flared suddenly stronger and began to weave itself into fantastic suggestions of shape which each spectator later described differently, there came from poor tethered Hero such a sound as no man before or since ever heard from a horse. Every person in that low-pitched sitting-room stopped his ears, and Ammi turned away from the window in horror and nausea. Words could not convey it—when Ammi looked out again the hapless beast lay huddled inert on the moonlit ground between the splintered shafts of the buggy. That was the last of Hero till they buried him next day. But the present was no time to mourn, for almost at this instant a detective silently called attention to something terrible in the very room with them. In the absence of the lamplight it was clear that a faint phosphorescence had begun to pervade the entire apartment. It glowed on the broad-planked floor and the fragment of rag carpet, and shimmered over the sashes of the small-paned windows. It ran up and down the exposed corner-posts, coruscated about the shelf and mantel, and infected the very doors and furniture. Each minute saw it strengthen, and at last it was very plain that healthy living things must leave that house.

Ammi shewed them the back door and the path up through the fields to the ten-acre pasture. They walked and stumbled as in a dream, and did not dare look back till they were far away on the high ground. They were glad of the path, for they could not have gone the front way, by that well. It was bad enough passing the glowing barn and sheds, and those shining orchard trees with their gnarled, fiendish contours; but thank heaven the branches did their worst twisting high up. The moon went under some very black clouds as they crossed the rustic bridge over Chapman's Brook, and it was blind groping from there to the open meadows.

When they looked back toward the valley and the distant Gardner place at the bottom they saw a fearsome sight. All the farm was shining with the hideous unknown blend of colour; trees, buildings, and even such grass and herbage as had not been wholly changed to lethal grey brittleness. The boughs were all straining skyward, tipped with tongues of foul flame, and lambent tricklings of the same monstrous fire were creeping about the ridgepoles of the house, barn, and sheds. It was a scene from a vision of Fuseli, and over all the rest reigned that riot of luminous amorphousness, that alien and undimensioned rainbow of cryptic poison from the well—seething, feeling, lapping, reaching, scintillating, straining, and malignly bubbling in its cosmic and unrecognisable chromaticism.

Then without warning the hideous thing shot vertically up toward the sky like a rocket or meteor, leaving behind no trail and disappearing through a round and curiously regular hole in the clouds before any man could gasp or cry out. No watcher can ever forget that sight, and Ammi stared blankly at the stars of Cygnus, Deneb twinkling above the others, where the unknown colour had melted into the Milky Way. But his gaze was the next moment called swiftly to earth by the crackling in the valley. It was just that. Only a wooden ripping and crackling, and not an explosion, as so many others of the party vowed. Yet the outcome was the same, for in one feverish, kaleidoscopic instant there burst up from that doomed and accursed farm a gleamingly eruptive cataclysm of unnatural sparks and substance; blurring the glance of the few who saw it, and sending forth to the zenith a bombarding cloud-burst of such coloured and fantastic fragments as our universe must needs disown. Through quickly re-closing vapours they followed the great morbidity that had vanished, and in another second they had vanished too. Behind and below was only a darkness to which the men dared not return, and all about was a mounting wind which seemed to sweep down in black, frore gusts from interstellar space. It shrieked and howled, and lashed the fields and distorted woods in a mad cosmic frenzy, till soon the trembling party realised it would be no use waiting for the moon to shew what was left down there at Nahum's.

Too awed even to hint theories, the seven shaking men trudged back toward Arkham by the north road. Ammi was worse than his fellows, and begged them to see him inside his own kitchen, instead of keeping straight on to town. He did not wish to cross the nighted, wind-whipped woods alone to his home on the main road. For he had had an added shock that the others were spared, and was crushed for ever with a brooding fear he dared not even mention for many years to come. As the rest of the watchers on that tempestuous hill had stolidly set their faces toward the road, Ammi had looked back an instant at the shadowed valley of desolation so lately sheltering his ill-starred friend. And from that stricken, far-away spot he had seen something feebly rise, only to sink down again upon the place from which the great shapeless horror had shot into the sky. It was just a colour—but not any colour of our earth or heavens. And because Ammi recognised that colour, and knew that this last faint remnant must still lurk down there in the well, he has never been quite right since.

Ammi would never go near the place again. It is over half a century now since the horror happened, but he has never been there, and will be glad when the new reservoir blots it out. I shall be glad, too, for I do not like the way the sunlight changed colour around the mouth of that abandoned well I passed. I hope the water will always be very deep—but even so, I shall never drink it. I do not think I shall visit the Arkham country hereafter. Three of the men who had been with Ammi returned the next morning to see the ruins by daylight, but there were not any real ruins. Only the bricks of the chimney, the stones of the cellar, some mineral and metallic litter here and there, and the rim of that nefandous well. Save for Ammi's dead horse, which they towed away and buried, and the buggy which they shortly returned to him, everything that had ever been living had gone. Five eldritch acres of dusty grey desert remained, nor has anything ever grown there since. To this day it sprawls open to the sky like a great spot eaten by acid in the woods and fields, and the few who have ever dared glimpse it in spite of the rural tales have named it "the blasted heath".

The rural tales are queer. They might be even queerer if city men and college chemists could be interested enough to analyse the water from that disused well, or the grey dust that no wind seems ever to disperse. Botanists, too, ought to study the stunted flora on the borders of that spot, for they might shed light on the country notion that the blight is spreading—little by little, perhaps an inch a year. People say the colour of the neighbouring herbage is not quite right in the spring, and that wild things leave queer prints in the light winter snow. Snow never seems quite so heavy on the blasted heath as it is elsewhere. Horses—the few that are left in this motor age—grow skittish in the silent valley; and hunters cannot depend on their dogs too near the splotch of greyish dust.

They say the mental influences are very bad, too. Numbers went queer in the years after Nahum's taking, and always they lacked the power to get away. Then the stronger-minded folk all left the region, and only the foreigners tried to live in the crumbling old homesteads.* They could not stay, though; and one sometimes wonders what insight beyond ours their wild, weird stories of whispered magic have given them. Their dreams at night, they protest, are very horrible in that grotesque country; and surely the very look of the dark realm is enough to stir a morbid fancy. No traveller has ever escaped a sense of strangeness in those deep ravines, and artists shiver as they paint thick woods whose mystery is as much of the spirit as of the eye. I myself am curious about the sensation I derived from my one lone walk before Ammi told me his tale. When twilight came I had vaguely wished some clouds would gather, for an odd timidity about the deep skyey voids above had crept into my soul.

Do not ask me for my opinion. I do not know—that is all. There was no one but Ammi to question; for Arkham people will not talk about the strange days, and all three professors who saw the aërolite and its coloured globule are dead. There were other globules—depend upon that. One must have fed itself and escaped, and probably there was another which was too late. No doubt it is still down the

* As editor, I considered deleting or muting the sometimes offensive terms Lovecraft uses to refer to racial and ethnic difference, but on balance I consider it better not to veil or bowdlerize Lovecraft's notorious racism.

well—I know there was something wrong with the sunlight I saw above that miasmal brink. The rustics say the blight creeps an inch a year, so perhaps there is a kind of growth or nourishment even now. But whatever daemon hatchling is there, it must be tethered to something or else it would quickly spread. Is it fastened to the roots of those trees that claw the air? One of the current Arkham tales is about fat oaks that shine and move as they ought not to do at night.

What it is, only God knows. In terms of matter I suppose the thing Ammi described would be called a gas, but this gas obeyed laws that are not of our cosmos. This was no fruit of such worlds and suns as shine on the telescopes and photographic plates of our observatories. This was no breath from the skies whose motions and dimensions our astronomers measure or deem too vast to measure. It was just a colour out of space—a frightful messenger from unformed realms of infinity beyond all Nature as we know it; from realms whose mere existence stuns the brain and numbs us with the black extra-cosmic gulfs it throws open before our frenzied eyes.

I doubt very much if Ammi consciously lied to me, and I do not think his tale was all a freak of madness as the townsfolk had forewarned. Something terrible came to the hills and valleys on that meteor, and something terrible—though I know not in what proportion—still remains. I shall be glad to see the water come. Meanwhile I hope nothing will happen to Ammi. He saw so much of the thing—and its influence was so insidious. Why has he never been able to move away? How clearly he recalled those dying words of Nahum's—"can't git away . . . draws ye . . . ye know summ'at's comin', but tain't no use . . ." Ammi is such a good old man—when the reservoir gang gets to work I must write the chief engineer to keep a sharp watch on him. I would hate to think of him as the grey, twisted, brittle monstrosity which persists more and more in troubling my sleep.

James Clerk Maxwell

Scottish scientist James Clerk Maxwell (1831–79) was responsible for the biggest advance in physics since Newton: his formulation of the classical theory of electromagnetic radiation, connecting electricity, magnetism, and light as different manifestations of the same phenomenon. In addition to his wide-ranging scientific work, Maxwell loved poetry, and published a number of poems of his own, mostly pastiches of other poets. This 'paradoxical ode' is styled 'after Shelley'. Hermann Stoffkraft is a fictional character who appears in Balfour Stewart and Peter Guthrie Tait's *Paradoxical Philosophy* (Macmillan, 1878), where he debates with other characters the possibilities of a 'fourth dimension'.

To Hermann Stoffkraft, Ph.D., A Paradoxical Ode (After Shelley)

I

My soul's an amphicheiral knot
Upon a liquid vortex wrought
By Intellect in the Unseen residing,
While thou dost like a convict sit
With marlinspike untwisting it
Only to find my knottiness abiding;
Since all the tools for my untying
In four-dimensioned space are lying,
Where playful fancy intersperses
Whole avenues of universes;
Where Klein and Clifford fill the void
With one unbounded, finite homaloid,
Whereby the Infinite is hopelessly destroyed.

II

But when thy Science lifts her pinions
In Speculation's wild dominions,
I treasure every dictum thou emittest;
While down the stream of Evolution
We drift, and look for no solution
But that of the survival of the fittest.
Till in that twilight of the gods
When earth and sun are frozen clods,

When, all its energy degraded,
Matter in æther shall have faded,
We, that is, all the work we've done,
As waves in æther, shall for ever run
In swift-expanding spheres, through heavens
    beyond the sun.

III

Great Principle of all we see,
Thou endless Continuity!
By thee are all our angles gently rounded;
Our misfits are by thee adjusted,
And as I still in thee have trusted,
So let my methods never be confounded!
O never may direct Creation
Break in upon my contemplation,
Still may the causal chain, ascending,
Appear unbroken and unending,
And, where that chain is lost to sight
Let viewless fancies guide my darkling flight
Through Æon-haunted worlds, in order infinite.

$$\frac{p}{t}$$

Arthur Conan Doyle

Though known today for his Sherlock Holmes short stories, Conan Doyle in fact wrote in a wide variety of genres including science fiction. 'The Horror of the Heights', first published like the Holmes stories in *The Strand Magazine*, manifests ingenuity of invention and Doyle's sure hand with mystery, but combines it with the chilling sense-of-wonder characteristic of the best SF. Today we take the stratosphere for granted, for flying has become a mass industry, a mundane matter for most of us. This story returns us to a time when the high sky was as unexplored and mysterious as the moon. Doyle's superbly eerie ecosystem populates the aery spaces with terror as well as wonder.

The Horror of the Heights
(Which Includes the Manuscript Known as the Joyce-Armstrong Fragment)

The idea that the extraordinary narrative which has been called the Joyce-Armstrong Fragment is an elaborate practical joke evolved by some unknown person, cursed by a perverted and sinister sense of humour, has now been abandoned by all who have examined the matter. The most *macabre* and imaginative of plotters would hesitate before linking his morbid fancies with the unquestioned and tragic facts which reinforce the statement. Though the assertions contained in it are amazing and even monstrous, it is none the less forcing itself upon the general intelligence that they are true, and that we must readjust our ideas to the new situation. This world of ours appears to be separated by a slight and precarious margin of safety from a most singular and unexpected danger. I will endeavour in this narrative, which reproduces the original document in its necessarily somewhat fragmentary form, to lay before the reader the whole of the facts up to date, prefacing my statement by saying that, if there be any who doubt the narrative of Joyce-Armstrong, there can be no question at all as to the facts concerning Lieutenant

Myrtle, R.N., and Mr Hay Connor, who undoubtedly met their end in the manner described.

The Joyce-Armstrong Fragment was found in the field which is called Lower Haycock, lying one mile to the westward of the village of Withyham, upon the Kent and Sussex border. It was on the fifteenth of September last that an agricultural labourer, James Flynn, in the employment of Mathew Dodd, farmer, of the Chauntry Farm, Withyham, perceived a briar pipe lying near the footpath which skirts the hedge in Lower Haycock. A few paces farther on he picked up a pair of broken binocular glasses. Finally, among some nettles in the ditch, he caught sight of a flat, canvas-backed book, which proved to be a notebook with detachable leaves, some of which had come loose and were fluttering along the base of the hedge. These he collected, but some, including the first, were never recovered, and leave a deplorable hiatus in this all-important statement. The notebook was taken by the labourer to his master, who in turn showed it to Dr J. H. Atherton, of Hartfield. This gentleman at once recognized the need for an expert examination, and the manuscript was forwarded to the Aero Club in London, where it now lies.

The first two pages of the manuscript are missing. There is also one torn away at the end of the narrative, though none of these affect the general coherence of the story. It is conjectured that the missing opening is concerned with the record of Mr Joyce-Armstrong's qualifications as an aeronaut, which can be gathered from other sources and are admitted to be unsurpassed among the air-pilots of England. For many years he has been looked upon as among the most daring and the most intellectual of flying men, a combination which has enabled him to both invent and test several new devices, including the common gyroscopic attachment which is known by his name. The main body of the manuscript is written neatly in ink, but the last few lines are in pencil and are so ragged as to be hardly legible – exactly, in fact, as they might be expected to appear if they were scribbled off hurriedly from the seat of a moving aeroplane. There are, it may be added, several stains, both on the last page and on the outside cover which have been pronounced by the Home Office experts to be blood – probably human and certainly mammalian. The fact that something closely resembling the organism of malaria was discovered in this blood, and that Joyce-Armstrong is known to have suffered from intermittent fever, is a remarkable example of the new weapons which modern science has placed in the hands of our detectives.

And now a word as to the personality of the author of this epoch-making statement. Joyce-Armstrong, according to the few friends who really knew something of the man, was a poet and a dreamer, as well as a mechanic and an inventor. He was a man of considerable wealth, much of which he had spent in the pursuit of his aeronautical hobby. He had four private aeroplanes in his hangars near Devizes, and is said to have made no fewer than one hundred and seventy ascents in the course of last year. He was a retiring man with dark moods, in which he would avoid the society of his fellows. Captain Dangerfield, who knew him better than anyone, says that there were times when his eccentricity threatened to develop into something more serious. His habit of carrying a shot-gun with him in his aeroplane was one manifestation of it.

Another was the morbid effect which the fall of Lieutenant Myrtle had upon his mind. Myrtle, who was attempting the height record, fell from an altitude of something over thirty thousand feet. Horrible to narrate, his head was entirely obliterated, though his body and limbs preserved their configuration. At every gathering of airmen, Joyce-Armstrong, according to Dangerfield, would ask, with an enigmatic smile: 'And where, pray, is Myrtle's head?'

On another occasion after dinner, at the mess of the Flying School on Salisbury Plain, he started a debate as to what will be the most permanent danger which airmen will have to encounter. Having listened to successive opinions as to air-pockets, faulty construction, and overbanking, he ended by shrugging his shoulders and refusing to put forward his own views, though he gave the impression that they differed from any advanced by his companions.

It is worth remarking that after his own complete disappearance it was found that his private affairs were arranged with a precision which may show that he had a strong premonition of disaster. With these essential explanations I will now give the narrative exactly as it stands, beginning at page three of the blood-soaked notebook:–

'Nevertheless, when I dined at Rheims with Coselli and Gustav Raymond I found that neither of them was aware of any particular danger in the higher layers of the atmosphere. I did not actually say what was in my thoughts, but I got so near to it that if they had any corresponding idea they could not have failed to express it. But then they are two empty, vainglorious fellows with no thought beyond seeing their silly names in the newspaper. It is interesting to note that neither of them had ever been much beyond the twenty-thousand-foot level. Of course, men have been higher than this both in balloons and in the ascent of mountains. It must be well above that point that the aeroplane enters the danger zone – always presuming that my premonitions are correct.

'Aeroplaning has been with us now for more than twenty years, and one might well ask: Why should this peril be only revealing itself in our day? The answer is obvious. In the old days of weak engines, when a hundred horse-power Gnome or Green was considered ample for every need, the flights were very restricted. Now that three hundred horse-power is the rule rather than the exception, visits to the upper layers have become easier and more common. Some of us can remember how, in our youth, Garros made a world-wide reputation by attaining nineteen thousand feet, and it was considered a remarkable achievement to fly over the Alps. Our standard now has been immeasurably raised, and there are twenty high flights for one in former years. Many of them have been undertaken with impunity. The thirty-thousand-foot level has been reached time after time with no discomfort beyond cold and asthma. What does this prove? A visitor might descend upon this planet a thousand times and never see a tiger. Yet tigers exist, and if he chanced to come down into a jungle he might be devoured. There are jungles of the upper air, and there are worse things than tigers which inhabit them. I believe in time they will map these jungles accurately out. Even at the present moment I could name two of them. One of them lies over the Pau-Biarritz district of France. Another is just over my head as I write here in my house in Wiltshire. I rather think there is a third in the Homburg–Wiesbaden district.

'It was the disappearance of the airmen that first set me thinking. Of course, everyone said that they had fallen into the sea, but that did not satisfy me at all. First, there was Verrier in France; his machine was found near Bayonne, but they never got his body. There was the case of Baxter also, who vanished, though his engine and some of the iron fixings were found in a wood in Leicestershire. In that case, Dr Middleton, of Amesbury, who was watching the flight with a telescope, declares that just before the clouds obscured the view he saw the machine, which was at an enormous height, suddenly rise perpendicularly upwards in a succession of jerks in a manner that he would have thought to be impossible. That was the last seen of Baxter. There was a correspondence in the papers, but it never led to anything. There were several other similar cases, and then there was the death of Hay Connor. What a cackle there was about an unsolved mystery of the air, and what columns in the halfpenny papers, and yet how little was ever done to get to the bottom of the business! He came down in a tremendous vol-plané from an unknown height. He never got off his machine and died in his pilot's seat. Died of what? "Heart disease," said the doctors. Rubbish! Hay Connor's heart was as sound as mine is. What did Venables say? Venables was the only man who was at his side when he died. He said that he was shivering and looked like a man who had been badly scared. "Died of fright," said Venables, but could not imagine what he was frightened about. Only said one word to Venables, which sounded like "Monstrous". They could make nothing of that at the inquest. But I could make something of it. Monsters! That was the last word of poor Harry Hay Connor. And he *did* die of fright, just as Venables thought.

'And then there was Myrtle's head. Do you really believe – does anybody really believe – that a man's head could be driven clean into his body by the force of a fall? Well, perhaps it may be possible, but I, for one, have never believed that it was so with Myrtle. And the grease upon his clothes – "all slimy with grease," said somebody at the inquest. Queer that nobody got thinking after that! I did – but, then, I had been thinking for a good long time. I've made three ascents – how Dangerfield used to chaff me about my shot-gun! – but I've never been high enough. Now, with this new, light Paul Veroner machine and its one hundred and seventy-five Robur, I should easily touch the thirty thousand tomorrow. I'll have a shot at the record. Maybe I shall have a shot at something else as well. Of course, it's dangerous. If a fellow wants to avoid danger he had best keep out of flying altogether and subside finally into flannel slippers and a dressing-gown. But I'll visit the air-jungle tomorrow – and if there's anything there I shall know it. If I return, I'll find myself a bit of a celebrity. If I don't, this notebook may explain what I am trying to do, and how I lost my life in doing it. But no drivel about accidents or mysteries, if *you* please.

'I chose my Paul Veroner monoplane for the job. There's nothing like a monoplane when real work is to be done. Beaumont found that out in very early days. For one thing, it doesn't mind damp, and the weather looks as if we should be in the clouds all the time. It's a bonny little model and answers my hand like a tender-mouthed horse. The engine is a ten-cylinder rotary Robur working up to one hundred and seventy-five. It has all the modern improvements – enclosed fuselage, high-curved landing skids, brakes, gyroscopic steadiers, and three speeds, worked by an alteration of the angle of the planes upon the Venetian-blind principle. I took a shot-gun with me and a dozen cartridges filled with buck-shot. You should have seen the face of Perkins, my old mechanic, when I directed him to put them in. I was dressed like an Arctic explorer, with two jerseys under my overalls, thick socks inside my padded boots, a storm-cap with flaps, and my talc goggles. It was stifling outside the hangars, but I was going for the summit of the Himalayas, and had to dress for the part. Perkins knew there was something on and implored me to take him with me. Perhaps I should if I were using the biplane, but a monoplane is a one-man show – if you want to get the last foot of lift out of it. Of course, I took an oxygen bag; the man who goes for the altitude record without one will either be frozen or smothered – or both.

'I had a good look at the planes, the rudder-bar, and the elevating lever before I got in. Everything was in order so far as I could see. Then I switched on my engine and found that she was running sweetly. When they let her go she rose almost at once upon the lowest speed. I circled my home field once or twice just to warm her up, and then, with a wave to Perkins and the others, I flattened out my planes and put her on her highest. She skimmed like a swallow down wind for eight or ten miles until I turned her nose up a little and she began to climb in a great spiral for the cloud-bank above me. It's all-important to rise slowly and adapt yourself to the pressure as you go.

'It was a close, warm day for an English September, and there was the hush and heaviness of impending rain. Now and then there came sudden puffs of wind from the south-west – one of them so gusty and unexpected that it caught me napping and turned me half-round for an instant. I remember the time when gusts and whirls and air-pockets used to be things of danger – before we learned to put an overmastering power into our engines. Just as I reached the cloud-banks, with the altimeter marking three thousand, down came the rain. My word, how it poured! It drummed upon my wings and lashed against my face, blurring my glasses so that I could hardly see. I got down on to a low speed, for it was painful to travel against it. As I got higher it became hail, and I had to turn tail to it. One of my cylinders was out of action – a dirty plug, I should imagine, but still I was rising steadily with plenty of power. After a bit the trouble passed, whatever it was, and I heard the full, deep-throated purr – the ten singing as one. That's where the beauty of our modern silencers comes in. We can at last control our engines by ear. How they squeal and squeak and sob when they are in trouble! All those cries for help were wasted in the old days, when every sound was swallowed up by the monstrous racket of the machine. If only the early aviators could come back to see the beauty and perfection of the mechanism which have been bought at the cost of their lives!

'About nine-thirty I was nearing the clouds. Down below me, all blurred and shadowed with rain, lay the vast expanse of Salisbury Plain. Half a dozen flying machines were doing hackwork at the thousand-foot level, looking like little black swallows against the green background. I dare say they were wondering what I was doing up in cloud-land. Suddenly a grey curtain drew across beneath me and the wet folds of vapours were swirling round my face. It was clammily cold and miserable. But I was above the hail-storm, and that was something gained. The cloud was as dark and thick as a London fog. In my anxiety to get clear, I cocked her nose up until the automatic alarm-bell rang, and I actually began to slide backwards. My sopped and dripping wings had made me heavier than I thought, but presently I was in lighter cloud, and soon had cleared the first layer. There was a second – opal-coloured and fleecy – at a great height above my head, a white, unbroken ceiling above, and a dark, unbroken floor below, with the monoplane labouring upwards upon a vast spiral between them. It is deadly lonely in these cloud-spaces. Once a great flight of some small water-birds went past me, flying very fast to the westwards. The quick whir of their wings and their musical cry were cheery to my ear. I fancy that they were teal, but I am a wretched zoologist. Now that we humans have become birds we must really learn to know our brethren by sight.

'The wind down beneath me whirled and swayed the broad cloud-plain. Once a great eddy formed in it, a whirlpool of vapour, and through it, as down a funnel, I caught sight of the distant world. A large white biplane was passing at a vast depth beneath me. I fancy it was the morning mail service betwixt Bristol and London. Then the drift swirled inwards again and the great solitude was unbroken.

'Just after ten I touched the lower edge of the upper cloud-stratum. It consisted of fine diaphanous vapour drifting swiftly from the westward. The wind had been steadily rising all this time and it was now blowing a sharp breeze – twenty-eight an hour by my gauge. Already it was very cold, though my altimeter only marked nine thousand. The engines were working beautifully, and we went droning steadily upwards. The cloud-bank was thicker than I had expected, but at last it thinned out into a golden mist before me, and then in an instant I had shot out from it, and there was an unclouded sky and a brilliant sun above my head – all blue and gold above, all shining silver below, one vast, glimmering plain as far as my eyes could reach. It was a quarter past ten o'clock, and the barograph needle pointed to twelve thousand eight hundred. Up I went and up, my ears concentrated upon the deep purring of my motor, my eyes busy always with the watch, the revolution indicator, the petrol lever, and the oil pump. No wonder aviators are said to be a fearless race. With so many things to think of there is no time to trouble about oneself. About this time I noted how unreliable is the compass when above a certain height from earth. At fifteen thousand feet mine was pointing east and a point south. The sun and the wind gave me my true bearings.

'I had hoped to reach an eternal stillness in these high altitudes, but with every thousand feet of ascent the gale grew stronger. My machine groaned and trembled in every joint and rivet as she faced it, and swept away like a sheet of paper when I banked her on the turn, skimming down wind at a greater pace, perhaps, than ever mortal man has moved. Yet I had always to turn again and tack up in the wind's eye, for it was not merely a height record that I was after. By all my calculations it was above little Wiltshire that my air-jungle lay, and all my labour might be lost if I struck the outer layers at some farther point.

'When I reached the nineteen-thousand-foot level, which was about midday, the wind was so severe that I looked with some anxiety to the stays of my wings, expecting momentarily to see them snap or slacken. I even cast loose the parachute behind me, and fastened its hook into the ring of my leathern belt, so as to be ready for the worst. Now was the time when a bit of scamped work by the mechanic is paid for by the life of the aeronaut. But she held together bravely. Every cord and strut was humming and vibrating like so many harp-strings, but it was glorious to see how, for all the beating and the buffeting, she was still the conqueror of Nature and the mistress of the sky. There is surely something divine in man himself that he should rise so superior to the limitations which Creation seemed to impose – rise, too, by such unselfish, heroic devotion as this air-conquest has shown. Talk of human degeneration! When has such a story as this been written in the annals of our race?

'These were the thoughts in my head as I climbed that monstrous, inclined plane with the wind sometimes beating in my face and sometimes whistling behind my ears, while the cloud-land beneath me fell away to such a distance that the folds and hummocks of silver had all smoothed out into one flat, shining plain. But suddenly I had a horrible and unprecedented experience. I have known before what it is to be in what our neighbours have called a *tourbillon*, but never on such a scale as this. That huge, sweeping river of wind of which I have spoken had, as it appears, whirlpools within it which were as monstrous as itself. Without a moment's warning I was dragged suddenly into the heart of one. I spun round for a minute or two with such velocity that I almost lost my senses, and then fell suddenly, left wing foremost, down the vacuum funnel in the centre. I dropped like a stone, and lost nearly a thousand feet. It was only my belt that kept me in my seat, and the shock and breathlessness left me hanging half-insensible over the side of the fuselage. But I am always capable of a supreme effort – it is my one great merit as an aviator. I was conscious that the descent was slower. The whirlpool was a cone rather than a funnel, and I had come to the apex. With a terrific wrench, throwing my weight all to one side, I levelled my planes and brought her head away from the wind. In an instant I had shot out of the eddies and was skimming down the sky. Then, shaken but victorious, I turned her nose up and began once more my steady grind on the upward spiral. I took a large sweep to avoid the danger-spot of the whirlpool, and soon I was safely above it. Just after one o'clock I was twenty-one thousand feet above the sea-level. To my great joy I had topped the gale, and with every hundred feet of ascent the air grew stiller. On the other hand, it was very cold, and I was conscious of that peculiar nausea which goes with rarefaction of the air. For the first time I unscrewed the mouth of my oxygen bag and took an occasional whiff of the glorious gas. I could feel it running like a cordial through my veins, and I was exhilarated almost to the point of drunkenness. I shouted and sang as I soared upwards into the cold, still outer world.

'It is very clear to me that the insensibility which came upon Glaisher, and in a lesser degree upon Coxwell, when, in 1862, they ascended in a balloon to the height of thirty thousand feet, was due to the extreme speed with which a perpendicular ascent is made. Doing it at an easy gradient and accustoming oneself to the lessened barometric pressure by slow degrees, there are no such dreadful symptoms. At the same great height I found that even without my oxygen inhaler I could breathe without undue distress. It was bitterly cold, however, and my thermometer was at zero, Fahrenheit. At one-thirty I was nearly seven miles above the surface of the earth, and still ascending steadily. I found, however, that the rarefied air was giving markedly less support to my planes, and that my angle of ascent had to be considerably lowered in consequence. It was already clear that even with my light weight and strong engine-power there was a point in front of me where

I should be held. To make matters worse, one of my sparking-plugs was in trouble again and there was intermittent misfiring in the engine. My heart was heavy with the fear of failure.

'It was about that time that I had a most extraordinary experience. Something whizzed past me in a trail of smoke and exploded with a loud, hissing sound, sending forth a cloud of steam. For the instant I could not imagine what had happened. Then I remembered that the earth is for ever being bombarded by meteor stones, and would be hardly inhabitable were they not in nearly every case turned to vapour in the outer layers of the atmosphere. Here is a new danger for the high-altitude man, for two others passed me when I was nearing the forty-thousand-foot mark. I cannot doubt that at the edge of the earth's envelope the risk would be a very real one.

'My barograph needle marked forty-one thousand three hundred when I became aware that I could go no farther. Physically, the strain was not as yet greater than I could bear, but my machine had reached its limit. The attenuated air gave no firm support to the wings, and the least tilt developed into side-slip, while she seemed sluggish on her controls. Possibly, had the engine been at its best, another thousand feet might have been within our capacity, but it was still misfiring, and two out of the ten cylinders appeared to be out of action. If I had not already reached the zone for which I was searching then I should never see it upon this journey. But was it not possible that I had attained it? Soaring in circles like a monstrous hawk upon the forty-thousand-foot level I let the monoplane guide herself, and with my Mannheim glass I made a careful observation of my surroundings. The heavens were perfectly clear; there was no indication of those dangers which I had imagined.

'I have said that I was soaring in circles. It struck me suddenly that I would do well to take a wider sweep and open up a new air-tract. If the hunter entered an earth-jungle he would drive through it if he wished to find his game. My reasoning had led me to believe that the air-jungle which I had imagined lay somewhere over Wiltshire. This should be to the south and west of me. I took my bearings from the sun, for the compass was hopeless and no trace of earth was to be seen – nothing but the distant, silver cloud-plain. However, I got my direction as best I might and kept her head straight to the mark. I reckoned that my petrol supply would not last for more than another hour or so, but I could afford to use it to the last drop, since a single magnificent vol-plané could at any time take me to the earth.

'Suddenly I was aware of something new. The air

in front of me had lost its crystal clearness. It was full of long, ragged wisps of something which I can only compare to very fine cigarette-smoke. It hung about in wreaths and coils, turning and twisting slowly in the sunlight. As the monoplane shot through it, I was aware of a faint taste of oil upon my lips, and there was a greasy scum upon the woodwork of the machine. Some infinitely fine organic matter appeared to be suspended in the atmosphere. There was no life there. It was inchoate and diffuse, extending for many square acres and then fringing off into the void. No, it was not life. But might it not be the remains of life? Above all, might it not be the food of life, of monstrous life, even as the humble grease of the ocean is the food for the mighty whale? The thought was in my mind when my eyes looked upwards and I saw the most wonderful vision that ever man has seen. Can I hope to convey it to you even as I saw it myself last Thursday?

'Conceive a jelly-fish such as sails in our summer seas, bell-shaped and of enormous size – far larger, I should judge, than the dome of St Paul's. It was of a light pink colour veined with a delicate green, but the whole huge fabric so tenuous that it was but a fairy outline against the dark blue sky. It pulsated with a delicate and regular rhythm. From it there depended two long, drooping, green tentacles, which swayed slowly backwards and forwards. This gorgeous vision passed gently with noiseless dignity over my head, as light and fragile as a soap-bubble, and drifted upon its stately way.

'I had half-turned my monoplane, that I might look after this beautiful creature, when, in a moment, I found myself amidst a perfect fleet of them, of all sizes, but none so large as the first. Some were quite small, but the majority about as big as an average balloon, and with much the same curvature at the top. There was in them a delicacy of texture and colouring which reminded me of the finest Venetian glass. Pale shades of pink and green were the prevailing tints, but all had a lovely iridescence where the sun shimmered through their dainty forms. Some hundreds of them drifted past me, a wonderful fairy squadron of strange, unknown argosies of the sky – creatures whose forms and substance were so attuned to these pure heights that one could not conceive anything so delicate within actual sight or sound of earth.

'But soon my attention was drawn to a new phenomenon – the serpents of the outer air. These were long, thin, fantastic coils of vapour-like material, which turned and twisted with great speed, flying round and round at such a pace that the eyes could hardly follow them. Some of these ghost-like creatures were twenty or thirty feet long, but it was difficult to tell their girth, for their outline was so hazy that it seemed to fade away into the air around them. These air-snakes were of a very light grey or smoke colour, with some darker lines within, which gave the impression of a definite organism. One of them whisked past my very face, and I was conscious of a cold, clammy contact, but their composition was so unsubstantial that I could not connect them with any thought of physical danger, any more than the beautiful bell-like creatures which had preceded them. There was no more solidity in their frames than in the floating spume from a broken wave.

'But a more terrible experience was in store for me. Floating downwards from a great height there came a purplish patch of vapour, small as I saw it first, but rapidly enlarging as it approached me, until it appeared to be hundreds of square feet in size. Though fashioned of some transparent, jelly-like substance, it was none the less of much more definite outline and solid consistence than anything which I had seen before. There were more traces, too, of a physical organization, especially two vast, shadowy, circular plates upon either side, which may have been eyes, and a perfectly solid white projection between them which was as curved and cruel as the beak of a vulture.

'The whole aspect of this monster was formidable and threatening, and it kept changing its colour from a very light mauve to a dark, angry purple so thick that it cast a shadow as it drifted between my monoplane and the sun. On the upper curve of its huge body there were three great projections which I can only describe as enormous bubbles, and I was convinced as I looked at them that they were charged with some extremely light gas which served to buoy up the misshapen and semi-solid mass in the rarefied air. The creature moved swiftly along, keeping pace easily with the monoplane, and for twenty miles or more it formed my horrible escort, hovering over me like a bird of prey which is waiting to pounce. Its method of progression – done so swiftly that it was not easy to follow – was to throw out a long, glutinous streamer in front of it, which in turn seemed to draw forward the rest of the writhing body. So elastic and gelatinous was it that never for two successive minutes was it the same shape, and yet each change made it more threatening and loathsome than the last.

'I knew that it meant mischief. Every purple flush of its hideous body told me so. The vague, goggling eyes which were turned always upon me were cold and merciless in their viscid hatred. I dipped the nose of my monoplane downwards to escape it. As I did so, as quick as a flash there shot out a long tentacle from this mass of floating blubber, and it fell as light and sinuous as a whip-lash across the front of my machine. There was a loud hiss as it lay for a moment across the hot engine, and it whisked itself into the air again, while the huge, flat body drew itself together as if in sudden pain. I dipped to a vol-piqué, but again a tentacle fell over the monoplane and was shorn off by the propeller as easily as it might have cut through a smoke wreath. A long, gliding, sticky, serpent-like coil came from behind and caught me round the waist, dragging me out of the fuselage. I tore at it, my fingers sinking into the smooth, glue-like surface, and for an instant I disengaged myself, but only to be caught round the boot by another coil, which gave me a jerk that tilted me almost on to my back.

'As I fell over I blazed off both barrels of my gun, though, indeed, it was like attacking an elephant with a pea-shooter to imagine that any human weapon could cripple that mighty bulk. And yet I aimed better than I knew, for, with a loud report, one of the great blisters upon the creature's back exploded with the puncture of the buck-shot. It was very clear that my conjecture was right, and that these vast, clear bladders were distended with some lifting gas, for in an instant the huge, cloud-like body turned sideways, writhing desperately to find its balance, while the white beak snapped and gaped in horrible fury. But already I had shot away on the steepest glide that I dared to attempt, my engine still full on, the flying propeller and the force of gravity shooting me downwards like an aerolite. Far behind me I saw a dull, purplish smudge growing swiftly smaller and merging into the blue sky behind it. I was safe out of the deadly jungle of the outer air.

'Once out of danger I throttled my engine, for nothing tears a machine to pieces quicker than running on full power from a height. It was a glorious, spiral vol-plané from nearly eight miles of altitude – first, to the level of the silver cloud-bank, then to that of the storm-cloud beneath it, and finally, in beating rain, to the surface of the earth. I saw the Bristol Channel beneath me as I broke from the clouds, but, having still some petrol in my tank, I got twenty miles inland before I found myself stranded in a field half a mile from the village of Ashcombe. There I got three tins of petrol from a passing motor-car, and at ten minutes past six that evening I alighted gently in my own home meadow at Devizes, after such a journey as no mortal upon earth has ever yet taken and lived to tell the tale. I have seen the beauty and I have seen the horror of the heights – and greater beauty or greater horror than that is not within the ken of man.

'And now it is my plan to go once again before I

give my results to the world. My reason for this is that I must surely have something to show by way of proof before I lay such a tale before my fellow-men. It is true that others will soon follow and will confirm what I have said, and yet I should wish to carry conviction from the first. Those lovely iridescent bubbles of the air should not be hard to capture. They drift slowly upon their way, and the swift monoplane could intercept their leisurely course. It is likely enough that they would dissolve in the heavier layers of the atmosphere, and that some small heap of amorphous jelly might be all that I should bring to earth with me. And yet something there would surely be by which I could substantiate my story. Yes, I will go, even if I run a risk by doing so. These purple horrors would not seem to be numerous. It is probable that I shall not see one. If I do I shall dive at once. At the worst there is always the shot-gun and my knowledge of . . .'

Here a page of the manuscript is unfortunately missing. On the next page is written, in large, straggling writing:

'Forty-three thousand feet. I shall never see earth again. They are beneath me, three of them. God help me; it is a dreadful death to die!'

Such in its entirety is the Joyce-Armstrong Fragment. Of the man nothing has since been seen.

Pieces of his shattered monoplane have been picked up in the preserves of Mr Budd-Lushington upon the borders of Kent and Sussex, within a few miles of the spot where the notebook was discovered. If the unfortunate aviator's theory is correct that this air-jungle, as he called it, existed only over the south-west of England, then it would seem that he had fled from it at the full speed of his monoplane, but had been overtaken and devoured by these horrible creatures at some spot in the outer atmosphere above the place where the grim relics were found. The picture of that monoplane skimming down the sky, with the nameless terrors flying as swiftly beneath it and cutting it off always from the earth while they gradually closed in upon their victim, is one upon which a man who valued his sanity would prefer not to dwell. There are many, as I am aware, who still jeer at the facts which I have here set down, but even they must admit that Joyce-Armstrong has disappeared, and I would commend to them his own words: 'This notebook may explain what I am trying to do, and how I lost my life in doing it. But no drivel about accidents or mysteries, if *you* please.'

Rokeya Sakhawat Hossain

Bengali writer Rokeya Sakhawat Hossain (1880–1932) published feminist utopian story 'Sultana's Dream' in *The Indian Ladies' Magazine* in 1905. She wrote it in part to practise her English – a second utopian tale, *Padmarag* (1924), was written in her native Bengali, and is set inside a protective 'keep' in which confined women cultivate their sense of community. A 'sultana' is a female sultan, and 'zenana' is the Hindi word for a part of a house reserved for high-caste women, in which women are segregated away from men. There is real wit and charm, as well as focused satirical penetration, in Hossain's imagined society.

One evening I was lounging in an easy chair in my bedroom and thinking lazily of the condition of Indian womanhood. I am not sure whether I dozed off or not. But, as far as I remember, I was wide awake. I saw the moonlit sky sparkling with thousands of diamondlike stars, very distinctly.

All on a sudden a lady stood before me; how she came in, I do not know. I took her for my friend, Sister Sara.

"Good morning," said Sister Sara. I smiled inwardly as I knew it was not morning, but starry night. However, I replied to her, saying, "How do you do?"

"I am all right, thank you. Will you please come out and have a look at our garden?"

I looked again at the moon through the open window, and thought there was no harm in going out at that time. The menservants outside were fast asleep just then, and I could have a pleasant walk with Sister Sara.

I used to have my walks with Sister Sara, when we were at Darjeeling. Many a time did we walk hand in hand and talk lightheartedly in the botanical gardens there. I fancied Sister Sara had probably come to take me to some such garden, and I readily accepted her offer and went out with her.

When walking I found to my surprise that it was a fine morning. The town was fully awake and the streets alive with bustling crowds. I was feeling very shy, thinking I was walking in the street in broad daylight, but there was not a single man visible.

Some of the passersby made jokes at me. Though I could not understand their language, yet I felt sure they were joking. I asked my friend, "What do they say?"

"The women say you look very mannish."

"Mannish?" said I. "What do they mean by that?"

"They mean that you are shy and timid like men."

"Shy and timid like men?" It was really a joke. I became very nervous when I found that my companion was not Sister Sara, but a stranger. Oh, what a fool had I been to mistake this lady for my dear old friend Sister Sara.

She felt my fingers tremble in her hand, as we were walking hand in hand.

"What is the matter, dear, dear?" she said affectionately.

"I feel somewhat awkward," I said, in a rather

apologizing tone, "as being a purdahnashin woman I am not accustomed to walking about unveiled."

"You need not be afraid of coming across a man here. This is Ladyland, free from sin and harm. Virtue herself reigns here."

By and by I was enjoying the scenery. Really it was very grand. I mistook a patch of green grass for a velvet cushion. Feeling as if I were walking on a soft carpet, I looked down and found the path covered with moss and flowers.

"How nice it is," said I.

"Do you like it?" asked Sister Sara. (I continued calling her "Sister Sara," and she kept calling me by my name.)

"Yes, very much; but I do not like to tread on the tender and sweet flowers."

"Never mind, dear Sultana. Your treading will not harm them; they are street flowers."

"The whole place looks like a garden," said I admiringly. "You have arranged every plant so skillfully."

"Your Calcutta could become a nicer garden than this, if only your countrymen wanted to make it so."

"They would think it useless to give so much attention to horticulture, while they have so many other things to do."

"They could not find a better excuse," said she with a smile.

I became very curious to know where the men were. I met more than a hundred women while walking there, but not a single man.

"Where are the men?" I asked her.

"In their proper places, where they ought to be."

"Pray let me know what you mean by 'their proper places.'"

"Oh, I see my mistake, you cannot know our customs, as you were never here before. We shut our men indoors."

"Just as we are kept in the zenana?"

"Exactly so."

"How funny." I burst into a laugh. Sister Sara laughed too.

"But, dear Sultana, how unfair it is to shut in the harmless women and let loose the men."

"Why? It is not safe for us to come out of the zenana, as we are naturally weak."

"Yes, it is not safe so long as there are men about the streets, nor is it so when a wild animal enters a marketplace."

"Of course not."

"Suppose some lunatics escape from the asylum and begin to do all sorts of mischief to men, horses, and other creatures: in that case what will your countrymen do?"

"They will try to capture them and put them back into their asylum."

"Thank you! And you do not think it wise to keep sane people inside an asylum and let loose the insane?"

"Of course not!" said I, laughing lightly.

"As a matter of fact, in your country this very thing is done! Men, who do or at least are capable of doing no end of mischief, are let loose and the innocent women shut up in the zenana! How can you trust those untrained men out of doors?"

"We have no hand or voice in the management of our social affairs. In India man is lord and master. He has taken to himself all powers and privileges and shut up the women in the zenana."

"Why do you allow yourselves to be shut up?"

"Because it cannot be helped as they are stronger than women."

"A lion is stronger than a man, but it does not enable him to dominate the human race. You have neglected the duty you owe to yourselves, and you have lost your natural rights by shutting your eyes to your own interests."

"But my dear Sister Sara, if we do everything by ourselves, what will the men do then?"

"They should not do anything, excuse me; they are fit for nothing. Only catch them and put them into the zenana."

"But would it be very easy to catch and put them inside the four walls?" said I. "And even if this were done, would all their business—political and commercial—also go with them into the zenana?"

Sister Sara made no reply. She only smiled sweetly. Perhaps she thought it was useless to argue with one who was no better than a frog in a well.

By this time we reached Sister Sara's house. It was situated in a beautiful heart-shaped garden. It was a bungalow with a corrugated iron roof. It was cooler and nicer than any of our rich buildings. I cannot describe how neat and nicely furnished and how tastefully decorated it was.

We sat side by side. She brought out of the parlor a piece of embroidery work and began putting on a fresh design.

"Do you know knitting and needlework?"

"Yes: we have nothing else to do in our zenana."

"But we do not trust our zenana members with embroidery!" she said laughing, "as a man has not patience enough to pass thread through a needlehole even!"

"Have you done all this work yourself?" I asked

her, pointing to the various pieces of embroidered teapoy cloths.

"Yes."

"How can you find time to do all these? You have to do the office work as well, have you not?"

"Yes. I do not stick to the laboratory all day long. I finish my work in two hours."

"In two hours! How do you manage? In our land the officers, magistrates, for instance, work seven hours daily."

"I have seen some of them doing their work. Do you think they work all the seven hours?"

"Certainly they do!"

"No, dear Sultana, they do not. They dawdle away their time in smoking. Some smoke two or three choroots during the office time. They talk much about their work, but do little. Suppose one choroot takes half an hour to burn off, and a man smokes twelve choroots daily; then, you see, he wastes six hours every day in sheer smoking."

We talked on various subjects; and I learned that they were not subject to any kind of epidemic disease, nor did they suffer from mosquito bites as we do. I was very much astonished to hear that in Ladyland no one died in youth except by rare accident.

"Will you care to see our kitchen?" she asked me.

"With pleasure," said I, and we went to see it. Of

course the men had been asked to clear off when I was going there. The kitchen was situated in a beautiful vegetable garden. Every creeper, every tomato plant, was itself an ornament. I found no smoke, nor any chimney either in the kitchen—it was clean and bright; the windows were decorated with flower garlands. There was no sign of coal or fire.

"How do you cook?" I asked.

"With solar heat," she said, at the same time showing me the pipe through which passed the concentrated sunlight and heat. And she cooked something then and there to show me the process.

"How did you manage to gather and store up the sun heat?" I asked her in amazement.

"Let me tell you a little of our past history, then. Thirty years ago, when our present Queen was thirteen years old, she inherited the throne. She was Queen in name only, the Prime Minister really ruling the country.

"Our good Queen liked science very much. She circulated an order that all the women in her country should be educated. Accordingly a number of girls' schools were founded and supported by the Government. Education was spread far and wide among women. And early marriage also was stopped. No woman was to be allowed to marry before she was twenty-one. I must tell you that, before this change, we had been kept in strict purdah."

"How the tables are turned," I interposed with a laugh.

"But the seclusion is the same," she said. "In a few years we had separate universities, where no men were admitted.

"In the capital, where our Queen lives, there are two universities. One of these invented a wonderful balloon, to which they attached a number of pipes. By means of this captive balloon, which they managed to keep afloat above the cloudland, they could draw as much water from the atmosphere as they pleased. As the water was incessantly being drawn by the university people, no cloud gathered and the ingenious Lady Principal stopped rain and storms thereby."

"Really! Now I understand why there is no mud here!" said I. But I could not understand how it was possible to accumulate water in the pipes. She explained to me how it was done; but I was unable to understand her, as my scientific knowledge was very limited. However, she went on:

"When the other university came to know of this, they became exceedingly jealous and tried to do something more extraordinary still. They invented an instrument by which they could collect as much sun heat as they wanted. And they kept the heat stored up to be distributed among others as required.

"While the women were engaged in scientific researches, the men of this country were busy increasing their military power. When they came to know that the female universities were able to draw water from the atmosphere and collect heat from the sun, they only laughed at the members of the universities and called the whole thing 'a sentimental nightmare'!"

"Your achievements are very wonderful indeed! But tell me how you managed to put the men of your country into the zenana. Did you entrap them first?"

"No."

"It is not likely that they would surrender their free and open air life of their own accord and confine themselves within the four walls of the zenana! They must have been overpowered."

"Yes, they have been!"

"By whom?—by some lady warriors, I suppose?"

"No, not by arms."

"Yes, it cannot be so. Men's arms are stronger than women's. Then?"

"By brain."

"Even their brains are bigger and heavier than women's. Are they not?"

"Yes, but what of that? An elephant also has got a bigger and heavier brain than a man has. Yet man can enchain elephants and employ them, according to his own wishes."

"Well said, but tell me, please, how it all actually happened. I am dying to know it!"

"Women's brains are somewhat quicker than men's. Ten years ago, when the military officers called our scientific discoveries 'a sentimental nightmare,' some of the young ladies wanted to say something in reply to those remarks. But both the Lady Principals restrained them and said they should reply not by word but by deed, if ever they got the opportunity. And they had not long to wait for that opportunity."

"How marvelous!" I heartily clapped my hands.

"And now the proud gentlemen are dreaming sentimental dreams themselves.

"Soon afterward certain persons came from a neighboring country and took shelter in ours. They were in trouble, having committed some political offense. The King, who cared more for power than for good government, asked our kindhearted Queen to hand them over to his officers. She refused, as it was against her principle to turn out refugees. For this refusal the king declared war against our country.

"Our military officers sprang to their feet at once and marched out to meet the enemy.

"The enemy, however, was too strong for them. Our soldiers fought bravely, no doubt. But in spite of all their bravery the foreign army advanced step by step to invade our country.

"Nearly all the men had gone out to fight; even a boy of sixteen was not left home. Most of our warriors were killed, the rest driven back, and the enemy came within twenty-five miles of the capital.

"A meeting of a number of wise ladies was held at the Queen's palace to advise as to what should be done to save the land.

"Some proposed to fight like soldiers; others objected and said that women were not trained to fight with swords and guns, nor were they accustomed to fighting with any weapons. A third party regretfully remarked that they were hopelessly weak of body.

"'If you cannot save your country for lack of physical strength,' said the Queen, 'try to do so by brain power.'

"There was a dead silence for a few minutes. Her Royal Highness said again, 'I must commit suicide if the land and my honor are lost.'

"Then the Lady Principal of the second university (who had collected sun heat), who had been silently thinking during the consultation, remarked that they were all but lost; and there was little hope left for them. There was, however, one plan that she would like to try, and this would be her first and last effort; if she failed in this, there would be nothing left but to commit suicide. All present solemnly vowed that they would never allow themselves to be enslaved, no matter what happened.

"The Queen thanked them heartily, and asked the Lady Principal to try her plan.

"The Lady Principal rose again and said, 'Before we go out the men must enter the zenanas. I make this prayer for the sake of purdah.' "'Yes, of course,' replied Her Royal Highness.

"On the following day the Queen called upon all men to retire into zenanas for the sake of honor and liberty.

"Wounded and tired as they were, they took that order rather for a boon! They bowed low and entered the zenanas without uttering a single word of protest. They were sure that there was no hope for this country at all.

"Then the Lady Principal with her two thousand students marched to the battlefield, and arriving there directed all the rays of the concentrated sun light and heat toward the enemy.

"The heat and light were too much for them to

bear. They all ran away panic-stricken, not knowing in their bewilderment how to counteract that scorching heat. When they fled away, leaving their guns and other ammunitions of war, they were burned down by means of the same sun heat.

"Since then no one has tried to invade our country any more."

"And since then your countrymen never tried to come out of the zenana?"

"Yes, they wanted to be free. Some of the Police Commissioners and District Magistrates sent word to the Queen to the effect that the Military Officers certainly deserved to be imprisoned for their failure; but they had never neglected their duty and therefore they should not be punished, and they prayed to be restored to their respective offices.

"Her Royal Highness sent them a circular letter, intimating to them that if their services should ever be needed they would be sent for, and that in the meanwhile they should remain where they were.

"Now that they are accustomed to the purdah system and have ceased to grumble at their seclusion, we call the system *mardana* instead of zenana."

"But how do you manage," I asked Sister Sara, "to do without the police or magistrates in case of theft or murder?"

"Since the mardana system has been established,

there has been no more crime or sin; therefore we do not require a policeman to find out a culprit, nor do we want a magistrate to try a criminal case."

"That is very good, indeed. I suppose if there were any dishonest person, you could very easily chastise her. As you gained a decisive victory without shedding a single drop of blood, you could drive off crime and criminals too without much difficulty!"

"Now, dear Sultana, will you sit here or come to my parlor?" she asked me.

"Your kitchen is not inferior to a queen's boudoir!" I replied with a pleasant smile. "But we must leave it now; for the gentlemen may be cursing me for keeping them away from their duties in the kitchen so long." We both laughed heartily.

"How my friends at home will be amused and amazed, when I go back and tell them that in the far-off Ladyland, ladies rule over the country and control all social matters, while gentlemen are kept in the mardanas to mind babies, to cook, and to do all sorts of domestic work; and that cooking is so easy a thing that it is simply a pleasure to cook!"

"Yes, tell them about all that you see here."

"Please let me know how you carry on land cultivation and how you plow the land and do other hard manual work."

"Our fields are tilled by means of electricity,

which supplies motive power for other hard work as well, and we employ it for our aerial conveyances too. We have no railroad nor any paved streets here."

"Therefore neither street nor railway accidents occur here," said I. "Do not you ever suffer from want of rainwater?" I asked.

"Never since the 'water balloon' has been set up. You see the big balloon and pipes attached thereto. By their aid we can draw as much rainwater as we require. Nor do we ever suffer from flood or thunderstorms. We are all very busy making nature yield as much as she can. We do not find time to quarrel with one another as we never sit idle. Our noble Queen is exceedingly fond of botany; it is her ambition to convert the whole country into one grand garden."

"The idea is excellent. What is your chief food?"

"Fruits."

"How do you keep your country cool in hot weather? We regard the rainfall in summer as a blessing from heaven."

"When the heat becomes unbearable, we sprinkle the ground with plentiful showers drawn from the artificial fountains. And in cold weather we keep our rooms warm with sun heat."

She showed me her bathroom, the roof of which was removable. She could enjoy a shower or bath whenever she liked, by simply removing the roof (which was like the lid of a box) and turning on the tap of the shower pipe.

"You are a lucky people!" ejaculated I. "You know no want. What is your religion, may I ask?"

"Our religion is based on Love and Truth. It is our religious duty to love one another and to be absolutely truthful. If any person lies, she or he is . . ."

"Punished with death?"

"No, not with death. We do not take pleasure in killing a creature of God—especially a human being. The liar is asked to leave this land for good and never to come to it again."

"Is an offender never forgiven?"

"Yes, if that person repents sincerely."

"Are you not allowed to see any man, except your own relations?"

"No one except sacred relations."

"Our circle of sacred relations is very limited; even first cousins are not sacred."

"But ours is very large; a distant cousin is as sacred as a brother."

"That is very good. I see Purity itself reigns over your land. I should like to see the good Queen, who is so sagacious and farsighted and who has made all these rules."

"All right," said Sister Sara.

Then she screwed a couple of seats on to a square piece of plank. To this plank she attached two smooth and well-polished balls. When I asked her what the balls were for, she said they were hydrogen balls and they were used to overcome the force of gravity. The balls were of different capacities, to be used according to the different weights desired to be overcome. She then fastened to the air-car two wing-like blades, which, she said, were worked by electricity. After we were comfortably seated she touched a knob and the blades began to whirl, moving faster and faster every moment. At first we were raised to the height of about six or seven feet and then off we flew. And before I could realize that we had commenced moving, we reached the garden of the Queen.

My friend lowered the air-car by reversing the action of the machine, and when the car touched the ground the machine was stopped and we got out.

I had seen from the air-car the Queen walking on a garden path with her little daughter (who was four years old) and her maids of honor.

"Halloo! You there!" cried the Queen, addressing Sister Sara. I was introduced to Her Royal Highness and was received by her cordially without any ceremony.

I was very much delighted to make her acquaintance. In the course of the conversation I had with her, the Queen told me that she had no objection to permitting her subjects to trade with other countries. "But," she continued, "no trade was possible with countries where the women were kept in the zenanas and so unable to come and trade with us. Men, we find, are rather of lower morals and so we do not like dealing with them. We do not covet other people's land, we do not fight for a piece of diamond though it may be a thousandfold brighter than the Koh-i-Noor,* nor do we begrudge a ruler his Peacock Throne.** We dive deep into the ocean of knowledge and try to find out the precious gems that Nature has kept in store for us. We enjoy Nature's gifts as much as we can."

After taking leave of the Queen, I visited the famous universities, and was shown over some of their factories, laboratories, and observatories.

* The Koh-i-Noor ("mountain of light") is the name of a large and exceptionally brilliant diamond in the possession of the Mughal rulers of India, currently part of the British Crown Jewels. To Indians, it is a symbol of great wealth.

** The Peacock Throne is a famous jewel-encrusted throne built for the Mughal Emperor Shah Jahan, also known for the Taj Mahal. It was carried away from Delhi by the Persian invader Nadir Shah. Its current location is the cause of much speculation. Many think that one of the thrones displayed in the Istanbul Museum is the Peacock Throne. It is a long-standing symbol of royal power and splendour to Indians.

After visiting the above places of interest, we got again into the air-car, but as soon as it began moving I somehow slipped down and the fall startled me out of my dream. And on opening my eyes, I found myself in my own bedroom still lounging in the easy chair!

Ambrose Bierce

Ambrose Bierce was a prolific journalist and short-story writer who has been called nineteenth-century America's most brilliant satirist. Despite lifelong severe asthma he served in the Union Army during the Civil War, suffering a bad head wound that left him prone to fainting and choleric mood swings. His three children predeceased him in tragic circumstances. None of this prevented him from travelling widely and writing extensively. In 1913 he went to Chihuahua, Mexico, to report on the Mexican Revolution. He disappeared. There were rumours that he had joined the rebel army, but he was never seen again. Presumably he died in the fighting there, although if he did not, he will be 180 years old in 2022, the year this present collection was first published.

A Psychological Shipwreck

In the summer of 1874 I was in Liverpool, whither I had gone on business for the mercantile house of Bronson & Jarrett, New York. I am William Jarrett; my partner was Zenas Bronson. The firm failed last year, and unable to endure the fall from affluence to poverty he died.

Having finished my business, and feeling the lassitude and exhaustion incident to its dispatch, I felt that a protracted sea voyage would be both agreeable and beneficial, so instead of embarking for my return on one of the many fine passenger steamers I booked for New York on the sailing vessel *Morrow*, upon which I had shipped a large and valuable invoice of the goods I had bought. The *Morrow* was an English ship with, of course, but little accommodation for passengers, of whom there were only myself, a young woman and her servant, who was a middle-aged negress. I thought it singular that a traveling English girl should be so attended, but she afterward explained to me that the woman had been left with her family by a man and his wife from South Carolina, both of whom had died on the same day at the house of the young lady's father in Devonshire—a circumstance in itself sufficiently uncommon to remain rather distinctly in my memory, even had it not afterward transpired in conversation with the young lady that the name of the man was William Jarrett, the same as my own. I knew that a branch of my family had settled in South Carolina, but of them and their history I was ignorant.

The *Morrow* sailed from the mouth of the Mersey on the 15th of June and for several weeks we had fair breezes and unclouded skies. The skipper, and admirable seaman but nothing more, favored us with very little of his society, except at his table; and the young woman, Miss Janette Harford, and I became very well acquainted. We were, in truth, nearly always together, and being of an introspective turn of mind I often endeavored to analyze and define the novel feeling with which she inspired me—a secret, subtle, but powerful attraction which constantly impelled me to seek her; but the attempt was hopeless. I could only be sure that at least it was not love. Having assured myself of this and being certain that she was quite as whole-hearted, I ventured one evening (I remember it was on the 3d of July) as we sat on deck to ask her, laughingly, if she could assist me to resolve my psychological doubt.

For a moment she was silent, with averted face, and I began to fear I had been extremely rude and indelicate; then she fixed her eyes gravely on my own. In an instant my mind was dominated by as strange a fancy as ever entered human consciousness. It seemed as if she were looking at me, not *with*, but *through*, those eyes—from an immeasurable distance behind them—and that a number of other persons, men, women and children, upon whose faces I caught strangely familiar evanescent expressions, clustered about her, struggling with gentle eagerness to look at me through the same orbs. Ship, ocean, sky—all had vanished. I was conscious of nothing but the figures in this extraordinary and fantastic scene. Then all at once darkness fell upon me, and anon from out of it, as to one who grows accustomed by degrees to a dimmer light, my former surroundings of deck and mast and cordage slowly resolved themselves. Miss Harford had closed her eyes and was leaning back in her chair, apparently asleep, the book she had been reading open in her lap. Impelled by surely I cannot say what motive, I glanced at the top of the page; it was a copy of that rare and curious work, "Denneker's Meditations," and the lady's index finger rested on this passage:

"To sundry it is given to be drawn away, and to be apart from the body for a season; for, as concerning rills which would flow across each other the weaker is borne along by the stronger, so there be certain of kin whose paths intersecting, their souls do bear company, the while their bodies go fore-appointed ways, unknowing."

Miss Harford arose, shuddering; the sun had sunk below the horizon, but it was not cold. There was not a breath of wind; there were no clouds in the sky, yet not a star was visible. A hurried tramping sounded on the deck; the captain, summoned from below, joined the first officer, who stood looking at the barometer. "Good God!" I heard him exclaim.

An hour later the form of Janette Harford, invisible in the darkness and spray, was torn from my grasp by the cruel vortex of the sinking ship, and I fainted in the cordage of the floating mast to which I had lashed myself.

It was by lamplight that I awoke. I lay in a berth amid the familiar surroundings of the stateroom of a steamer. On a couch opposite sat a man, half undressed for bed, reading a book. I recognized the face of my friend Gordon Doyle, whom I had met in Liverpool on the day of my embarkation, when he was himself about to sail on the steamer *City of Prague*, on which he had urged me to accompany him.

After some moments I now spoke his name. He simply said, "Well," and turned a leaf in his book without removing his eyes from the page.

"Doyle," I repeated, "did they save *her?*"

He now deigned to look at me and smiled as if amused. He evidently thought me but half awake.

"Her? Whom do you mean?"

"Janette Harford."

His amusement turned to amazement; he stared at me fixedly, saying nothing.

"You will tell me after a while," I continued; "I suppose you will tell me after a while."

A moment later I asked: "What ship is this?"

Doyle stared again. "The steamer *City of Prague*, bound from Liverpool to New York, three weeks out with a broken shaft. Principal passenger, Mr. Gordon Doyle; ditto lunatic, Mr. William Jarrett. These two distinguished travelers embarked together, but they are about to part, it being the resolute intention of the former to pitch the latter over-board."

I sat bolt upright. "Do you mean to say that I have been for three weeks a passenger on this steamer?"

"Yes, pretty nearly; this is the 3d of July."

"Have I been ill?"

"Right as a trivet all the time, and punctual at your meals."

"My God! Doyle, there is some mystery here; do have the goodness to be serious. Was I not rescued from the wreck of the ship *Morrow?*"

Doyle changed color, and approaching me, laid his fingers on my wrist. A moment later, "What do you know of Janette Harford?" he asked very calmly.

"First tell me what *you* know of her?"

Mr. Doyle gazed at me for some moments as if thinking what to do, then seating himself again on the couch, said:

"Why should I not? I am engaged to marry Janette Harford, whom I met a year ago in London. Her family, one of the wealthiest in Devonshire, cut up rough about it, and we eloped—are eloping rather, for on the day that you and I walked to the landing stage to go aboard this steamer she and her faithful servant, a negress, passed us, driving to the ship *Morrow*. She would not consent to go in the same vessel with me, and it had been deemed best that she take a sailing vessel in order to avoid observation and lessen the risk of detection. I am now alarmed lest this cursed breaking of our machinery may detain us so long that the *Morrow* will get to New York before us, and the poor girl will not know where to go."

I lay still in my berth—so still I hardly breathed. But the subject was evidently not displeasing to Doyle, and after a short pause he resumed:

"By the way, she is only an adopted daughter of the Harfords. Her mother was killed at their place by being thrown from a horse while hunting, and her father, mad with grief, made away with himself the same day. No one ever claimed the child, and after a reasonable time they adopted her. She has grown up in the belief that she is their daughter."

"Doyle, what book are you reading?"

"Oh, it's called 'Denneker's Meditations.' It's a rum lot, Janette gave it to me; she happened to have two copies. Want to see it?"

He tossed me the volume, which opened as it fell. On one of the exposed pages was a marked passage:

"To sundry it is given to be drawn away, and to be apart from the body for a season; for, as concerning rills which would flow across each other the weaker is borne along by the stronger, so there be certain of kin whose paths intersecting, their souls do bear company, the while their bodies go foreappointed ways, unknowing."

"She had—she has—a singular taste in reading," I managed to say, mastering my agitation.

"Yes. And now perhaps you will have the kindness to explain how you knew her name and that of the ship she sailed in."

"You talked of her in your sleep," I said.

A week later we were towed into the port of New York. But the *Morrow* was never heard from.

The Door in the Wall

H. G. WELLS

I

One confidential evening, not three months ago, Lionel Wallace told me this story of the Door in the Wall. And at the time I thought that so far as he was concerned it was a true story.

He told it to me with such a direct simplicity of conviction that I could not do otherwise than believe in him. But in the morning, in my own flat, I woke to a different atmosphere, and as I lay in bed and recalled the things he had told me, stripped of the glamour of his earnest slow voice, denuded of the focussed shaded table light, the shadowy atmosphere that wrapped about him and the pleasant bright things, the dessert and glasses and napery of the dinner we had shared, making them for the time a bright little world quite cut of from every-day realities, I saw it all as frankly incredible. "He was mystifying!" I said, and then: "How well he did it! . . . It isn't quite the thing I should have expected him, of all people, to do well."

Afterwards, as I sat up in bed and sipped my morning tea, I found myself trying to account for the flavour of reality that perplexed me in his impossible reminiscences, by supposing they did in some way suggest, present, convey—I hardly know which word to use—experiences it was otherwise impossible to tell.

Well, I don't resort to that explanation now. I have got over my intervening doubts. I believe now, as I believed at the moment of telling, that Wallace did to the very best of his ability strip the truth of his secret for me. But whether he himself saw, or only thought he saw, whether he himself was the possessor of an inestimable privilege, or the victim of a fantastic dream, I cannot pretend to guess. Even the facts of his death, which ended my doubts forever, throw no light on that. That much the reader must judge for himself.

I forget now what chance comment or criticism of mine moved so reticent a man to confide in me. He was, I think, defending himself against an imputation of slackness and unreliability I had made in relation to a great public movement in which he had disappointed me. But he plunged suddenly. "I have" he said, "a preoccupation—"

"I know," he went on, after a pause that he devoted to the study of his cigar ash, "I have been negligent. The fact is—it isn't a case of ghosts or apparitions—but—it's an odd thing to tell of, Redmond—I am haunted. I am haunted by something—that rather takes the light out of things, that fills me with longings . . ."

He paused, checked by that English shyness that so often overcomes us when we would speak of moving or grave or beautiful things. "You were at Saint Athelstan's all through," he said, and for a moment that seemed to me quite irrelevant. "Well"—and he paused. Then very haltingly at first, but afterwards more easily, he began to tell of the thing that was hidden in his life, the haunting memory of a beauty and a happiness that filled his heart with insatiable longings that made all the interests and spectacle of worldly life seem dull and tedious and vain to him.

Now that I have the clue to it, the thing seems written visibly in his face. I have a photograph in which that look of detachment has been caught and intensified. It reminds me of what a woman once said of him—a woman who had loved him greatly. "Suddenly," she said, "the interest goes out of him. He forgets you. He doesn't care a rap for you—under his very nose . . ."

Yet the interest was not always out of him, and when he was holding his attention to a thing Wallace could contrive to be an extremely successful man. His career, indeed, is set with successes. He left me behind him long ago; he soared up over my head, and cut a figure in the world that I couldn't cut—anyhow. He was still a year short of forty, and they say now that he would have been in office and very probably in the new Cabinet if he had lived. At school he always beat me without effort—as it were by nature. We were at school together at Saint Athelstan's College in West Kensington for almost all our school time. He came into the school as my co-equal, but he left far above me, in a blaze of scholarships and brilliant performance. Yet I think I made a fair average running. And it was at school I heard first of the Door in the Wall—that I was to hear of a second time only a month before his death.

To him at least the Door in the Wall was a real door leading through a real wall to immortal realities. Of that I am now quite assured.

And it came into his life early, when he was a little fellow between five and six. I remember how, as he sat making his confession to me with a slow gravity, he reasoned and reckoned the date of it. "There was," he said, "a crimson Virginia creeper in it—all one bright uniform crimson in a clear amber sunshine against a white wall. That came into the impression somehow, though I don't clearly remember how, and there were horse-chestnut leaves upon the clean pavement outside the green door. They were blotched yellow and green, you know, not brown nor dirty, so that they must have been new fallen. I take it that means October. I look out for horse-chestnut leaves every year, and I ought to know.

"If I'm right in that, I was about five years and four months old."

He was, he said, rather a precocious little boy—he learned to talk at an abnormally early age, and he was so sane and "old-fashioned," as people say, that he was permitted an amount of initiative that most children scarcely attain by seven or eight. His mother died when he was born, and he was under the less vigilant and authoritative care of a nursery governess. His father was a stern, preoccupied lawyer, who gave him little attention, and expected great things of him. For all his brightness he found life a little grey and dull I think. And one day he wandered.

He could not recall the particular neglect that enabled him to get away, nor the course he took among the West Kensington roads. All that had faded among the incurable blurs of memory. But the white wall and the green door stood out quite distinctly.

As his memory of that remote childish experience ran, he did at the very first sight of that door experience a peculiar emotion, an attraction, a desire to get to the door and open it and walk in. And at the same time he had the clearest conviction that either it was unwise or it was wrong of him—he could not tell which—to yield to this attraction. He insisted upon it as a curious thing that he knew from the very beginning—unless memory has played him the queerest trick—that the door was unfastened, and that he could go in as he chose.

I seem to see the figure of that little boy, drawn and repelled. And it was very clear in his mind, too, though why it should be so was never explained, that his father would be very angry if he went through that door.

Wallace described all these moments of hesitation to me with the utmost particularity. He went right past the door, and then, with his hands in his pockets, and making an infantile attempt to whistle, strolled right along beyond the end of the wall. There he recalls a number of mean, dirty shops, and particularly that of a plumber and decorator, with a dusty disorder of earthenware pipes, sheet lead ball taps, pattern books of wall paper, and tins of enamel. He stood pretending to examine these things, and coveting, passionately desiring the green door.

Then, he said, he had a gust of emotion. He made a run for it, lest hesitation should grip him again, he went plump with outstretched hand through the green door and let it slam behind him. And so, in a trice, he came into the garden that has haunted him all his life.

It was very difficult for Wallace to give me his full sense of that garden into which he came.

There was something in the very air of it that exhilarated, that gave one a sense of lightness and good happening and well being; there was something in the sight of it that made all its colour clean and perfect and subtly luminous. In the instant of coming into it one was exquisitely glad—as only in rare moments and when one is young and joyful one can be glad in this world. And everything was beautiful there . . .

Wallace mused before he went on telling me. "You see," he said, with the doubtful inflection of a man who pauses at incredible things, "there were two great panthers there . . . Yes, spotted panthers. And I was not afraid. There was a long wide path with marble-edged flower borders on either side, and these two huge velvety beasts were playing there with a ball. One looked up and came towards me, a little curious as it seemed. It came right up to me, rubbed its soft round ear very gently against the small hand I held out and purred. It was, I tell you, an enchanted garden. I know. And the size? Oh! it stretched far and wide, this way and that. I believe there were hills far away. Heaven knows where West

Kensington had suddenly got to. And somehow it was just like coming home.

"You know, in the very moment the door swung to behind me, I forgot the road with its fallen chestnut leaves, its cabs and tradesmen's carts, I forgot the sort of gravitational pull back to the discipline and obedience of home, I forgot all hesitations and fear, forgot discretion, forgot all the intimate realities of this life. I became in a moment a very glad and wonder-happy little boy—in another world. It was a world with a different quality, a warmer, more penetrating and mellower light, with a faint clear gladness in its air, and wisps of sun-touched cloud in the blueness of its sky. And before me ran this long wide path, invitingly, with weedless beds on either side, rich with untended flowers, and these two great panthers. I put my little hands fearlessly on their soft fur, and caressed their round ears and the sensitive corners under their ears, and played with them, and it was as though they welcomed me home. There was a keen sense of home-coming in my mind, and when presently a tall, fair girl appeared in the pathway and came to meet me, smiling, and said 'Well?' to me, and lifted me, and kissed me, and put me down, and led me by the hand, there was no amazement, but only an impression of delightful rightness, of being reminded of happy things that had in some strange way been overlooked. There were broad steps, I remember, that came into view between spikes of delphinium, and up these we went to a great avenue between very old and shady dark trees. All down this avenue, you know, between the red chapped stems, were marble seats of honour and statuary, and very tame and friendly white doves . . .

"And along this avenue my girl-friend led me, looking down—I recall the pleasant lines, the finely-modelled chin of her sweet kind face—asking me questions in a soft, agreeable voice, and telling me things, pleasant things I know, though what they were I was never able to recall . . . And presently a little Capuchin monkey, very clean, with a fur of ruddy brown and kindly hazel eyes, came down a tree to us and ran beside me, looking up at me and grinning, and presently leapt to my shoulder. So we went on our way in great happiness . . ."

He paused.

"Go on," I said.

"I remember little things. We passed an old man musing among laurels, I remember, and a place gay with paroquets, and came through a broad shaded colonnade to a spacious cool palace, full of pleasant fountains, full of beautiful things, full of the quality and promise of heart's desire. And there were many things and many people, some that still seem to stand out clearly and some that are a little vague, but all these people were beautiful and kind. In some way—I don't know how—it was conveyed to me that they all were kind to me, glad to have me there, and filling me with gladness by their gestures, by the touch of their hands, by the welcome and love in their eyes. Yes—"

He mused for awhile. "Playmates I found there. That was very much to me, because I was a lonely little boy. They played delightful games in a grass-covered court where there was a sun-dial set about with flowers. And as one played one loved . . .

"But—it's odd—there's a gap in my memory. I don't remember the games we played. I never remembered. Afterwards, as a child, I spent long hours trying, even with tears, to recall the form of that happiness. I wanted to play it all over again—in my nursery—by myself. No! All I remember is the happiness and two dear playfellows who were most with me . . . Then presently came a sombre dark woman, with a grave, pale face and dreamy eyes, a sombre woman wearing a soft long robe of pale purple, who carried a book and beckoned and took me aside with her into a gallery above a hall—though my playmates were loth to have me go, and ceased their game and stood watching as I was carried away. 'Come back to us!' they cried. 'Come back to us soon!' I looked up at her face, but she heeded them not at all. Her face was very gentle and grave. She took me to a seat in the gallery, and I stood beside her, ready to look at her book as she opened it upon her knee. The pages fell open. She pointed, and I looked, marvelling, for in the living pages of that book I saw myself; it was a story about myself, and in it were all the things that had happened to me since ever I was born . . .

"It was wonderful to me, because the pages of that book were not pictures, you understand, but realities."

Wallace paused gravely—looked at me doubtfully.

"Go on," I said. "I understand."

"They were realities—yes, they must have been; people moved and things came and went in them; my dear mother, whom I had near forgotten; then my father, stern and upright, the servants, the nursery, all the familiar things of home. Then the front door and the busy streets, with traffic to and fro: I looked and marvelled, and looked half doubtfully again into the woman's face and turned the pages over, skipping this and that, to see more of this book, and more, and so at last I came to myself hovering and hesitating outside the green door in the long white wall, and felt again the conflict and the fear.

"'And next?' I cried, and would have turned on, but the cool hand of the grave woman delayed me.

"'Next?' I insisted, and struggled gently with her hand, pulling up her fingers with all my childish strength, and as she yielded and the page came over she bent down upon me like a shadow and kissed my brow.

"But the page did not show the enchanted garden, nor the panthers, nor the girl who had led me by the hand, nor the playfellows who had been so loth to let me go. It showed a long grey street in West Kensington, on that chill hour of afternoon before the lamps are lit, and I was there, a wretched little figure, weeping aloud, for all that I could do to restrain myself, and I was weeping because I could not return to my dear play-fellows who had called after me, 'Come back to us! Come back to us soon!' I was there. This was no page in a book, but harsh reality; that enchanted place and the restraining hand of the grave mother at whose knee I stood had gone—whither have they gone?"

He halted again, and remained for a time, staring into the fire.

"Oh! the wretchedness of that return!" he murmured.

"Well?" I said after a minute or so.

"Poor little wretch I was—brought back to this

grey world again! As I realised the fulness of what had happened to me, I gave way to quite ungovernable grief. And the shame and humiliation of that public weeping and my disgraceful home-coming remain with me still. I see again the benevolent-looking old gentleman in gold spectacles who stopped and spoke to me—prodding me first with his umbrella. 'Poor little chap,' said he; 'and are you lost then?'—and me a London boy of five and more! And he must needs bring in a kindly young policeman and make a crowd of me, and so march me home. Sobbing, conspicuous and frightened, I came from the enchanted garden to the steps of my father's house.

"That is as well as I can remember my vision of that garden—the garden that haunts me still. Of course, I can convey nothing of that indescribable quality of translucent unreality, that difference from the common things of experience that hung about it all; but that—that is what happened. If it was a dream, I am sure it was a day-time and altogether extraordinary dream . . . H'm!—naturally there followed a terrible questioning, by my aunt, my father, the nurse, the governess—everyone . . .

"I tried to tell them, and my father gave me my first thrashing for telling lies. When afterwards I tried to tell my aunt, she punished me again for my wicked persistence. Then, as I said, everyone was forbidden to listen to me, to hear a word about it. Even my fairy tale books were taken away from me for a time—because I was 'too imaginative.' Eh? Yes, they did that! My father belonged to the old school . . . And my story was driven back upon myself. I whispered it to my pillow—my pillow that was often damp and salt to my whispering lips with childish tears. And I added always to my official and less fervent prayers this one heartfelt request: 'Please God I may dream of the garden. Oh! take me back to my garden! Take me back to my garden!'

"I dreamt often of the garden. I may have added to it, I may have changed it; I do not know . . . All this you understand is an attempt to reconstruct from fragmentary memories a very early experience. Between that and the other consecutive memories of my boyhood there is a gulf. A time came when it seemed impossible I should ever speak of that wonder glimpse again."

I asked an obvious question.

"No," he said. "I don't remember that I ever attempted to find my way back to the garden in those early years. This seems odd to me now, but I think that very probably a closer watch was kept on my movements after this misadventure to prevent my going astray. No, it wasn't until you knew me that I tried for the garden again. And I believe there was a period—incredible as it seems now—when I forgot the garden altogether—when I was about eight or nine it may have been. Do you remember me as a kid at Saint Athelstan's?"

"Rather!"

"I didn't show any signs did I in those days of having a secret dream?"

II

He looked up with a sudden smile.

"Did you ever play North-West Passage with me? . . . No, of course you didn't come my way!"

"It was the sort of game," he went on, "that every imaginative child plays all day. The idea was the discovery of a North-West Passage to school. The way to school was plain enough; the game consisted in finding some way that wasn't plain, starting off ten minutes early in some almost hopeless direction, and working one's way round through unaccustomed streets to my goal. And one day I got entangled among some rather low-class streets on the other side of Campden Hill, and I began to think that for once the game would be against me and that I should get to school late. I tried rather desperately a street that seemed a *cul de sac*, and found a passage at the end. I hurried through that with renewed hope. 'I shall do it yet,' I said, and passed a row of frowsy little shops that were inexplicably familiar to me, and behold! there was my long white wall and the green door that led to the enchanted garden!

"The thing whacked upon me suddenly. Then, after all, that garden, that wonderful garden, wasn't a dream! . . ."

He paused.

"I suppose my second experience with the green door marks the world of difference there is between the busy life of a schoolboy and the infinite leisure of a child. Anyhow, this second time I didn't for a moment think of going in straight away. You see . . . For one thing my mind was full of the idea of getting to school in time—set on not breaking my record for punctuality. I must surely have felt *some* little desire at least to try the door—yes, I must have felt that . . . But I seem to remember the attraction of the door mainly as another obstacle to my overmastering determination to get to school. I was immediately interested by this discovery I had made, of course—I went on with my mind full of it—but I went on. It didn't check me. I ran past tugging out my watch, found I had ten minutes still to spare, and then I was going downhill into familiar surroundings. I got to school, breathless, it is true, and wet with perspiration, but in time. I can remember hanging up my coat and hat . . . Went right by it and left it behind me. Odd, eh?"

He looked at me thoughtfully. "Of course, I didn't know then that it wouldn't always be there. School boys have limited imaginations. I suppose I thought it was an awfully jolly thing to have it there, to know my way back to it, but there was the school tugging at me. I expect I was a good deal distraught and inattentive that morning, recalling what I could of the beautiful strange people I should presently see again. Oddly enough I had no doubt in my mind that they would be glad to see me . . . Yes, I must have thought of the garden that morning just as a jolly sort of place to which one might resort in the interludes of a strenuous scholastic career.

"I didn't go that day at all. The next day was a half holiday, and that may have weighed with me. Perhaps, too, my state of inattention brought down impositions upon me and docked the margin of time necessary for the detour. I don't know. What I do know is that in the meantime the enchanted garden was so much upon my mind that I could not keep it to myself.

"I told—What was his name?—a ferrety-looking youngster we used to call Squiff."

"Young Hopkins," said I.

"Hopkins it was. I did not like telling him, I had

a feeling that in some way it was against the rules to tell him, but I did. He was walking part of the way home with me; he was talkative, and if we had not talked about the enchanted garden we should have talked of something else, and it was intolerable to me to think about any other subject. So I blabbed.

"Well, he told my secret. The next day in the play interval I found myself surrounded by half a dozen bigger boys, half teasing and wholly curious to hear more of the enchanted garden. There was that big Fawcett—you remember him?—and Carnaby and Morley Reynolds. You weren't there by any chance? No, I think I should have remembered if you were . . .

"A boy is a creature of odd feelings. I was, I really believe, in spite of my secret self-disgust, a little flattered to have the attention of these big fellows. I remember particularly a moment of pleasure caused by the praise of Crawshaw—you remember Crawshaw major, the son of Crawshaw the composer?—who said it was the best lie he had ever heard. But at the same time there was a really painful undertow of shame at telling what I felt was indeed a sacred secret. That beast Fawcett made a joke about the girl in green—."

Wallace's voice sank with the keen memory of that shame. "I pretended not to hear," he said.

"Well, then Carnaby suddenly called me a young liar and disputed with me when I said the thing was true. I said I knew where to find the green door, could lead them all there in ten minutes. Carnaby became outrageously virtuous, and said I'd have to—and bear out my words or suffer. Did you ever have Carnaby twist your arm? Then perhaps you'll understand how it went with me. I swore my story was true. There was nobody in the school then to save a chap from Carnaby though Crawshaw put in a word or so. Carnaby had got his game. I grew excited and red-eared, and a little frightened, I behaved altogether like a silly little chap, and the outcome of it all was that instead of starting alone for my enchanted garden, I led the way presently—cheeks flushed, ears hot, eyes smarting, and my soul one burning misery and shame—for a party of six mocking, curious and threatening school-fellows.

"We never found the white wall and the green door . . ."

"You mean?—"

"I mean I couldn't find it. I would have found it if I could.

"And afterwards when I could go alone I couldn't find it. I never found it. I seem now to have been always looking for it through my school-boy days, but I've never come upon it again."

"Did the fellows—make it disagreeable?"

"Beastly . . . Carnaby held a council over me for wanton lying. I remember how I sneaked home and upstairs to hide the marks of my blubbering. But when I cried myself to sleep at last it wasn't for Carnaby, but for the garden, for the beautiful afternoon I had hoped for, for the sweet friendly women and the waiting playfellows and the game I had hoped to learn again, that beautiful forgotten game . . .

"I believed firmly that if I had not told— . . . I had bad times after that—crying at night and wool-gathering by day. For two terms I slackened and had bad reports. Do you remember? Of course you would! It was *you*—your beating me in mathematics that brought me back to the grind again."

III

For a time my friend stared silently into the red heart of the fire. Then he said: "I never saw it again until I was seventeen.

"It leapt upon me for the third time—as I was driving to Paddington on my way to Oxford and a scholarship. I had just one momentary glimpse. I was leaning over the apron of my hansom smoking a cigarette, and no doubt thinking myself no end of a man of the world, and suddenly there was the door, the wall, the dear sense of unforgettable and still attainable things.

"We clattered by—I too taken by surprise to stop my cab until we were well past and round a corner. Then I had a queer moment, a double and divergent movement of my will: I tapped the little door in the roof of the cab, and brought my arm down to pull out my watch. 'Yes, sir!' said the cabman, smartly. 'Er—well—it's nothing,' I cried. '*My* mistake! We haven't much time! Go on!' and he went on . . .

"I got my scholarship. And the night after I was told of that I sat over my fire in my little upper room, my study, in my father's house, with his praise—his rare praise—and his sound counsels ringing in my ears, and I smoked my favourite pipe—the formidable bulldog of adolescence—and thought of that door in the long white wall. 'If I had stopped,' I thought, 'I should have missed my scholarship, I should have missed Oxford—muddled all the fine career before me! I begin to see things better!' I fell musing deeply, but I did not doubt then this career of mine was a thing that merited sacrifice.

"Those dear friends and that clear atmosphere seemed very sweet to me, very fine, but remote. My grip was fixing now upon the world. I saw another door opening—the door of my career."

He stared again into the fire. Its red lights picked

out a stubborn strength in his face for just one flickering moment, and then it vanished again.

"Well," he said and sighed, "I have served that career. I have done—much work, much hard work. But I have dreamt of the enchanted garden a thousand dreams, and seen its door, or at least glimpsed its door, four times since then. Yes—four times. For a while this world was so bright and interesting, seemed so full of meaning and opportunity that the half-effaced charm of the garden was by comparison gentle and remote. Who wants to pat panthers on the way to dinner with pretty women and distinguished men? I came down to London from Oxford, a man of bold promise that I have done something to redeem. Something—and yet there have been disappointments . . .

"Twice I have been in love—I will not dwell on that—but once, as I went to someone who, I know, doubted whether I dared to come, I took a short cut at a venture through an unfrequented road near Earl's Court, and so happened on a white wall and a familiar green door. 'Odd!' said I to myself, 'but I thought this place was on Campden Hill. It's the place I never could find somehow—like counting Stonehenge—the place of that queer day dream of mine.' And I went by it intent upon my purpose. It had no appeal to me that afternoon.

"I had just a moment's impulse to try the door, three steps aside were needed at the most—though I was sure enough in my heart that it would open to me—and then I thought that doing so might delay me on the way to that appointment in which I thought my honour was involved. Afterwards I was sorry for my punctuality—I might at least have peeped in, I thought, and waved a hand to those panthers, but I knew enough by this time not to seek again belatedly that which is not found by seeking. Yes, that time made me very sorry . . .

"Years of hard work after that and never a sight of the door. It's only recently it has come back to me. With it there has come a sense as though some thin tarnish had spread itself over my world. I began to think of it as a sorrowful and bitter thing that I should never see that door again. Perhaps I was suffering a little from overwork—perhaps it was what I've heard spoken of as the feeling of forty. I don't know. But certainly the keen brightness that makes effort easy has gone out of things recently, and that just at a time with all these new political developments—when I ought to be working. Odd, isn't it? But I do begin to find life toilsome, its rewards, as I come near them, cheap. I began a little while ago to want the garden quite badly. Yes—and I've seen it three times."

"The garden?"

"No—the door! And I haven't gone in!"

He leaned over the table to me, with an enormous sorrow in his voice as he spoke. "Thrice I have had my chance—*thrice*! If ever that door offers itself to me again, I swore, I will go in out of this dust and heat, out of this dry glitter of vanity, out of these toilsome futilities. I will go and never return. This time I will stay . . . I swore it and when the time came—*I didn't go.*

"Three times in one year have I passed that door and failed to enter. Three times in the last year.

"The first time was on the night of the snatch division on the Tenants' Redemption Bill, on which the Government was saved by a majority of three. You remember? No one on our side—perhaps very few on the opposite side—expected the end that night. Then the debate collapsed like eggshells. I and Hotchkiss were dining with his cousin at Brentford, we were both unpaired, and we were called up by telephone, and set off at once in his cousin's motor. We got in barely in time, and on the way we passed my wall and door—livid in the moonlight, blotched with hot yellow as the glare of our lamps lit it, but unmistakable. 'My God!' cried I. 'What?' said Hotchkiss. 'Nothing!' I answered, and the moment passed.

"'I've made a great sacrifice,' I told the whip as I got in. 'They all have,' he said, and hurried by.

"I do not see how I could have done otherwise then. And the next occasion was as I rushed to my father's bedside to bid that stern old man farewell. Then, too, the claims of life were imperative. But the third time was different; it happened a week ago. It fills me with hot remorse to recall it. I was with Gurker and Ralphs—it's no secret now you know that I've had my talk with Gurker. We had been dining at Frobisher's, and the talk had become intimate between us. The question of my place in the reconstructed ministry lay always just over the boundary of the discussion. Yes—yes. That's all settled. It needn't be talked about yet, but there's no reason to keep a secret from you . . . Yes—thanks! thanks! But let me tell you my story.

"Then, on that night things were very much in the air. My position was a very delicate one. I was keenly anxious to get some definite word from Gurker, but was hampered by Ralphs' presence. I was using the best power of my brain to keep that light and careless talk not too obviously directed to the point that concerns me. I had to. Ralphs' behaviour since has more than justified my caution . . . Ralphs, I knew, would leave us beyond the Kensington High Street, and then I could surprise Gurker by a sudden frankness. One has sometimes to resort to these little devices . . . And then it was that in the margin of my field of vision I became aware once more of the white wall, the green door before us down the road.

"We passed it talking. I passed it. I can still see the shadow of Gurker's marked profile, his opera hat tilted forward over his prominent nose, the many folds of his neck wrap going before my shadow and Ralphs' as we sauntered past.

"I passed within twenty inches of the door. 'If I say good-night to them, and go in,' I asked myself, 'what will happen?' And I was all a-tingle for that word with Gurker.

"I could not answer that question in the tangle of my other problems. 'They will think me mad,' I thought. 'And suppose I vanish now!—Amazing disappearance of a prominent politician!' That weighed with me. A thousand inconceivably petty worldlinesses weighed with me in that crisis."

Then he turned on me with a sorrowful smile, and, speaking slowly; "Here I am!" he said.

"Here I am!" he repeated, "and my chance has gone from me. Three times in one year the door has been offered me—the door that goes into peace, into delight, into a beauty beyond dreaming, a kindness no man on earth can know. And I have rejected it, Redmond, and it has gone—"

"How do you know?"

"I know. I know. I am left now to work it out, to stick to the tasks that held me so strongly when my moments came. You say, I have success—this vulgar, tawdry, irksome, envied thing. I have it." He had a walnut in his big hand. "If that was my success," he said, and crushed it, and held it out for me to see.

"Let me tell you something, Redmond. This loss is destroying me. For two months, for ten weeks nearly now, I have done no work at all, except the most necessary and urgent duties. My soul is full of inappeasable regrets. At nights—when it is less likely I shall be recognised—I go out. I wander. Yes. I wonder what people would think of that if they knew. A Cabinet Minister, the responsible head of that most vital of all departments, wandering alone—grieving—sometimes near audibly lamenting—for a door, for a garden!"

IV

I can see now his rather pallid face, and the unfamiliar sombre fire that had come into his eyes. I see him very vividly to-night. I sit recalling his words, his tones, and last evening's *Westminster Gazette* still lies on my sofa, containing the notice of his death. At lunch to-day the club was busy with him and the strange riddle of his fate.

They found his body very early yesterday morning in a deep excavation near East Kensington Station. It is one of two shafts that have been made in connection with an extension of the railway southward. It is protected from the intrusion of the public by a hoarding upon the high road, in which a small doorway has been cut for the convenience of some of the workmen who live in that direction. The doorway was left unfastened through a misunderstanding between two gangers, and through it he made his way . . .

My mind is darkened with questions and riddles.

It would seem he walked all the way from the House that night—he has frequently walked home during the past Session—and so it is I figure his dark form coming along the late and empty streets, wrapped up, intent. And then did the pale electric lights near the station cheat the rough planking into a semblance of white? Did that fatal unfastened door awaken some memory?

Was there, after all, ever any green door in the wall at all?

I do not know. I have told his story as he told it to me. There are times when I believe that Wallace was no more than the victim of the coincidence between a rare but not unprecedented type of hallucination and a careless trap, but that indeed is not my profoundest belief. You may think me superstitious if you will, and foolish; but, indeed, I am more than half convinced that he had, in truth, an abnormal gift, and a sense, something—I know not what—that in the guise of wall and door offered him an outlet, a secret and peculiar passage of escape into another and altogether more beautiful world. At any rate, you will say, it betrayed him in the end. But did it betray him? There you touch the inmost mystery of these dreamers, these men of vision and the imagination. We see our world fair and common, the hoarding and the pit. By our daylight standard he walked out of security into darkness, danger and death. But did he see like that?

Permissions Acknowledgements

The lines by Isaac Asimov on p. 21 are from *Before the Golden Age* (Doubleday, 1974), p. 625.

'A Martian Odyssey' reproduced with kind permission from Eric Leif Davin, literary executor of the Stanley G. Weinbaum estate.

'The Colour out of Space' by H. P. Lovecraft courtesy of S. T. Joshi, *H. P. Lovecraft: Collected Fiction Volume 2 (1926–1930): A Variorum Edition* (Hippocampus Press, 2017).

Rokeya Sakhawat Hossain, 'Sultana's Dream' from *Sultana's Dream: A Feminist Utopia and Selections from the Secluded Ones*, edited and translated by Roushan Jahan. Translation copyright © 1988 by Roushan Jahan (footnotes are reproduced from the source edition). Reprinted with the permission of the publishers, www.feministpress.org. All rights reserved.

M

MACMILLAN COLLECTOR'S LIBRARY

Own the world's great works of literature [illegible]

[illegible]

[illegible]

Beautifully produced [illegible]

[illegible]

[illegible]

[illegible]